1 MINUTE TO MIDNIGHT

Midnight Trilogy Book 3

L.M. HATCHELL

1 Minute to Midnight
Midnight Trilogy Book 3

First published by ALX Publishing 2022

Cover Design by CBC Designs
Editing by Three Point Author Services

Paperback ISBN: 9781916365124

This novel is entirely a work of fiction. The names, characters and incidents portrayed in it are the work of the author's imagination. Any resemblance to actual

L.M. Hatchell asserts the moral right to be identified as the author of this work.

For Ian and Ali, who sacrificed many hours with me so that this series might come to life

Images flashed before Cassandra's eyes. They were the same images that had haunted her for the past millennium: red hair like flames, unnaturally green eyes, death. This time it was different, however. This time there was more.

A heartbeat. The rhythmic sound of hope.

An impatient clearing of the throat broke through the fog that clouded her mind, and the visions blurred, mixing with reality. The leather chair was rough beneath her. The lights in the room, while dim, caused her to wince. Her body felt raw, as if it had been scraped repeatedly with a razor blade, and the light chiffon of her dress grazed against skin which was now oversensitive and painful even to the gentlest touch. Her mind struggled to remember where she was. When she was.

Five pairs of eyes regarded her warily from across a large oak boardroom table. No, wait … That wasn't right. There were only four pairs of eyes now. The witch was no longer among them. It was only her essence that Cassandra saw, the memory of her.

Diana's death hadn't been a surprise. She'd foreseen the witch's fate long before Diana had succumbed to her final breath, but Cassandra had borne the vision in silence. Even as the brutality of what she'd seen destroyed a little piece of her own soul, she'd known that it must come to pass. That was her curse: to see and to know.

Fate was often a cruel thing. Not by design, but out of necessity. One suffered so that others may live, and one lived so that many may suffer. Millions of threads weaving together. She'd learned long ago the cost of intervening in even the smallest of those threads. She'd learned to endure the visions in silence until, after more than two thousand years, she hardly knew what was real any longer.

Yet here she was, sitting in front of the Council once more. Because this was bigger than her, bigger than them all. The very existence of her people was at their mercy, and she could only pray that they'd make the right decisions.

"What have you seen?" Méabh sat back in her chair, shrewd gaze watching her closely. The cunning that lay behind those green eyes could easily have been overlooked in the shadow of the fae's sultry pout and luscious curves, but Cassandra saw it. She saw everything.

"Two hearts beat as one." The words left her mouth in a whisper, the rhythm of the heartbeat still thrumming through her. "From their love a new possibility is born."

William slammed his palms on the table and stood. "What the hell does that even mean?"

The werewolf's Scottish accent was thickened by his frustration, and tension rippled across his shoulders as he turned to pace the length of the boardroom. Cassandra knew that he, out of all the Council members, was the least likely to ever cause her harm, but still she shrank back, eyeing him like one might a wild animal.

"Cassandra." Kam's tone was soothing as he drew her attention to where he sat on the opposite side of the table. "Can you tell us exactly what you saw?"

She tilted her head and looked at the shifter with the kind eyes. His Asian features had always fascinated her. They brought to mind faraway lands and magical adventures. She never let herself dwell on such thoughts for long, however; they were not her adventures to have. And she never let herself be fooled by his kind eyes.

When her response wasn't immediately forthcoming, there was another impatient clearing of the throat from Vlad at the furthest end of the table. The vampire's face was fixed in a scowl, and though he was the picture of composure, she was almost certain his ridiculously shiny black shoe was tapping the floor impatiently beneath the table. Overcome by a sudden urge to stick her tongue out at him, Cassandra bit back the childish giggle that tried to slip past her lips. His scowl deepened.

"The girl has triggered the prophecy," she said, after taking a moment to compose herself. "But she also holds the means to stop it."

The images played before her eyes once more, and they, not the room she was in, became her reality. "A new life grows from their love. A chance to end the prophecy. The child must live. Or we all will die."

The images shattered, and she came back to the present with a gasp.

Méabh leaned forward, her red-tipped nails clutching the table like claws. "The child? You're saying the hybrid is pregnant?"

Cassandra stayed silent. She'd said too much already. Anything she said had the power to influence the future, and the balance was already precarious. She couldn't risk saying more; not now. So, she fixed her gaze firmly on the frosted glass that covered one entire wall of the room and pinched her lips together.

William's pacing ceased abruptly, and he glared at Vlad. "I guess it's a bloody good thing we didn't kill her then, isn't it!"

"The child is no guarantee. The Seer said it herself." Vlad waved a hand dismissively. "The hybrid's death ensures our safety."

"We gave our word to give them time."

"We also gave our word to protect our people. Or have you forgotten that?"

William growled low in his throat and leaned over the table towards Vlad. "Don't try to pretend it's 'our people' that you're worried about."

Vlad pushed back his chair and stood.

"Enough," Kam ordered quietly. Both wolf and vampire paused but didn't take their eyes from each other. "This hybrid child, will it prevent the Horsemen from returning to our plane of existence?"

Cassandra looked at him once more, debating how much she could safely say. "If it survives, they will not be able to return in their true form."

"Well then, we need to ensure it does."

Kam turned to the figure sitting in the corner behind Cassandra, the one who had been observing their discussion in silence. She'd been aware of the man's presence but had purposely avoided looking in his direction. Every instinct told her that the man was important, that his presence here would change everything. She hadn't looked at him yet because there were some things even she didn't want to see.

"Vicktor," Kam addressed the man, "perhaps the Council Liaison Office may be able to act as a contact between the hybrid and the Council? It's important that we assist her in whatever manner we can, but I fear, given recent events, that she may be less than amenable to dealing with us directly."

The conversation faded into the background as Cassandra finally gave in to the compulsion that had been tugging at the deepest part of her mind. Slowly, she turned to look as the man in the neat grey suit stood and nodded.

An icy chill shot through her as the vision came. Flashes of red. Screams of agony. Fires hotter than the depths of hell. He would bring death to them all.

2

The nausea kicked in at the worst possible moment. Phoenix scrunched her eyes tight and tried to slowly breathe through it. The small ball of light she held in her hands flickered and winked out.

"Dammit." She bit back a scream of frustration. It had taken her half an hour to get that far. The makeshift target she'd been aiming for mocked her from where it stood, untouched, fifty feet away.

Her stomach lurched, and the image of a small boat on roiling seas came to mind. She hunkered down on the ground and let her head hang between her knees. Was this what it felt like to be hungover? Dammit, it would be easier if she just got sick already. But no, her body insisted on torturing her with relentless, unproductive nausea instead.

All around her the familiar sounds of fighting continued. The field that the Donegal pack used as their main training ground was huge. Thick, lush forests bordered it on all sides, and rich green grass covered the open space. Groups of werewolves dotted the field around her, some in their wolf shape, some in their human one. Cormac, their Alpha, yelled training drills at them, and they obeyed with lethal grace and efficiency.

To her left she could hear Sasha's hearty laugh as Abi unexpectedly flipped her. While Nate had started Abi's self-defence training, Ethan's sister had taken it upon herself to help Phoenix's very human, very breakable best friend up her game. She was adamant that given guidance, Abi could be every bit as skilled as the Supes she was surrounded by, and Abi had taken to the training with an enthusiasm that made Phoenix proud.

On the other side of her, by the forest treeline, Lucas and Shade were deep in discussion. Shade had been spending quite a bit of time with her father's Sire ever since Lucas had arrived to save them all from almost certain death at the hands of the Council's assassins. Of course, the Mists didn't answer to the Council anymore, thanks to her. She wasn't quite sure who they answered to now. They'd disappeared after striking a tenuous truce with her, but not before making the ominous promise to return when they were needed.

With the sun high in the midday sky, Lucas and Shade kept close to the shadows provided by the trees. Lucas was old enough to withstand the sun, but Shade was still severely weakened by it. Every few minutes, she would hear a sharp hiss from their direction as Shade stepped into its bright rays and gritted his teeth while Lucas counted, providing intermittent instructions and encouragement as Shade worked to build his resistance.

It was the sounds of training that she focused on now, the familiar routine that had become her life in the three weeks since the Mist attack. At first it had been strange not having someone try to kill her anymore. The Council had agreed to a stay of execution – temporarily at least. And Darius, well, he needed her alive in order for his stupid prophecy to be fulfilled. The gold-gilded note he'd sent to her with a single red rose had reminded her as much.

After the last few months, it all seemed almost anticlimactic, but she took the reprieve while she could because she knew it wouldn't last.

A few slow breaths later, and the nausea subsided enough for her to rise to her feet. Ethan's mother, Fia, had assured her this was normal in the early stages of pregnancy, even more so with the accelerated growth of Supes. If that was the case, Phoenix couldn't help but wonder why women willingly signed themselves up for it.

A niggle of guilt immediately followed the thought, and she placed her hand on her still-flat stomach. "Sorry, munchkin, I don't mean it, really."

She sighed and straightened her shoulders, focusing her attention on the wooden target. *Small ball of light, pinpoint control,* she reminded herself yet again.

The heat resting in the centre of her chest was strengthened by the sun on her bare arms. It was warm for March, and the cloudless sky was a welcome reprieve from the recent crazy weather that had varied from sudden snowstorms to sun showers in a single day. Given that she was half vampire and the pregnancy had brought with it an inconvenient aversion to blood or any food heavy in iron, the elemental fae half of her genetics was having to do a lot of heavy lifting to make up for the shortfall in sustenance. The sunny day was a much needed chance to replenish her energy.

Focusing her thoughts, she directed the heat into her arms and down to her open palms, cupped together in front of her. The spark of light was hesitant at first, her power confused by the willing barrier she placed on it. Sure, she could blast the target with a huge ball of light in the blink of an eye, but that would only get her so far. She needed to start learning real control of her fae powers instead of just blowing shit up and blinding everyone around her.

Gently, Phoenix urged the spark of light to grow, mesmerised by the tiny ball of light that radiated the sun's heat back up at her. It was getting easier to draw on the power of the sun, the connection as natural to her as breathing once she'd finally embraced it. She smiled. She could do this; she could be a force to be reckoned with, even if she had to stop to retch every once in a while.

She coaxed the light to grow until it was almost the size of a tennis ball. It began to emit a tremendous amount of heat as she focused the energy into the small space. She raised her eyes and zeroed in on her target.

Head? No, that was too adventurous to start with. A larger body part, maybe. The chest? That was doable, wasn't it? She just ... needed ... to ... concentrate ...

The image of the ball striking the wooden figure dead centre held in her mind, she released the power. An ear-splitting *BOOM* sounded, and she was flung backwards, landing with a heavy thud on the ground.

The field around her grew completely silent. Phoenix shook her head in confusion and looked at the target.

Only it wasn't there. In its place was a muddy crater in the ground where the target had once been.

The front door flung open as Ethan stepped out of the kitchen and into the hallway, steaming cup of tea in hand. Phoenix stomped into his parents' house, her vibrant red hair in disarray, dirt on her clothes, and her shoulders tense. He froze, gaping at her. "What —"

She cut off his question with a warning glare and stormed up the stairs without a word. A couple of leaves fell from her top as she went, and Ethan looked from the stairs to the front door and back again. What the hell had happened at training?

He moved to follow her but hesitated with his foot on the first step as he remembered the look on her face. Her mood had been rather unpredictable after training sessions recently. The battle with the Mists had taken a lot out of her, and for a time she'd worried that she had burned out her fae powers entirely. He'd tried pointing out that her body was under a lot of pressure, what with the pregnancy and all that, but his suggestion that she maybe take it easy for a while had been met with a snarl that would rival any wolf in his pack.

She hadn't seemed injured. Maybe she wanted to be alone?

Before he could make a decision on whether or not to check on her, Nate appeared in the hallway, eyes glued to the tablet in his hand. "You got a minute?"

Ethan gave a final glance at the empty staircase and sighed, following Nate into the living room. A low fire simmered in the stone fireplace even with the sun streaming through the large picture windows that covered one wall of the room. He placed his cup of tea on one of the small oak side tables and settled into the oversized sofa facing the window and the view of the rolling hills that made up the pack lands.

Nate sat down beside him, still distracted by whatever was on the screen. Ethan couldn't help but notice the dark circles under the young shifter's amber eyes, and the unkempt appearance of his clothes. Ever since Lily's death a few weeks prior, Nate's usual cheeky sparkle had been missing. It was understandable given Nate's feelings for Lily, yet Ethan couldn't help but worry that he wasn't coping well with the loss.

"What did you want to talk to me about?"

Nate flipped the tablet around to give him a clear view of the screen. Ethan frowned.

"What the hell is that?" He squinted at what looked like a rough sketch of a vaguely human shape composed almost entirely of writhing insects.

"Greed. At least the only visual depiction I've been able to find of him. Unlikely to be his true form, of course." Nate flicked to another image that looked disturbingly like a person devouring his own flesh. "My research suggests he's the lowest ranking of the Horsemen, but still one scary motherfucker. Anyone he touches is consumed by an insatiable hunger that ultimately leads to –" He waved a hand at the screen with a grimace. "Well, you can see for yourself."

Ethan shuddered, unable to look away from the images. "What about the other three Horsemen?"

"All I've managed to find on Envy are the articles collating the aftermath: an unprecedented increase in child abductions, people murdering their next-door neighbours for their possessions, whole communities wiping each other out to gain access to their resources. It doesn't make for good bedtime reading. I'm drawing a pretty big blank with Fear and Hatred."

Ethan blew out a slow breath and tried to ignore the growing knot of unease twisting around his gut. "Makes sense. It's been millennia since the Horsemen were free to wreak their destruction here. If the stories are to be believed, survivors were a rarity wherever they went so there wouldn't have been anyone to pass on the information about them."

"The very first Council were charged with banishing them and creating the barrier. Surely they must have more information than this. Can't your dad contact William? I've gotten as much as I can from the online archives, but maybe the Council have physical records or something. At the very least we're going to need details of the banishment spell."

A heavy weight settled in Ethan's chest at the mention of the Council and his father's cousin. Not too long ago he'd have gone straight to William himself without hesitation. But after everything that had happened in recent weeks, maybe Cormac had been right when he said William would put the Council before blood. Could they really take the risk of turning to him for help now?

"That'll have to be a last resort. Now that Phoenix has broken their edicts and is pregnant … We can't take the chance that they'll come for her, even with the truce."

Something darkened in Nate's amber eyes and he nodded. Once more Ethan was struck by the strain that was visible on the young shifter's face. Not too long ago he'd seen a similar strain on Lily's face as she attempted to bury the grief of her sister's death. That hadn't ended well.

"Nate, do me a favour?" Ethan stood, an inexplicable sense of exhaustion settling over him. "Take a break from this. Clear your head and do something to blow off steam. We have time to figure this out." At least he hoped they did.

3

The werewolf snarled, white foam dripping from one side of his mouth. He wrenched against the silver bonds that held him in the centre of the sterile white room. Muscles corded along his naked body, and veins protruded as his face turned a dangerous shade of red.

Darius glanced sideways at Sean. The Omega's face was pinched and beaded with sweat as he watched the suffering of the bound wolf. Sean's very nature allowed him to calm and ease the pain of other wolves – a discovery that had been invaluable in the early stages of testing – but Darius had no patience for this bleeding-heart reaction.

"You might want to get a better hold on your wolf, Omega, or this is not going to be pleasant."

Sean's jaw and fists clenched in response to Darius's order. His body trembled as he fought to calm the shackled werewolf. "He can't take any more," he ground out. "You need to stop."

As if to prove the point, the other man suddenly went rigid. His head flung back, and his spine bowed at such an unnatural angle that Darius expected to hear it snap. To their left, the witch's low chanting grew faster, more urgent. The air became charged, and the growing power raised the hairs on Darius's arms.

"Why would I want to stop? If this transfer fails, you'll just have to select another wolf until we find a match." A low whine came from the Omega wolf at his side, and Darius resisted the urge to strike him. It wouldn't do to break Sean's concentration while he was assisting with the transfer – albeit under duress.

It had been unfortunate that the last test had been a failure, but that was the difficulty in trying to find the correct combination of Supe and demon. So far they'd only successfully managed the transfer with vampire subjects. The barrier between worlds wasn't yet weak enough for the higher-level demons to come through, even with the magical assistance of the witches. Success balanced on a knife edge of timing, power, and compatibility. It was a frustrating but necessary process.

Patience, he reminded himself. Soon he would have his army and stand at the side of the Horsemen. Soon he would return the Lore to its true glory.

Electricity crackled over Darius's skin as the energy built to bursting point within the square chamber. Sean dropped to his knees with an agonised groan, and an inhuman scream ripped from the wolf he was trying to control.

Darius could feel the exact point when the fabric tore around them. The power waiting within the void was breathtaking. It was alive and straining to break free from its confines. Not long now.

15

There was a hollow *POP* and the energy disappeared. The barrier knitted back together, and the power became little more than an echoing memory. But it was there, waiting until the moment that the veil came crashing down entirely.

A clang of chains drew Darius's attention back to the centre of the room. Low growls rumbled from the bound wolf's throat, and his fangs elongated to vicious points. The sinewy muscle covering his body tensed as if poised to attack. Wild yellow eyes darted around the room without seeming to focus on anything.

A minute passed. Then two. There was no noticeable change in the wolf that Darius could see.

No sooner had he finished his observation than the werewolf started to thrash about. The yellow eyes went wide with fear as the skin on the left side of its body darkened, growing almost black in places. Darius watched with morbid fascination as small patches of skin appeared to rot and decay. Pus oozed from the wounds and a rancid odour filled the room.

Another failure, he noted with a clinical disappointment, and prepared to turn for the door.

The wolf's eyes flashed red. As quickly as it had started, the thrashing stopped. The pattern of decay slowly faded. When the skin was once again smooth, the wolf grew deathly still.

He raised red eyes to meet Darius's, and a vicious grin split his mouth.

Darius took the secure elevator to the upper level of the Club of Night, musing on the progress of the testing. Another demon-Supe match confirmed. It was a step in the right direction, but it still wasn't enough. He had less than nine months before the prophecy would reach its conclusion. Less than nine months to build an army fit for the right hand of the Horsemen. The fabric was failing too slowly; he needed more power if he was to pull through higher-level demons.

His head of security awaited him when he entered his office. Darius joined him at the panoramic window that provided a one-way viewing platform to the heaving dancefloor below. The stocky vampire stood with his hands clasped behind his back as he observed the crowd in detached assessment.

"It's busy tonight," Erik commented.

Darius didn't respond. He'd known long before setting up this little enterprise that there would be a rabid market for the services he offered. On the face of it, the club was simply an underground hotspot that allowed Supes to blow off some steam without the need to hide; any human within its walls knew well what they were walking into. But the true heart of the club's thriving balance sheet was funded by the darker services available to select patrons.

Sordid and depraved individuals, all of them. Of course, the humans were no better. They came here serving themselves up on a silver platter, blinded by some ridiculous fantasy that had been implanted in their head by Hollywood. They made his job far too easy.

He turned from the viewing window and went to the mahogany bar built into the wall behind his desk. He poured a dram of whiskey from the crystal decanter and settled on the plush velvet sofa that faced the bank of monitors covering the opposite wall of the room. Each screen showed one of the private rooms available to the club's elite members. Barely past midnight and already the rooms were fully occupied.

The images before him showcased a variety of depravities, ranging from temptingly sensual to unspeakably brutal. All of the participants had entered under their own free will. But not all would leave.

He took a sip of his drink, relishing the burn as the liquid slid down his throat. "Have you found him yet?"

"According to our sources at the Council Liaison Office, Vicktor has been away at a private meeting in Brussels. He's due back this evening. I have men stationed to apprehend him as soon as he returns."

So, he'd been with the Council. Darius mused on this, debating just how much risk the weasel posed to him. Yes, it was very possible that Vicktor could have informed the Council about Darius's plans to nudge the prophecy along, but that would mean admitting to his own culpability, given he'd previously assisted Darius's endeavours.

The CLO rep was too much of a coward to take a stand against him. That didn't change the fact that he'd become a dangerous loose end, however. In the wake of Diana's untimely demise, the Council would be looking closely at everything that was happening around them. He could no longer rely on Vicktor's sense of self-preservation to ensure his loyalty.

"Good. See to it that he's brought here immediately." Darius stood and surveyed the horde of writhing bodies below. "I'm going to find someone to eat."

4

Phoenix eyed the steaks in the middle of the large oak table with a strange mix of longing and revulsion. Her mouth watered even as her stomach somersaulted. The dining room was buzzing with conversation as everyone settled down for dinner. It had been their daily ritual ever since they'd arrived at Ethan's family home – no matter what else happened during the day, they all made an effort to eat dinner together. Of course, for Phoenix eating had become a rather loose term of late.

She looked up as Ethan pulled out the chair beside her and sat down.

"How are you feeling?"

She eyed the amazing spread of food and gave a martyred sigh. "Like I got the short end of the stick with this pregnancy business."

His brown eyes glinted, and he attempted to look suitably apologetic but failed miserably. "It could be worse. You could be the one listening to you complain."

She glared at him and raised her fork threateningly, but she couldn't help the smile that tugged at her lips when he started laughing.

"Dig in, folks," Cormac ordered, placing two more steaming dishes in the centre of the already packed table before taking his seat beside Fia.

Phoenix assessed her options as one might the coloured wires on a live bomb. She couldn't even bring herself to look at the rare slabs of meat that had once been her preference. The vegetables were all homegrown and provided a rainbow of colours that were full of the nutrients the baby needed, so naturally her body rejected that option with a surge of nausea. Which just left the potatoes.

She leaned over to reach for the bowl of mashed potatoes only for it to rise into the air and float towards her. Her eyes widened in surprise before she belatedly noticed the pale hand holding it and looked up into Lucas's grey eyes. She gave him a sheepish grin and accepted the offered bowl.

Her father's Sire had been the main reason they'd all survived when the Council had sent their deadliest assassins, the Mists, to kill Phoenix and anyone that helped her. Lucas had sent his vampires back to England once the dust had settled but had decided to stay behind himself in case he could be of further use. She'd had mixed feelings about that at first, given the role he'd played in her parents' banishment, but in a strange way it had been nice to have some connection to her family.

"I have to say, Phoenix, pregnancy suits you." Lucas relinquished his hold on the bowl with a kind smile.

Beside him, Shade snorted, not even bothering to look at her with his icy blue eyes. "He's full of shit. You look like hell. Get some blood into you before you turn any paler."

Before she had a chance to retort, a hand snaked around behind Shade and gave him a clatter in the back of the head. "Never tell a pregnant woman she looks like shit," Fia warned, pointing a finger at him before turning towards Phoenix. "How are you feeling? Have you had any luck keeping any blood down?"

Heat burned Phoenix's cheeks as all eyes turned to her. Did they really need to be discussing her blood drinking habits over dinner?

Seated on her left-hand side, Abi glanced at her, clearly realising her discomfort. Her friend plastered a huge smile on her face and interjected. "Oh my god, did I tell you all about the deadly new move Sasha taught me today?"

The attention shifted to Ethan's twin sister, Sasha, as she animatedly began describing Abi's new-found prowess with throwing knives. Grateful, Phoenix reached out to squeeze Abi's hand under the table and gave her a small smile. It still amazed her how well her friend had fit into their insane world. By all accounts Abi was putting her past experience in dealing with drunk pub customers to good use and was embracing some of the more violent forms of expression that were necessary in the Lore. Looking at her now, Phoenix could almost believe that Abi didn't miss her old pub at all, but that was just wishful thinking and a vain attempt to ease her own guilt over its destruction.

Phoenix contemplated the remaining mashed potato on her plate as the dishes around her were scraped clean of every last morsel of food. It was only when she noticed the sudden absence of laughter that she looked up and noticed the mood had turned sombre.

"Did the witches get the ward finished?" Ethan asked his father.

Cormac had been working with the local witch coven to restore and reinforce security around the pack lands ever since the Mists had shattered the original wards. Wolves had been stationed to guard the perimeter in the interim, but they couldn't take any risks; it was only a matter of time before Darius or the Council decided to target them again.

"They finished the last binding this morning," Cormac answered, leaning back in his chair and placing his hands on his stomach with a satisfied sigh. "Going forward, only pack members, or people invited by the pack, can cross onto our land."

"Let's hope they did a better job of it this time," Ethan muttered under his breath.

Phoenix jabbed him in the ribs with her elbow and frowned. He shrugged, looking suitably chastised. They both knew he didn't really blame the witches for what had happened; none of them had expected to face opponents as strong as the Mists. The thought sobered her.

It was possible they hadn't even faced their strongest opponents yet. If the prophecy was fulfilled …

A shiver ran through Phoenix and she placed a protective hand on her belly. She couldn't contemplate that possibility right now.

"Phoenix? I was hoping we might speak."

Phoenix looked up in surprise to find Lucas standing in the doorway of the living room. She'd been so mesmerised by the flames blazing in the stone fireplace that she hadn't realised he was standing there. Would it be rude to say no? She so rarely got a moment alone now that so many of them were staying with Ethan's parents that she was sorely tempted to make an excuse.

Instead, she bit back a resigned sigh and gave him what she hoped was a friendly smile as she motioned for him to join her. "To what do I owe the pleasure?"

He closed the door behind him and settled beside her on the sofa. His posture remained poised despite the soft cushions behind him, but he managed to make himself look powerfully composed rather than stiff and unapproachable.

"How are you feeling?" he asked. "While I stand by my earlier assessment that pregnancy suits you, I see you're still suffering with some rather unpleasant side effects."

Phoenix snorted. He was ever so polite, her father's Sire. "Fia assures me it's normal and should pass once I'm over the earliest stage of the pregnancy. Whenever that might be."

And that was the million-dollar question, wasn't it? How long exactly would her pregnancy be? And would it be soon enough to save them? Even for pure werewolves, the length of each pregnancy varied. The mix of wolf and human genetics meant full term could be anything from a wolf's sixty-odd days to a human's forty weeks. The average often fell somewhere in between the two, which would give her plenty of time to have her bun cooked before the prophecy reached its endpoint at midnight on thirty-first December.

But that was the simplified timeline, if they only took into account Ethan's contribution to the gene pool. Her own contribution was a little more complicated since they hadn't yet been able to establish the gestation period for fae. And vampires supposedly couldn't have babies – a fact her own existence highly called into question.

"That was actually part of what I wanted to speak to you about."

"Huh?" She looked at him in confusion.

"It's true we haven't known each other for a very long time, and I've been hesitant to overstep any boundaries, but I wondered if you've considered reaching out to your mother's family?"

Phoenix couldn't help the wall that slammed down at his words. She sat back farther into the cushions, trying hard to keep her expression composed. "And have them report me to the Council for breaching the same edict that my parents were banished for?"

A shadow darkened Lucas's grey eyes, but he accepted her words without flinching. "It's possible that they now regret their decision as I do."

"With all due respect, Lucas, you may have turned my father into a vampire, and you may have been friends with him for a very long time, but you weren't blood. My mother's *parents* banished her. They turned their back on

25

their own daughter because of an outdated, prejudiced law that makes absolutely no sense." Phoenix swallowed, surprised at the sudden burning in her throat as the anger swelled inside of her.

The vampire looked down at his hands, lines tightening the corners of his eyes. "I could argue that I loved Marcus as if he were my own blood, but that only makes my actions even more unforgivable. I can only say that I tried to do what was best for my clan. Perhaps Aria's parents also carried the same burden for their people."

"What do you mean 'their people'?" The phrasing was odd enough that it momentarily distracted her from her anger.

He looked up at her, grey eyes seeming to assess her, but for what she wasn't sure. "How much did your mother tell you of your fae heritage?"

Sweet fuck all because it hurt her too much to ever speak of it. Phoenix bit back the retort. "Not much."

"Your mother's family descend from a great lineage. I guess you could say they are considered royalty among the fae."

Her jaw dropped. "Royalty?"

Lucas nodded. "Not exactly in the human sense, but yes, royalty of sorts. They are descended from the Tuatha Dé Danann, the original rulers of the fae. The political structure has changed significantly over the millennia, but your family still hold a great level of power and responsibility over the courts. As such, they would be expected to uphold a certain level of … ideals."

"Why are you telling me this?" Phoenix wrapped her arms around herself, not quite sure what to make of the information or why it should change how she felt.

"I guess I'm trying to explain why your mother's family might now, as people, be regretting the choice they made then as leaders."

She bit her lower lip. A detached part of her could understand his reasoning, but the part that had witnessed her parents' pain at their banishment wasn't so willing to listen to logic. Whatever regret her mother's family had was their burden to bear. She wouldn't risk the safety of her child on the assumption that they'd had a change of heart, not even for more information on fae reproduction.

"There have to be other ways to get the answers we need."

"In truth, information around your pregnancy is only one of the reasons I feel it may be worthwhile reaching out to your family."

She raised an eyebrow but stayed quiet.

"I wasn't alive when the Horsemen last roamed this plane, but I am old enough to have heard rumours about their banishment. It was said that the magic of the Tuatha Dé Danann was used to forge the fabric that keeps them at bay. Fae magic is unlike the magic of any other species in the Lore. It's an ancient magic that existed long before much of humanity. Back when demons ruled our world."

Back when demons did what now? Phoenix shook her head, trying to clear her reeling thoughts. Even if what he was saying was true and her family had some connection to the magic that bound the Horsemen, why would …

27

She froze. Her stomach clenched with something other than her usual pregnancy nausea as the realisation hit her. "You think we'll need that magic to banish them again."

It wasn't a question, and his suggestion shouldn't have been a surprise. Lucas was only voicing what they all secretly feared. She grew cold despite the fire that blazed in the hearth.

"I think we'll need to be prepared for that possibility. Your baby is a miracle, Phoenix. A beautiful miracle. But it is innocent, and it should be us protecting the baby from the world, not the baby protecting us."

5

Darius stared at the screen in the centre of the bank of monitors. The image showcased an empty, square space, containing only a metal table and a lone figure seated before it. Even from the visual on the screen, Darius could detect the man's pompous air. His posture was rigid despite the chains that held him in place, and his nose was turned up in distaste as he stared directly ahead.

"Did you have much trouble acquiring him?" Darius asked Erik.

"No, though he was adamant that we would pay for our insubordination."

A sliver of satisfaction ran through Darius. He would show the little weasel what insubordination really looked like. "I'll be sure to give him my deepest apologies."

He stood and removed his suit jacket, rolling up the sleeves of his crisp white shirt. "Cancel my next meeting," he ordered, before striding from the viewing room.

The music was a dull thudding bass as he made his way through the darkened hallways that ran along the rear of the club. Blue lights bordered either side of the black carpet, casting an eerie glow as he passed the windowless doors of the private rooms. At the end of the hall, he stopped in front of one such door.

Vicktor's glare was the first thing he noticed as he entered the room, and he smiled wide in greeting. "Vicktor. It's been a while."

"What the hell do you think you're playing at, Darius?" The CLO rep shifted on the metal chair, setting his chains clinking. His eyes darted to the questionable stains on the table and he licked his lips.

"Playing? Oh, I don't believe this is a game."

"The Council know it was you who killed Diana. They have witnesses who saw you heading to her quarters. If something happens to me, they'll —"

"They'll what? Come avenge your death?" Darius sneered. "Don't fool yourself. Even if they cared to expend the energy — which I highly doubt — it won't change the fact you're dead, will it?"

Vicktor swallowed and a vein pulsed at his temple.

"But I don't want to kill you, Vicktor." Darius walked a slow circle around the table, coming to a stop behind the chair. He placed his hands on the other man's shoulders and smiled when Vicktor tensed. "I just want to know what your meeting with the Council was about."

"Why should I tell you anything?"

Darius shrugged and continued his circle until he was once more standing in front of the table. "You shouldn't. Though I'd hate to have to reconsider my decision to keep you alive."

Vicktor licked his lips again. His grey eyes flitted from side to side, searching for an escape that didn't exist.

The restraints in all of the private rooms were of the highest quality and could be easily tailored to suit any species of Supe. The doors were magically reinforced, and a building full of highly trained vampires stood between Vicktor's chair and freedom. There was no escaping.

Clearly coming to the same conclusion, Vicktor swallowed audibly. "If I tell you, I want your word that you'll let me live."

Darius brushed the demand off with a wave of his hand. "You have my word."

"The Seer has had another vision. It seems there's a possible solution to the prophecy."

Darius became deathly still. The only *solution* was for the prophecy to be fulfilled. Any other alternative was unacceptable.

"The hybrid is pregnant," Vicktor continued. "If she births the child before the prophecy endpoint, the balance will be restored."

"What do you mean she's pregnant?"

Vicktor grimaced. "Another abomination to the Lore."

Darius paced the small confines of the room as he considered this development. Every day the fabric was growing weaker; he could already see signs of it as they managed to pull stronger demons through with each transfer they conducted. But the Horsemen were a different story; they were more than mere demons. The fabric would need to fail entirely for them to pass over.

"Did the Seer happen to offer the odds on this outcome?" It wasn't unusual for a scenario to have many possible paths. Perhaps this was just the Council clinging desperately to the sinking ship.

"It was unclear. It seems the future balances precariously on a series of key events."

"Indeed."

"The Council will protect the hybrid now that they know. It doesn't matter that she's broken their edict; they'll do everything in their power to ensure the baby is born."

"I fear you overestimate your dear Council. As you so rightly pointed out, one of their own has already met an untimely demise. Without the Mists to do their bidding, they are little more than an inconvenience." Darius stopped once more in front of the table and leaned forward until his face was mere inches from Vicktor's. "The prophecy will come to pass. I promise you that much. It's just a shame you won't be here to see it."

Vicktor jerked back, his pinched features paling. "You gave your word that you wouldn't kill me."

"Oh, I'm not going to kill you. I'm going to do something much worse." Turning away, Darius pulled his mobile phone from his trouser pocket and pressed the first number on his speed dial. "Erik, I believe we've found ourselves our next test subject."

Darius headed for the stainless-steel lift at the end of the corridor, Vicktor's protests and fruitless threats still ringing in his ears. He had debated with himself over recent months whether or not to keep the CLO rep alive.

Vicktor had long ago outlived his usefulness when it came to getting information about key Council actions, but Darius hadn't wanted to take the risk in drawing attention to himself too soon, should the weasel have a failsafe in place. Now it seemed patience would bring its own reward.

In all their testing to date, they hadn't yet managed to find a suitable demon match for shifters. While not the rarest of the Supe species, myths about their skin being able to transfer the shifting magic to the wearer of same had led to the species being hunted. As a result, they were notoriously private and less inclined than their wolfen counterparts to live in groups. It had meant fewer opportunities to test them than he'd have liked.

Vicktor would make an ideal candidate. If the transfer was successful, it would move their testing along even further. And if it didn't? Well then, the weasel would be out of his hair once and for all. And since it would technically be the demon that killed him, Darius would have even kept his word.

He paused in front of the retina scanner and the lift doors opened with a hiss. There was only one button and it deposited him five floors underground, in the complex that been built below the club.

Significantly smaller than the space they'd previously used at the Dublin clan's lair, he'd felt it prudent to move the most vital of their operations after Phoenix and her little band of do-gooders had breached the lair's security a couple of months previous. The space at the club allowed for a well-equipped laboratory, a testing chamber, and a number of holding cells for the subjects. The remainder of their operations had been moved to the pharmaceutical complex that had been the starting point for the testing, and now also accommodated his ever-growing army of demon-Supe hybrids.

Stepping from the lift, Darius strode past tables laden with tubes, computers, and strange gadgets that meant little to him. A technician in a white lab coat bustled about, preparing for Vicktor's transfer, while a witch readied himself for the ritual on the opposite side of the room.

Darius vaguely recognised the sharp, pale features of the man who stood with his head bowed, chanting in a low voice over a bowl that was coated in a tar-like substance. A streak of white ran through the witch's mousy brown hair and that, more than any personal knowledge of the man, was what triggered Darius's memory.

Though he wasn't always present for the transfers, it was unusual for Darius to see any of the witches more than once. The spell to weaken the barrier, even temporarily, drained a significant amount of energy and burned many of the weaker witches out entirely. Of course, that was the benefit of having the Dublin coven at his disposal; he always had another witch on hand when needed. The coven's greed had long ago left them beholden to him, and now that they floundered without a strong leader, it was even easier to bend them to his will.

Satisfied that all was in hand for the transfer, he made his way to the heavy steel door at the far end of the room. Two feet thick, the door offered much needed soundproofing from the cells that lay beyond it. He

34

stepped up to a second retina scanner, and there was a moment's pause before the door crept open. Immediately, his senses were assaulted by the howls of pain and the stench of days-old filth. He grimaced in distaste before stepping through to the waiting darkness.

Metal bars ran the length of the room on either side of him, and perpendicular sets of bars sectioned each side into smaller cells. The segregation had become necessary when some of the first test subjects had torn each other to shreds in a rather undignified manner.

He passed the first few cells with only a cursory glance at their occupants. A werewolf coated in his own dried blood. A shifter curled in the foetal position, mumbling incoherently as he clawed obsessively at his skin. A vampire so starved he could almost see her skeleton. A witch that did little more than stare at him with eyes that flickered repeatedly between red and a wide-eyed green. Dejected figures, each in a varying state of disrepair.

New candidates for the trials were held in the pharmaceutical complex until their genetic manipulation and psychological conditioning were complete. Only then could they be considered for progression to the next stage – demon transfer. Occasionally candidates didn't take well to the treatment. Or they progressed to the second stage, but the demon transfer still failed due to an incompatible match. Rejects were housed here until it could be decided what to do with them. Sometimes he released them into the general population for his amusement, others were destroyed depending on his mood. It was an unfortunate waste given the time spent on bending each subject to his will, but only the strongest would suffice for his army.

A guttural growl came from the last cell on the left, followed immediately by a sharp yelp and hushed words. Even in the dim light, Darius could see Sean crouching by the silver-coated bars. He was speaking in a low, soothing tone, but the wolf occupying the cage was far past the point of listening.

There was a clang as the wolf hurled himself against the bars. It roared in pain as it came into contact with the silver. *Stupid mutt.*

Sean tensed at Darius's approach, not taking his eyes from the wolf. "He just needs time," he said, his voice strained.

"I'm not concerned with your rabid pup." Darius eyed the werewolf in the cage as he approached. Crazed red eyes stared back, a mix of fear and desperation haunting their depths.

According to Erik's report, the transfer hadn't gone well with this subject. Whether it was due to weakness on the witch's part or a natural rejection of the demon, they didn't know. It was clear from looking at the wolf that they would be adding another number to their tally of failures, something that did not put him in a good mood.

They needed to refine the process. And the witch involved would have to pay for their ineptitude, of course.

But that wasn't why he'd come. "I have a job for you," he informed Sean. "I need you to go back to Donegal and retrieve the hybrid."

Sean's blue eyes flashed in the darkness before he managed to rein in his emotions. He swallowed before answering. "They'll never let me waltz in there and take her."

"On the contrary. You're part of the pack. If anyone here can do just that, it's you."

"The hybrid is of no threat to you. Why not just leave her be?"

Darius levelled his gaze on the Omega. Fear for the other wolves had been more than enough to keep the man in line before now, but ever since Sean had returned from his last visit to Donegal there'd been a change in him. Perhaps it was time to remind him just who his Alpha was now.

"You will go to Donegal. And you will bring me back the hybrid, alive and unharmed. Take one of the other wolves with you." He turned to walk back towards the metal door, casting a final disparaging glance over his shoulder. "Oh, and Sean? Kill the mutt before you leave."

6

A strange thudding noise broke through Phoenix's consciousness and she peeled one eyelid open gingerly. Her body was leaden, and it exhausted her to do even that much. Sunlight filled the bedroom she was sharing with Abi and she squinted against the glare. It took a moment before the knocking registered in her muddled brain.

Before she could call out – or pull the duvet over her head and hide – the door opened a crack and Ethan peeked his head in. "Hey."

"Hey," she mumbled, ducking her head under the covers when she suddenly noticed the thin line of drool running from the corner of her mouth to the pillow. "What time is it?"

"Nearly noon," he said, stepping into the room and closing the door behind him. "We all thought you could use a lie-in."

Noon? Wow, she'd slept twelve hours straight. She'd never done that – not even after a heavy night working behind the bar. The munchkin growing inside her was really wearing her out.

With what felt like monumental effort, she sat up and patted the bed beside her. Ethan's brown eyes sparkled with a cheeky glint, his mouth opening to say something that would no doubt get him into trouble. She glared a warning at him even as her cheeks heated and a smile tugged at her lips.

Obediently, he came to sprawl next to her on the double bed and with a flourish of his hand, he produced a chocolate bar – her favourite dark Belgian kind.

She grabbed it and eagerly tore at the wrapper. "You're the –"

Before she could even raise the luscious chocolate slab to her mouth, the heady aroma of cocoa reached her nose and her stomach lurched. Her eyes widened and she glared at the bar accusingly. "No!" She shook her head in denial.

Her body chose that moment to revolt with another wave of nausea. She shoved the bar back at Ethan before burying her face in her pillow with a wail. "This sucks!"

The mattress beneath her shifted as Ethan jumped up. A soft thud signalled his swift eviction of the chocolate bar from the room, then his weight returned again, causing her to roll into the dip he created in the mattress.

"Sorry. I thought the sugar hit might help your energy levels. My mam's downstairs brewing some strange concoction that she says will help calm your stomach. It's some ancient family recipe apparently. I thought the chocolate seemed like a better idea."

Phoenix peeked an eye out from her behind her pillow. Fia was making a family recipe for her?

A strange feeling that she couldn't quite clarify caused her chest to tighten. She'd grown very fond of Ethan's mother in the short time she'd known her. Fia only ever treated her with respect. Never once had she made Phoenix feel like an abomination because of her hybrid nature. And even when the unexpected pregnancy quite clearly confirmed that Phoenix had led her one and only son astray – an act punishable by death under their laws – she was downstairs preparing a family recipe rather than condemning her.

She looked up to see concern shadowing Ethan's gaze as he watched her. He'd been careful not to put pressure on her or smother her over the past few weeks, but he'd always been there if she needed help. What was it like for him? Did it feel real to him that they were having a baby together? Because it still didn't to her, and she was the one growing it.

"We haven't really had much chance to spend time alone since we've gotten here," he said, breaking the silence. She arched an eyebrow at him and he laughed, shaking his head. "I don't mean like that. All of this has been pretty sudden, what with the pregnancy and everything. I just realised we've never even had a first date."

A sound of surprise slipped past her lips. A date? That was definitely not what she'd expected him to say. "Are you asking me out?"

He grinned. "Well, I feel it's only the gentlemanly thing to do. What d'ye say? Mam will make her magic herbs, and I'll get a picnic ready in case you feel up to eating something?"

A nervous flutter tickled her belly as she forced her expression to stay carefully neutral. She pretended to contemplate his offer for a full minute before putting him out of his misery. "I suppose I can grace you with my presence."

Ethan stood and gave her a mock bow. "I'm honoured … I'm sure." With a wink, he turned to leave, calling back over his shoulder. "Meet me in the forest clearing in half an hour."

She watched the broad expanse of his back as he retreated. Their first date. She gave herself and surreptitious sniff. Maybe she could squeeze in a quick shower before she went to find Fia.

Phoenix gritted her teeth as she yanked the brush through her unruly hair. With a frustrated sigh, she flung the brush on the bed and turned away from the mirror. This was stupid. Ethan had seen her at her absolute worst more than once; if he was put off by her uncooperative hair, then this was all pointless anyway.

Refusing to allow herself a final glance at her reflection, she left the bedroom and went in search of Fia. The strong aroma of herbs hit her the second she stepped out into the hallway. The fresh scent of ginger was particularly familiar given she'd all but taken to chewing on the stuff to help her nausea. Beneath that was a lighter, flowery scent. Chamomile maybe? She shrugged and followed her nose to the kitchen. If it helped, she'd try anything.

Fia turned from the pot she was stirring at the stove and gave her a warm smile. "An old family recipe. It looks awful, but I promise you it doesn't taste that bad. It was a godsend when I was pregnant. I was waiting for the last herbs to grow, otherwise I'd have made it for you sooner."

With a final stir, she poured the contents of the pot into a plain white mug and held it out in offering. Phoenix wrinkled her nose as she assessed the highly questionable brown liquid but took the mug with what she hoped was a grateful smile.

Best to do it quickly, she decided, and closed her eyes, knocking back the mystery concoction before she could second guess herself. The flavours came in waves: the light taste of chamomile was followed by an uncomfortable burn, then eased to a cool aftertaste of mint.

Satisfied, Fia took the empty mug from her, and nudged her towards the door. "Go. Have fun," she ordered.

The afternoon was unseasonably sunny for March, and Phoenix paused outside the house to soak in the warmth of the sun. Her cells tingled at its touch, and a spark of power flared to life in her solar plexus. The freshness of the calm air brought with it spring's promise of new life, a promise of possibilities. The distant sound of laughter reached her from the back of the house where she knew Cormac was tending the garden with some of the pack's younger pups. With a smile and a nervous flutter of anticipation, she headed for the forest at the far side of the garden.

The bright light of day faded and was replaced by leafy shadows. The moss was springy beneath her feet, and the privacy afforded by the trees was blissful. Even the birds were leaving her to her moment of peace, their birdsong silent, undoubtedly due to the number of large predators nearby. She filled her lungs with the earthy scent of the forest as she wove her way through the oak trees to the small clearing.

There was no sign of Ethan when she got there and she had to push back the involuntary pang of disappointment. She was early, that's all. Sunlight filtered in through the trees and the lush green grass looked as tempting as any picnic blanket. So with nothing to do but wait, she picked a spot and settled down to do just that.

She let her eyes drift closed and noticed that, for the first time in weeks, the permanent threat of nausea didn't seem to be lurking under the surface, waiting to pounce at the most inopportune moment. Damn, maybe Fia's family recipe really did work. She'd happily drink all the brown sludge in the world if that was the case.

A soft rustle sounded behind her and she stilled, suddenly aware that she wasn't alone. Her senses picked up the signature of a wolf, but she knew instantly that it wasn't Ethan. She frowned, turning to look behind her. Surely he wouldn't have sent one of the other wolves if he planned to cancel on her?

The wolf who stood at the edge of the clearing was taller than Ethan, his frame leaner. His long white hair partially obscured his eyes, which were a stunning shade of blue, and there was a roughness to his features that made him seem almost feral. But despite the wild edge to his appearance, his energy felt calming. Which was odd, given that wolves were predators and naturally triggered an innate survival instinct buried deep within a person's genome. Even a human who was oblivious to the existence of werewolves would feel an inexplicable sense of unease in the presence of one.

"Did Ethan send you?" She cringed inwardly at the edge of accusation in her tone. If Ethan *had* decided to stand her up, it wasn't this wolf's fault that he'd been sent to deal with the dirty work of telling her.

The man was quiet for a moment, his gaze piercing. "He asked me to get you. There's been a change of plans." His voice was hoarse, as if he was unused to speaking, and he glanced around uneasily.

Phoenix narrowed her eyes and took a closer look at him. Had she seen him around before? They hadn't been here that long, but she was pretty sure she'd met most of the pack and this wolf wasn't familiar to her.

"I'm sorry, I didn't catch your name?"

The wolf hesitated. "It's Sean."

7

Feeling very pleased with himself, Ethan loaded up a cooler box with succulent cuts of meat, fresh fruit, and freshly baked scones. He could already imagine the look on Phoenix's face when she discovered his hidden talent for baking. Hopefully his mother's herbal remedy had done the trick and she'd even be able to enjoy some of the food.

With a final check to make sure he had everything, he threw a blanket over his shoulder and left the kitchen. He had the front door opened when Nate called his name. Ethan groaned inwardly but tried to keep impatience from showing on his face as he turned.

"You got a minute?" Nate didn't wait for an answer before shoving an iPad in his direction. "Look." He jabbed his finger at the newspaper article on the screen.

Ethan scanned the words while at the same time wondering just how pissed Phoenix was going to be at him for being late. A bold headline cited, "An unexplained surge in crime," and he noted plenty of buzzwords to highlight the point: *aggravated assault, petty larceny, arson, vicious murder.*

"What am I supposed to take from this?" he asked with a resigned sigh.

Nate jabbed the screen emphatically. "It's getting worse. There are headlines like this popping up all over the place, and the dark web is full of talk about demon sightings. Their influence is beginning to affect anyone they come into contact with."

A now all-too-familiar sense of apprehension settled over Ethan, dulling his good mood. Frustration welled up inside him, and he handed the iPad back to Nate.

He wasn't going to do this. For a just a few bloody hours, he was going to focus on something positive. "We already know there are demons breaking through. The fabric is weak, but we'll find a way to repair it."

"I want to go to Belfast. The most recent headlines are all centred around there. If I can capture one of the demons, I might –"

"What?" Ethan cut him off more forcefully than he'd intended. "Are you insane?"

Nate shoved his messy brown hair back off his face and Ethan noticed again the dark shadows around the shifter's eyes. "It's still only minor demons coming through. If I can catch one, I can study it. Maybe I can figure out a way for us to fight them."

Ethan let out a sharp laugh, remembering all too clearly what it was like to fight a minor demon. Hell, he and Phoenix had barely escaped with their lives. "How exactly do you plan on capturing one? We are out of the amulets, and now that Lily's gone, we have no one to make more."

He regretted the words immediately. The brief flash of pain that passed across Nate's face sent a pang through his own heart.

"I might know someone who can help us," Nate said quietly, averting his gaze.

Ethan sighed and put a hand on the shifter's shoulder. "Let's talk about this later when everyone's together. Maybe my dad can spare a few wolves to go with you, just to check it out. Now's not the time for taking unnecessary risks, Nate."

Nate gave only a brief nod before turning away. Ethan watched, torn. Then, with a sigh, he walked through the doorway and pulled the front door closed behind him. Nate may have missed his chance with Lily, and Ethan was sorry that he was hurting, but he wasn't going to make the same mistake with Phoenix.

Phoenix stared at the white-haired wolf, transfixed. She'd only ever heard the name Sean mentioned in one context in relation to the pack. And it wasn't a context that resulted in a living, breathing wolf standing before her.

She should be afraid, the sane part of her knew that. Instead, she got to her feet and gave him what she hoped was an amiable smile. "So, what's this change of plans?"

He assessed her somewhat warily as she moved towards him but didn't respond. His nostrils flared and his blue eyes widened with surprise. He took a step back, shaking his head. "You're – He didn't tell me – I can't –"

She wrinkled her brow in confusion, but before she could ask what he meant, a large black crow burst through the trees, startling them both. Phoenix recognised the oil-slick feathers and red eyes as soon as the bird landed beside her, and when the it issued a warning *"Caw!"* her pulse ricocheted. She shot a nervous glance back towards Sean and her mouth went dry.

Another man had somehow appeared at Sean's side without making a sound. He was a solid wall of muscle and had a square jaw that looked like it could easily take more than one punch. But it was his eyes that struck her the most. They were so dark they appeared almost black in the shadows of the trees. However, when he shifted into the light of the sun, she could see blood-red swirling in their depths.

Heat left her body in a rush, and an icy fear slithered through her. His signature felt like a wolf's, but it was murkier, almost slimy. And those eyes …

The crow let out another *"Caw!"* but this time the warning was unnecessary.

"It would be best if you come with us," the other wolf growled, placing his hand on Sean's shoulder.

A pained look flashed across Sean's face and his fists clenched at his sides. "Let's just leave it," he pleaded in a quiet voice.

The hand resting on his shoulder tightened. As Phoenix watched, the skin on the back of the hand turned a dark, brownish-grey and began to split. Cracks formed along the surface, and a wriggling maggot slid from between one of the gaps. Followed by another. And another.

The stench of decay hit her, and her stomach lurched.

"Need I remind you of the consequences should you fail, Omega?" The wolf spoke to Sean, but his grin was all for her – a gruesome smile which showcased rotten teeth and a mouth crawling with maggots.

Phoenix swallowed back a scream. Then she blinked, and somehow the image disappeared. The hand on Sean's shoulder was blemish-free, and no maggots crawled from his menacing grin. She shook her head in confusion.

Sean's blue eyes screamed at her to run, even as he stood silent and pale beneath the other man's bruising grip. Heat flared in her chest and her fingers twitched. The power was there to be called, but doubt mingled with her fear.

She took a step back. Then another. The two wolves just watched her, one with a pained look, the other with a confident grin.

Without warning, the large crow took flight. There was a blur of feathers, followed by a yell of surprise. Phoenix didn't pause to see what happened; she turned and bolted.

Her blood pounded so loudly in her ears that she couldn't tell if anyone was following her or not. She stumbled through the trees, almost tripping over the tangle of roots that had broken through the soil in her haste to get away. She swerved left and then curved right. Within moments she'd lost her sense of orientation but was too terrified to stop.

The large werewolf lunged from her left and barrelled into her. The force of impact sent her colliding into a tree, and her breath left her in a gasp. Rough hands grabbed her in a bruising grip.

"Let's not make this harder than it has to be." Red eyes flashed a warning at her, and her skin crawled as she stared into their swirling depths.

She opened her mouth to scream, but the sound was smothered by a large hand. The wolf smashed her head against the tree, and the world around her swam.

"Don't worry," the wolf assured her. "He won't kill you. Just your baby."

Terror flooded her at the mention of her unborn child, and heat burst from her chest in an involuntary flare of power. The flash of light sent the wolf flying to the ground in a roar of pain. Not waiting to see if he got up, she pushed from the tree and ran.

Where was the other one? Where was Sean?

The thought had barely entered her mind when the Omega stepped out in front of her, and she slammed into his chest. He grabbed her shoulders to steady her, but before she could strike out at him, he let go of her and urged her on.

"Go. I'll hold him off as long as I can."

There was a rustle of movement behind her, and Phoenix turned to see the other man prowling towards them. The left side of his face was a scorched mess and his blood-red eyes blazed with fury.

"Go!" Sean roared and shifted into a huge white wolf.

The last thing Phoenix saw before she turned and ran was the huge white figure leaping through the air.

8

Ethan hurried towards the forest, wondering just how late he was. Dammit, knowing his luck Phoenix would've decided he'd stood her up and left. What a great bloody start to their first date. He broke into a light jog as he hit the trees and followed the short trail to the clearing.

He drew up short when he came upon the empty space. A patch of flattened grass was confirmation that someone had been here, but there was no sign of Phoenix. His heart plummeted. Surely he wasn't that late? He lowered the cooler box and blanket to the ground and looked around.

Okay, let's not blow this out of proportion just yet. He sniffed the air, intending to follow her trail, and froze.

Phoenix's scent was strong enough to confirm that she had indeed been there very recently, but that wasn't what gave him pause. Mingled with her scent was another, long-forgotten one.

Sean.

Ethan frowned. That couldn't be right – Sean was dead. But then a memory came to him, unbidden, of a white wolf that had saved him from Maj during the faithful battle against the Mists. He'd long since convinced himself that it had been his imagination playing tricks on him, that the illusions cast by the Mists had confused his memories. There was no way those blue eyes had belonged to his dead friend. But scents didn't lie.

Heart hammering in his chest, he followed his nose deeper into the forest. Both Sean and Phoenix's trail moved in the same direction until suddenly Sean's veered left. He eyed that path, torn, but continued straight on.

A third, unfamiliar scent intersected Phoenix's not long after Sean's disappeared. He'd sensed this one back at the clearing too, but had been too distracted to pay attention to it. Now he took a moment to examine it and frowned. His first thought was that it was from another werewolf, but there was something off about the scent; it left him with a strange, rotten taste in his mouth.

A twig snapped just ahead of him and a voice he recognised all too well yelled in pain. Adrenaline shot through him and he bolted through the trees, unusual scent forgotten. A flash of red caught his eye, and he made a beeline for it. The sounds of a struggle preceded yet another scream, and his wolf roared, forcing him onwards with mindless urgency.

He leapt over a fallen tree in his path and skidded to a stop when he came to a small break in the trees. His breath caught in his throat, and his body froze in fear as he saw Phoenix lying on the ground with a stocky man looming over her.

Her eyes were wide with terror as they met his, and Ethan took in the man's vicious grin as he pinned her to the ground with one knee pressing into her abdomen. Ice-cold rage washed over him. The man was going to die.

He leaped for the man, knocking him clear of Phoenix and sending them both tumbling across the ground. The man was on his feet before Ethan had a chance to rise. Ethan lunged upwards, slamming his shoulder into the man's gut. There was a jarring *thud* as the man's back slammed against a tree.

Ethan had a moment to notice something odd about the eyes that were gleaming back at him before the man grabbed him by the shoulders and flung him aside as if he weighed nothing. A sharp *crack* signalled Ethan's own collision with a tree and he slid to the ground, winded.

Phoenix crawled towards him, one arm clutching her abdomen. The man simply watched her, the relaxed look on his face making it clear he was in no hurry to end the fun.

"Get out of here," Ethan ordered, even as he knew by the stubborn set of her jaw that she wouldn't leave him.

"Sean. I think he's –"

"Later," he ground out, even as his gut clenched at the mention of his friend. Painfully, he rose to his feet and angled himself between Phoenix and the red-eyed wolf.

"I can take you to Sean," the man offered amicably. "You can get reacquainted while I get to know your girlfriend better."

A low snarl forced itself from Ethan's throat, courtesy of the wolf within him. He allowed his claws to extend but kept a tight hold on his inner beast as he held still and waited.

"No?" The man shrugged. The air around him changed and his body began to shift.

At that moment, a huge crow burst through the trees and slammed into him. There was a blur of feathers and furious roar before the werewolf caught hold of the bird and flung it away from him.

The crow landed to the right of Phoenix and the air shimmered around it. From one blink to the next, it changed from a bird into a huge black wolf, and with mesmerising grace, it launched itself at the man.

Ethan had no idea what the hell was going on, but it didn't matter – he was going to kill the man for hurting Phoenix. He moved to help the black wolf.

An apparition stepped between him and the fight, pulling him up short. White hair and blazing blue eyes were scarcely visible on a face that was covered in so much blood it was barely recognisable. But Ethan did recognise it. It was the face that had haunted all his nightmares ever since his friend's death.

For a moment their eyes met. The pack bond flared like a rope tethering them together. Then Sean tore his gaze away, and just as quickly the connection was gone.

"Get her out of here." The Omega didn't spare him a second glance as he shifted into his wolf form and dived into the fray.

Ethan's shock was shattered by a groan of pain behind him and he turned to find Phoenix on her knees, bent double and clutching her stomach. The memory of the man's knee on her abdomen flashed into Ethan's mind, and fear for her well-being pushed away all other emotions.

The fight raged mere feet from him, and instinct roared at him to help the friend he thought he'd lost. But an even stronger instinct demanded that he protect his mate and his child. Unable to do anything else, he sent an urgent call for help through the pack bond, praying that someone would be close by. Then he scooped Phoenix up into his arms and ran, leaving his friend to his fate once again.

Phoenix could focus on little else other than the fear for her baby as Ethan raced through the forest, holding her in his arms. At any other time, she'd have protested the show of chivalry, but the sharp pain shooting through her abdomen blocked out everything else.

Fia and Cormac met them at the edge of the forest, and without a word, ushered them back to the house and into the living room where the pack doctor was already setting up. She dimly wondered how they'd known to get the doctor as Ethan placed her gently on the sofa and brushed the hair away from her face with an unreadable expression. She watched as he turned to speak to his father in a low voice.

A sharp twinge in her belly elicited an involuntary gasp from her lips, and when she tried to sit up, Fia rushed to her side.

"Don't move," Ethan's mother urged, gently pressing her back against the soft cushions. "Not until the doctor checks you over."

"How did you know?"

Fia smiled, though it didn't reach her eyes. "Ethan sent out a distress call through the pack bond."

The mention of the pack brought the image of the white-haired wolf to Phoenix's mind, and she grabbed Fia's hand, panicked. "Sean —"

"I know," Fia assured her, pain shadowing her features. "We'll find him."

Before she could ask anything more, Ethan and Cormac finished their hushed conversation and Ethan crouched down beside her. "The doctor's ready to check you over, if that's okay?"

Phoenix swallowed. The worry she'd been trying in vain to ignore caused bile to rise in the back of her throat. She knew the pains in her abdomen couldn't be good. She knew exactly where the wolf's knee had pressed.

"He's sworn an oath of secrecy," Cormac assured her, taking her pause to be from reluctance. "Nothing he learns here will leave this room. You have my word."

Not trusting herself to speak, she bit her lip and nodded.

With her consent given, the doctor ushered Fia and Cormac from the room, only allowing Ethan to remain at her say-so. The doctor fired questions at her as he finished setting up an assortment of gadgets in a frighteningly efficient manner.

"Can I please clarify your species?"

She cleared her throat, hands suddenly clammy. "Half vampire, half fae."

No obvious reaction.

"Which is from your mother?"

"Fae."

57

A nod. "Species of the baby's father?"

Phoenix's cheeks heated with a shame she didn't want to feel. Ethan took her hand and gripped it with a reassuring squeeze before answering for her. "Werewolf."

"How far is the pregnancy?"

"Em, three weeks, maybe four?" Time had lost all meaning to her in the chaos of the recent weeks.

The doctor pulled on a pair of latex gloves, then looked at her with kind eyes. "Do I have your permission to examine you and the baby?"

She nodded, even as a knot of panic settled in her chest. Ethan released his grip on her hand and moved to the end of the sofa to give the doctor room to work, but stayed within eye line.

As the doctor raised her top to expose her stomach, a sharp hiss from Ethan made her look down. Mottled purple bruising marked her abdomen where the wolf had used his knee to pin her. The violent discolouration marked the exact spot where she often found herself unconsciously resting her hand, and tears pricked the back of her eyes. A sob threatened to tear itself from her throat and she bit down on her lip hard enough to draw blood in an attempt to hold it back.

She watched in numb fascination as the doctor smeared a clear substance on a wand-like contraption that was connected to a small machine. He placed the wand on her lower abdomen and there was an initial shock of cold as the jelly touched her skin. She winced as he applied gentle pressure, but stayed quiet.

A deafening silence filled the room, seeming to go on for an eternity. Then she heard it. A heartbeat.

It was like a freight train, strong and sure. And it was the most amazing thing she'd ever heard.

She looked at Ethan, and the awe on his face caused her own heart to skip a beat. She followed his line of sight, turning her gaze to the monitor beside her. The screen was small, but she could just about make out a small shape moving. "Is that …"

"Your baby." The doctor gave her a smile. "It's more developed than a human child would be at this stage, but that's not unusual for Supe pregnancies. Typically, we see more progress in the early stages, and then development can slow depending on the species. It's one of the reasons the pregnancy takes so much out of you in the beginning."

Phoenix squinted at the screen, trying to make out the shape. Was that the head? It looked like it could be a head … maybe. Shouldn't she be able to figure out what part of her baby was what? What kind of mother didn't know what her baby's head looked like? Her chest tightened in panic.

Ethan cast her a worried glance before addressing the doctor. "Is the baby okay?"

The doctor was quiet for one terrifying moment as he focused on the screen and adjusted the position of the wand. "I can't see any damage to the placenta. Blood flow to the cord appears to be good, and there's plenty of amniotic fluid around the baby. I'd like to monitor you a little while longer, but it looks like you have a strong one here."

His words brought with them an overwhelming sense of relief, but still there was another worry, a deeper sense of anxiety that gnawed at Phoenix. "Can you tell what the due date might be?" she asked quietly.

"I'm afraid not. With a mix like this it could be a few months, or even as long as a year."

She looked at Ethan, and the shadow that passed over his face mirrored her own thoughts. They didn't have a year.

9

The doctor was only just out the door when Abi rushed into the living room with Sasha hot on her heels. Both hurried to Phoenix's side, and it was all she could do to concentrate on their questions. The sound of her baby's heartbeat still rang in her ears, and although the cramping had subsided, fear still held her firmly in its grip.

Fia and Cormac followed close behind Sasha and Abi, and Ethan hurried to his father's side. "Did they find him?"

Cormac shook his head, frown lines creasing his forehead as he turned his attention to her. "I'm sorry, lass. I promised that you'd be safe here, and we failed you. I don't know how they managed to break the wards."

"They didn't." Nate appeared in the doorway, laptop in hand, face grim. "The wards recognised Sean as pack, so he was free to enter. As was anyone he invited."

A shiver ran down her spine at the thought of the red-eyed wolf. Sean's taste in company seemed to have gone downhill since he "died".

Sasha's face scrunched in pained confusion. "I don't understand. Why wouldn't he have come to us before now if he was alive? And what does he want now?"

Phoenix's heart broke as she saw the same look of pain mirrored on all the wolves' faces. "He was sent for me."

Ethan's eyes flashed yellow for the briefest moment as they met hers. "Darius sent him."

Sasha's frown deepened. "He's working for Darius?"

Phoenix thought back to the torn look on Sean's face. Whatever else he'd done, he'd helped to save her. "I'm not sure he has a choice."

"There's always a choice," Ethan snarled. He blew out a breath, grabbing his hair in a fist. "We need to find him."

Fia moved to his side and placed a hand on his shoulder. "We'll do what we can, Mo Faolán, but our priority right now is for the safety of Phoenix and the baby."

The room fell silent. No one said what they were all thinking: it wasn't safe here for her anymore.

Phoenix pushed her way up to sitting, ignoring Ethan's protests. She'd be damned if she was going to lie there all helpless while they discussed her safety. "The wolf with Sean, there was something odd about him. He didn't … feel right."

Ethan nodded. "His eyes were strange too. A deep blood red."

"Like a demon's."

Phoenix looked up in surprise and saw Lucas in the doorway of the living room, Shade standing behind him. Damn vampires could sneak up on anybody.

"What do you mean?" Nate asked, blowing a mop of hair out of his face.

Even before Lucas explained his thought process, Phoenix knew he was right. She remembered back to her previous demon encounters, and that same feeling of wrongness had been present. It had been muted this time, less obvious, but that could have been from the strength of the wolf signature or just the blinding fear.

"So Darius is somehow combining Supes and demons?" Nate said thoughtfully. "But how? None of the demons we've encountered so far have been strong enough to possess a Supe."

No one answered. Everyone in the room bore a similar look of apprehension, and Shade summed it up best when he whispered, "Well, fuck me to high hell."

A bone-deep weariness settled over Phoenix. She'd gotten complacent over the past few weeks. She'd almost forgotten what it was like to be in constant fear for her life. "What do we do now?"

Lucas moved to come to her side, but froze, becoming deathly still.

Beside her, Ethan's whole body tensed, and the hairs on the back of her neck stood up. Shifting awkwardly on the sofa to follow his gaze, she turned to look out the window behind her.

In the distance, she could see the forest, and from the trees, a huge black wolf emerged. The very same black wolf that had saved them from the demon-Supe hybrid.

It moved towards the house with an otherworldly grace that made all the other werewolves she knew seem clumsy in comparison.

Phoenix watched, mesmerised. The tension in the room cloyed at the back of her throat, and she knew from the reaction of the others that this wolf wasn't one of their own. Yet, none of the wolves that Cormac had ordered to stand guard in front of the house moved to attack as the black wolf drew closer.

The air around the wolf blurred, and without missing a step it transformed into a woman. Her pale skin seemed to glow in the light of the sun, and long black hair flowed behind her. Even from a distance Phoenix could see the miasma of colours that shimmered through the ebony strands. Purples, blues, and greens all reflected back at Phoenix, bringing with them a forgotten memory: Lily's Ritual of Passing, the wolf. She'd seen this woman before.

Without realising she'd moved, Phoenix found herself standing, staring out the window as the woman came to a stop in front of the house.

"Morrigan," Lucas whispered, drawing all eyes to him.

Phoenix gasped and looked from her father's Sire back to the woman who waited patiently at the bottom of the steps leading to the house. She walked out of the living room and made her way to the front door, ignoring the protests behind her.

An odd sense of calm settled over her as she pulled the door open and made her way down the steps to meet the woman she'd only ever known by name. Morrigan. Her mother's guardian.

She stopped a few feet away from the figure, conscious of the others stationed behind her, ready to react to the slightest twitch. "Your eyes aren't red anymore." The words left her mouth before she could think, and she cringed.

Morrigan laughed, a rich, musical sound that wrapped around Phoenix and made her skin tingle. "No child, they're not. It's a side-effect of the magic I use to shift." She paused, and a sad smile settled on her ethereal face. "You've grown into such a beautiful woman. I wish we might have met under different circumstances."

Phoenix said nothing, unsure of how to respond. Her mother had told her many stories about Morrigan when she was a child. The goddess who'd helped lead the fae to greatness in the midst of their darkest hours. The high being who heralded victory and doom alike. The woman who had watched over their family for many centuries. They were little more than fairy tales to her, and yet her mother had spoken of Morrigan as if she were a friend.

"You know who I am?" Morrigan asked.

"I do." Phoenix thought back to the various times in her life when an intervention from the large black crow had meant the difference between life and death. "You've been watching over me. Keeping me safe."

"When I can. Like all, I'm limited in the actions I can take without disrupting the natural order."

"Thank you."

Morrigan inclined her head, her dark eyes glistening. "Your mother meant a great deal to me, Phoenix. As do you. I wish I could do more to spare you the pain of what you are to face, but that is not my place. I've come here to offer you what little help I can."

A tremor of fear ran down Phoenix's spine as the words brought forth a premonition as yet unformed.

"You're not safe here, child. I'm sure that has already become apparent to you. The forces at work behind this prophecy will stop at nothing to ensure it is fulfilled. They will come for you again, and next time I fear they may succeed. You need to go somewhere that they cannot reach you."

"Where?"

"Faerie."

Phoenix barked out a harsh laugh. "Faerie? What makes you think I'd be any safer there?"

"Your mother was banished because she broke a Council edict that normally carries the punishment of death. Banishment was the minimum punishment that would have been deemed acceptable by the Courts. But propriety is very important to the fae, and it would be improper in their eyes for the fae, or your family, to apply that same judgement to you."

"Assuming they don't realise that history has repeated itself." Phoenix hated herself for the bitterness that laced her tone, but she couldn't help it; the fear for her baby was still so raw that she didn't give a shit about the Council or their edicts, or fae propriety.

There was no surprise in Morrigan's expression, only a hint of sorrow as she inclined her head in acknowledgement of the truth. "Your baby is vital to the survival of this world, but some prejudices are deeply ingrained. I will not lie and tell you Faerie is a safe place.

It will be filled with much treachery, and I fear I will not be able to assist you while you're there. But it is the only place that Darius cannot follow you, and for that reason alone it is the safest place for you right now."

"No!" Ethan stepped up to Phoenix's side, clearly done with staying quiet in the background. "We can protect her. There's no way she's going to Faerie."

Morrigan met his challenging glare with dark eyes filled with an ageless understanding. "You have done a valiant job in keeping her safe, wolf. And you will be the difference between life and death for her before this is over. But you can't protect her from what is coming. She must leave here if she is to live."

He opened his mouth to protest further, but Phoenix put a hand on his arm. Trepidation filled her and she wanted more than anything to argue alongside him, to stay here, safe with the people she loved. But some part of her knew that what Morrigan said was true. Darius wouldn't give up. And so long as she was here, she was putting them all in danger.

"How long would I have to go for?"

Ethan spun her to face him, eyes blazing. "Are you mad? You can't go to Faerie. What if they find out you're pregnant? You'll be all alone and –"

"She won't be alone," Morrigan interjected softly. "Tomorrow is the Equinox. The veil will be weak enough that, with my help, she'll be able to pull you across with her. But you must make the decision now, or it'll be too late."

Phoenix didn't take her eyes off Ethan as fear, doubt, and determination all warred behind his dark eyes. She knew that he would do everything in his power to protect their child, but he was right – they had no idea what might await them in Faerie. Was it fair to ask this of him? She didn't know; she just knew she couldn't stay.

"Will you come with me?" she asked, her heart halting its rhythm in her chest as she waited for the answer.

He opened his mouth and closed it again. Looked at his family, then back at her. For an agonizing moment she thought he might refuse. Then he blew out a long breath and ran a hand through his hair, shaking his head.

"It was getting a bit boring here anyway," he answered finally, his lip quirking up in the ghost of a grin.

"There's one more thing."

They groaned in unison and turned to look at Morrigan. She gave them an apologetic smile but continued anyway.

"Four ancient fae weapons were used in the original banishment of the Horsemen. Afterwards, the weapons were scattered so that no one could ever use them to undo what had been done. The time has come to unite them once more."

Phoenix frowned in confusion. "What's that got to do with us going to Faerie?"

"I need you to help gather the weapons." Morrigan held up her hand to halt the protest that was on Phoenix's lips. "One of the weapons is here in the human realm. Lia Fáil, the Stone of Destiny, sits on the Hill of Tara, and is easily accessible when the time comes to act. The second, Claíomh Solais, the Sword of Light, is already in your possession."

68

A collective gasp sounded as Phoenix's jaw dropped. *The Sword of Light?*

Realisation dawned. "My father's sword."

"Yes. Your mother gifted it to him as a sign of her devotion. The sword is a fae weapon and should have only answered to a fae, but her love allowed for a new bond to be formed. It created the possibility of a new future."

Phoenix let the information sink in as she thought back to the first time she'd ever wielded the sword. The pull she'd felt, and the power that had vibrated through the blade, was still fresh in her memory. After that one and only time, she'd put the blade away, afraid of the strange feeling it had triggered. But now she understood. It had called to her, recognised her as a fae.

She shook her head, trying to organise her thoughts. "You said there are four weapons?"

"The third weapon, the Spear of Lugh, remains in Faerie. I need you to find it. The weapons call to each other. If you bring Claíomh Solais with you, it will lead you to the spear."

"What about the fourth weapon?" Ethan asked.

"Dagda's Cauldron. It is safe. It was taken many millennia ago so that it wouldn't fall into the wrong hands. When the time comes, I will call on its guardians and they will bring it to us."

10

Darius stared at Sean in silence as fury scorched a path through his veins. It was bad enough that the Omega had disobeyed his order to retrieve Phoenix, but now the mutt dared to stand before him with his shoulders squared defiantly, no trace of fear on his face. Well, that would soon change.

"And why, pray tell, did you see fit to return empty-handed when I gave you a direct order?"

"She's pregnant," Sean ground out from between clenched teeth. As if those two words should explain everything.

"And?"

"I won't have the death of an innocent on my conscience. I don't care what you do to me, I won't help you with this."

Darius gave a humourless laugh. "My dear Sean, you and I both know you already have the deaths of many innocents on your conscience. And you're about to have even more." He pulled out his mobile phone and redialled the most recent number. "Erik, can you please gather any remaining wolves that haven't yet completed the transition? Our Omega has decided that they're not fit to continue the process and he'd like to oversee their termination himself."

Sean blanched, and the defiance that had moments ago dared to darken his blue eyes shifted to an agonised look of disbelief. He shook his head, but it was a futile denial. He would comply just like he always did because for every wolf that Darius hurt or killed to control him, there were always more that needed the Omega to save them.

Darius held Sean's gaze with a cruel smile and continued speaking to Erik. "When he's finished, see that he's made comfortable in one of the chambers. I shall inform the witches that there's another transfer to be done."

Thick, rich blood slid down the back of Darius's throat as he drained the last drops of precious life from the nameless woman. Her body lay limp in his arms, the weight an inconvenience now that he'd taken what he needed from her. With swift efficiency, he retracted his fangs and tossed her to the floor beside his mahogany desk like a discarded tissue.

The warm blood coursing through his veins did little to abate his fury. Sean's failure had put everything in jeopardy. Even now Phoenix was likely on the move, the failed abduction attempt giving her more than sufficient warning that she wasn't safe within the confines of the pack.

Licking an errant drop of blood from the corner of his mouth, he slipped his hand into his pocket and wrapped it around the silver coin resting there. His flesh burned where the precious metal made contact, and he forced his hand to grip it tighter. The pain was searing, but he focused on it, letting it clear his mind of all distractions.

The witches were already busy at work trying to track Phoenix. They'd had little trouble following her whereabouts in the past, and this time would be no different. It was inconvenient, but still only a minor setback. He'd have the hybrid under his control within twenty-four hours, and he'd deal with the abomination growing inside her.

He stood, stepping over the woman who lay in a heap on the floor beside him, and made his way from the office down to the lowest level of the club.

The laboratory was abuzz with activity as Darius stepped from the elevator. Preparations were being made for Sean's demon transfer, and it gave him no small sense of satisfaction to imagine the Omega's horror at the knowledge that pure evil would soon live inside him. It had been a nice little touch to the punishment, if Darius did say so himself.

He glanced around for a witch, intending to enquire on the progress of the tracking spell, and was surprised to once again recognise the sharp features of the witch with the white streak of hair. As when Darius had last seen him, the man was in the middle of preparing for the transfer. Despite his scrawny frame and pale features, the man seemed in no way weakened from having conducted the same spell only the previous day. Darius watched him with curiosity, a thought forming in the back of his mind.

"You," he said, when the witch's preparations seemed to be complete. "What's your name?"

The man straightened and met Darius's eyes without flinching. "Richard."

"What's your affinity?" Witches drew their power from the world around them, and while they could work various common spells, their individual strengths tended to have a more specialised focus. Darius had found that some affinities proved more useful than others when he required someone to do his bidding.

"I can control animals."

Oh, now that is interesting.

"Tell me, Richard." Darius placed a hand on the man's bony shoulder. "What are your ambitions in life?"

"What does any self-respecting man want?" Richard's beady eyes flashed. "I want to be the most powerful witch that history has ever known."

Darius smiled. This one would do.

"What if I told you I could help you with that? You do something for me, and I will give you power unlike anything you've ever known."

Richard regarded him closely, making a poor attempt to mask his interest. "What would I need to do?"

With a comforting pat on the shoulder, Darius led him towards the empty chamber that was being prepared for Sean's transfer. He gave a subtle nod to the scientist who was eyeing the interaction with curiosity and guided

Richard into the sterile white room. The door closed tightly behind them.

11

Phoenix stared at the rolling hills that zoomed past the car's window. It was easier to focus on the blur of green than the apprehension twisting itself into a complex knot in her stomach. She hadn't been back to Dunluce Castle since Lily's death, and the thought of returning to the place where she'd held the young witch's dying body filled her with a sickening dread.

It had been no real surprise when Morrigan told them the old castle was one of the main gateways to Faerie; Phoenix still remembered the power the place held, and how it had called to her. In truth, she wasn't quite sure how much of her trepidation about returning was because of Lily's death, and how much was fear of facing that power again.

But even on the Equinox they needed a place of great energy to enable her to pull Ethan through to Faerie with her. So, they'd left Donegal as soon as the sun had crested the horizon that morning, and Ethan had treated every speed sign as if it were a gentle suggestion rather than a legal limit in his haste to get them to the gateway where they'd meet Morrigan.

It was hard to believe that she'd finally get to see the place where her mother had been born. She'd never once had the urge to visit Faerie – had never even been sure if she could, given her hybrid nature – but now that she was going, she couldn't help but wonder what it'd be like. Of course, they weren't exactly going on a summer holiday. Morrigan had warned them more than once to be on their guard, and with time moving differently in Faerie than it did here, they'd have to make haste in their search for the Spear of Lugh.

For the umpteenth time, Phoenix glanced behind her to the back seat of the car and the long mahogany box that rested there. Intricate Celtic designs covered the wood protecting her father's sword, and she pictured the blade that lay cushioned inside. Claíomh Solais. Had her parents known? Did they know they'd someday need the sword to protect the world because of her?

She pushed the thought from her mind and asked Ethan, "Did you get a chance to speak to Nate?"

Ethan glanced sideways at her. "He pinkie-promised not to let Abi out of his sight. He's enlisted her to help with his research. I'm not sure that's a good thing for her, but he seems happy to have someone who's actually willing to listen to his tech waffle."

A tinge of sadness laced Phoenix's laughter. "She loves learning about our world and feeling useful. I just wish she'd gotten the chance under better circumstances."

"She will," he assured her, reaching over to give her hand a quick squeeze.

The warmth of his touch chased away some of the chill lingering deep inside her, and when he took his hand away, she felt its loss so acutely that she shivered. She wrapped her arms around herself, her abdomen still tender to the touch. The pack doctor hadn't been too happy to discover he wouldn't be able to monitor her further, but he'd grudgingly agreed that the baby seemed largely unharmed. Phoenix, for her part, took comfort in the memory of the strong heartbeat, and the soft flutters that let her know the munchkin was still with her.

"Are you nervous about meeting your family?" Ethan asked, when she lapsed into silence for a time.

"I've been trying not to think about it. They may be the least of our problems once we hit Faerie."

Morrigan believed that Phoenix's half-fae blood should be enough for them to avoid a direct attack once they crossed over, but all they really had to go on at this stage was supposition. They'd need to make their way to her family as quickly as possible if they were going to utilise the protection of her family name.

"Did your mother tell you much about them?"

"She didn't like to talk about them; it hurt her too much." Even now Phoenix could remember the look of pain on her mother's face when, as a child, she'd innocently asked about her family. She shook her head with a wry grin. "Hell, I didn't even know I came from royalty. I could have demanded that you address me as Princess all this time."

Ethan burst out laughing, a hearty chuckle that she couldn't help but join in with. "Keep dreaming!"

"How do you think we'll find …" She trailed off, squinting at the horizon. A heavy fog rolled towards them, the thick grey mass a striking contrast to the bright cloudless sky directly above.

"What the –" Ethan leaned forward over the steering wheel as he too noticed the strange sight.

The fog engulfed the landscape before them, muting the vivid greens of nature as if an unnatural grey veil had been dropped over everything. Ethan eased his foot off the accelerator, putting on the hazard lights as he slowed the car and pulled it to a stop at the side of the road.

"That's a pretty sudden change in weather," Phoenix noted, a nervous tingle running down her spine. She looked behind them and her unease was only increased at the sight of the sun shining high in the sky.

Ethan was quiet for a minute as he too watched the grey wall of fog move closer with each passing second. "There's no turnoff on this road for another mile."

That would take them straight into the fog.

Phoenix worried at the sleeve of her jacket. "We could turn back?"

"We're not far from the castle now. Besides," he added with what she assumed was false confidence, "it's not unusual for Ireland to have four seasons in one day."

She said nothing as he slowly pulled the car back onto the road, but a tightness settled in her chest. The air grew heavier as they moved forward. Her fingers twitched and she looked back at the mahogany box that held her father's sword.

In less than a minute the grey mist blanketed them, bringing with it a weighty silence that made it almost seem as if they were underwater. Visibility reduced to little more than a couple of feet in front of them, and even the car's fog lights struggled to pierce the veil.

They inched forward, tension building as they both acknowledged the creeping sensation that warned them this fog wasn't natural. The car jerked, and Phoenix's seat belt halted her forward momentum with bruising force. Ethan cursed loudly, slapping the steering wheel as they shuddered to a sudden stop.

"Wait here," he ordered, and jumped out of the car before she could respond.

Like hell was she staying there alone. She fumbled to unbuckle her seat belt and reached over to retrieve her father's sword from its box in the back seat. By the time she climbed out after him, Ethan was standing staring at the wheels on the driver's side with a grim frown.

Both tyres on her side hung limply around the alloy wheels, and a quick walk to where Ethan stood showed her the same. Deep gashes ran across each tyre, shredding them beyond repair. Phoenix looked in dismay from the tyres to Ethan.

"How –"

A loud "*Caw!*" broke through the muted silence of the fog, cutting her off. Morrigan's crow form swooped down towards them.

"What's she doing here? I thought we were meeting at the castle?" Phoenix had barely finished her question when chilling howls sounded in the distance. Her breath caught and she looked at Ethan with wide eyes.

In a single movement, the crow landed beside them and shifted into a woman. Morrigan grabbed Phoenix by the elbow, her eyes tight with tension. "Go. He's coming."

A primal fear ran through Ethan at the distant howls. He met Morrigan's dark eyes and recognised the unspoken order in their depths: *protect her*. He had no idea who was coming for them, or what could possibly have the goddess so on edge, but he wasn't about the ignore the warning.

As the air shimmered and the large crow propelled itself once more into the air, he grabbed Phoenix's hand, mentally calculating the distance to the castle. It had been less than twenty-four hours since she'd been hurt and the last thing he wanted to do was put her body under more stress, but injuries would be a moot point unless they survived.

"Can you run?"

She clutched her father's sword tighter and gave him a determined nod despite the fear that glistened in her green eyes.

They broke into a sprint, letting instinct rather than sight guide them as they moved deeper and deeper into the fog. It didn't matter how quickly they ran, however; the snarls and howls continued to grow closer. Not breaking his stride, Ethan risked a glance behind him. His stomach lurched.

Through the thick blanket of fog, he could see a blur of black on the horizon. As it grew closer, he could just about make out the shapes of huge black dogs. They moved faster than the wind, and the pounding of their paws was like thunder in the unnatural denseness of the fog.

Phoenix gasped as she too spotted their pursuers. Her steps faltered. He grabbed for her as she stumbled. "Just a little bit further," he urged, hoping like hell he was right.

Vicious snarls punctuated his words. But this time the sound didn't come from behind them. It came from in front of them.

Ethan skidded to a halt, pushing Phoenix behind him with a low curse. The blanket of fog parted and a tall, wiry man with sharp features stepped into their path. A streak of white ran through the man's mousey brown hair, and his eyes flickered from black to red as he smiled at them. Two huge Irish wolfhounds stood on either side of him, reaching almost to his shoulder. Acrid black smoke rolled off their dark grey coats, and they too had red eyes.

A sickening aura permeated the man and his dogs, the tainted sensation of black magic mixing with something otherworldly. Ethan's skin crawled, and even the beast within him shrank back to try to escape the magic's vile touch.

"Here, doggy," the man hissed and clicked his fingers.

A blinding pain ripped through Ethan. Ligaments tore away from bone as his body started to shift and change against his will. Claws ruptured from his fingertips, and fangs burst through his gums, filling his mouth with blood. His wolf howled.

He was dimly aware of Phoenix screaming his name as his knees buckled. The memory of another such violation of his will caused every cell in his body to roar in protest, but try as he might, he couldn't resist the shift any more now than he had the last time. Then something changed.

Phoenix's hand gripped his shoulder, and the warmth of her touch sent a jolt through him. A white light surrounded them, and he could feel the heat of the sun as his wolf latched onto her scent. He clung to it for all he was worth, drawing on her power to help fight back against the unnatural magic that tried to crush him to its will.

Sweat soaked his body as he visualised silver bars slamming down around his wolf, caging it within him. Inch by agonising inch, he forced his body to straighten, his limbs to realign.

"You dare defy me!" the witch roared, red eyes blazing. The wolfhounds at his side snarled and foaming saliva dripped from mouths filled with impossibly sharp teeth. They jerked forward, but the man stopped them with a snap of his fingers.

His face relaxed to a chilling calm. "I would've liked to add a wolf to my collection of pets. Never mind. I'll deliver your bitch to Darius and I'm sure he'll gladly provide me with one. Maybe even your white-haired friend."

Low growls began to emanate from all sides. Ethan's blood ran cold.

"Shit," Phoenix whispered, moving closer to him as he risked a glance away from the witch.

The swarm of black hounds that they'd seen on the horizon had finally reached them. Slowly and deliberately, the dogs formed a circle and caged them in. Pairs of red eyes shone like torches of fire through the heavy fog, and their blade-like teeth gleamed.

Ethan noticed the witch making minute gestures with his hands, and the hounds began to move with an eerie synchronicity. Beside him, Phoenix tensed, raising Claíomh Solais before her. The noose tightened around them and Ethan tensed for the attack.

A blur of black swooped down from the sky, and a cawing shriek shattered the tense bubble of silence. Morrigan swept past Ethan with a rush of air, her feathers skimming his cheek right before she collided with the witch.

The man stumbled backwards, hands flapping in a desperate attempt to keep her striking beak away from the soft flesh of his face. His momentary distraction broke the hold he had on the hounds and the red disappeared from their eyes in an instant. The dogs shuffled about in confusion, and a couple whined pitifully as they cowered down on the ground.

The two wolfhounds at the witch's side were a different story, however. Without their master to hold them back, they fixed their feral stares on Phoenix and Ethan and stalked forward. Acrid black smoke swirled around them, and fear choked Ethan as he looked into the emotionless depths of their eyes.

As one, the wolfhounds tensed and leapt. Phoenix slashed out with her sword and caught the one on the left with a glancing blow. A swipe of Ethan's still extended claws tore through the side of the one on the right, but the sheer weight of it leaping at him threw him backwards.

"Morrigan!" Phoenix yelled as they struggled to hold their ground against the wolfhounds.

A piercing shriek sounded from the witch, only to be abruptly cut off. The black crow shot through the air towards them, shifting mid-flight. When Morrigan struck the ground, she no longer bore the oil-slick feathers of the bird but instead took the form of a huge black horse.

The horse reared up on its hind legs before the wolfhounds, using its sheer size to drive the dogs back. It gave a sharp whinny as the front hooves struck the ground, and Ethan grabbed Phoenix. He got her up on the horse's back a fraction of a second before the wolfhounds regrouped.

He lashed out with his claws as the one on his right snapped vicious teeth towards him. He drew blood, but not nearly enough. The wolfhound on the left followed the attack, its teeth latching on to his shoulder. Fire blazed through him as the dog's canines locked onto bone and refused to let go.

A flash of metal came from above and Phoenix plunged the blade of her sword down into the wolfhound, who released its grip on Ethan's shoulder.

With his one remaining good arm, Ethan swung himself up behind her on the horse. "Go!" he roared.

12

Phoenix's heart thundered so hard she thought it would shatter her ribcage at any moment. She gripped the horse's oil slick mane with one hand and her father's sword with the other as the wind whipped at her face. The heavy fog didn't thin as they shot towards Dunluce Castle, and there were eerie cries in the distance, but Morrigan moved faster than the horrors that followed and nothing caught them before they reached the castle's boundaries.

A wave of power washed over Phoenix as the castle's jagged structure came into view, stealing her breath away. It called to the very core of her, and this time she recognised it for what it was: like calling to like. The power wasn't the only thing that came, however. Memories came too. She gritted her teeth and pushed them away. Thinking about Lily's death wouldn't help her now.

The black horse pounded up the dirt track and leapt over the metal barrier that blocked entry to the empty car park. Through the unnatural grey veil, the castle ruins loomed up from the edge of the cliff, the broken walls and crumbling stone somehow making it seem more imposing rather than less.

Only when they reached the entry wall to the castle did Morrigan come to a stop. Ethan dismounted in a single graceful movement behind her. Phoenix handed him the sword, relieved to see the wound on his shoulder already appeared to be healing despite the blood that soaked one side of his jumper. She swung her legs over to the right side and slid rather ungracefully to the ground.

The air shimmered and the horse disappeared, leaving the goddess with flowing black hair in its place. "We don't have much time," Morrigan said, eyeing the horizon as if she expected danger to appear at any second. "The witch isn't dead, or the fog would have lifted. He'll be coming for you." She urged them through the jagged arch that had once been a doorway and into the centre of the ruins.

The castle was just how Phoenix remembered. Colourful flowers dotted the lush green grass, their vibrancy in no way muted by the unnatural grey shroud surrounding them. Her gaze was drawn to the stone wall where Maj had once stood with that strange look of regret on her face. Some part of Phoenix still wondered at that look, and whether she'd made the right decision in freeing the Mists. The other part of her was just glad they'd decided not to stick around after the uneasy truce was struck.

She blew out a long breath and turned to face Morrigan and Ethan. "What now?"

"Now I'll show you how to cross the barrier to Faerie. As your guardian it is my job to watch over you and protect you in any way I can, but once you reach Faerie, I fear my hands will be tied. The rules that govern my power also serve to hold back others more powerful than me. If I overstep my boundaries while you're there, they will be allowed to overstep theirs. So, I urge you again to take care. I did not lie when I said Faerie is the safest place for you right now, but it is by no means a safe place."

Phoenix swallowed at the ominous warning and nodded her understanding.

"Keep the secret of your union close to you." Morrigan looked from her to Ethan with a sad smile. "It is a precious gift you carry, though others may not yet see that."

She held out her hands in invitation. Phoenix took the sword back from Ethan and gripped it tightly in her hand as she reached forward to place her other hand in Morrigan's. Ethan stepped forward next and placed his hand in the goddess's without hesitation.

"Time moves differently in Faerie. What seems like days there may be weeks, or even months, here. Waste no time in seeking the spear." With Morrigan's final words, the world around them disappeared.

Blinding white filled Phoenix's vision, and she groped desperately for Ethan. Her heart pounded and her head spun. She was both weightless and heavy at the same time, floating with nothing beneath her feet but infinity. A wave rippled through her body and she lurched forward. She gasped when a hand grabbed her, and only when her panic calmed enough to feel the familiar heat radiating from the touch did the tightness in her chest ease. Slowly the light faded from her vision, leaving specks of colour dancing before her eyes.

The boundaries of Dunluce Castle were gone, now just a memory etched into her eyelids from the light. Instead, trees surrounded them in all directions. Gnarled trunks twisted, their thick branches coated with an unusual mix of colours – greens so vibrant they were almost illuminous, azure blues which brought to mind the ocean, yellows that varied from the palest lemon to rich golden tones. Mushrooms and toadstools dotted the ground, making the tableau seem like an illustration from a children's book.

"Is it just me, or does all this feel a little cliché?" Ethan muttered, taking it all in with a look of disbelief.

Phoenix giggled, imagining little gnomes popping up from the grass to greet them. "It's kind of quaint."

"I guess we should try find a way out of here. It would have been helpful if Morrigan had supplied a map or something." He looked at her and stopped in his tracks, mouth gaping. "Where did you get that?"

"Huh?" She looked down, patting her torso in confusion. Her hands found a thick leather strap running diagonally across her body that hadn't been there before. She followed it up over her shoulder where she found the hilt of her father's sword within easy reach.

Ducking carefully, she pulled the strap over her head and stared at the simple black scabbard covering the sword's blade. She hadn't even realised the sword wasn't in her hand anymore. Where the hell had this come from?

She was about to voice the question aloud when a piercing shriek shook the trees, jerking her head up to meet Ethan's wide eyes. "Any chance that was my imagination?"

He shook his head, body instantly alert as he eyed the area around them. "We should get moving."

She drew Claíomh Solais from the scabbard and slung the leather strap across her back. The weight of the sword was comforting in her hand, but it didn't chase away the icy fear as they cut a careful path through the cheery landscape.

Something about that sound had tapped straight into her primal senses, and as they moved, Phoenix realised that her first impression of their surroundings had been subtly deceptive. The closer she looked, the more she realised that the forest around them was alive, and she had the creeping sense that it was watching them. Waiting.

As soon as the thought came to her mind, the lush green grass disappeared. In its place, twisting ropes of ivy covered the forest floor, writhing like snakes.

One of the vines edged towards her, slithering around her foot and up her leg. She jumped back with a yelp and kicked out at the space around her with a shudder. Yet more vines snaked their way down from a nearby tree to tenderly caress Ethan's cheek before moving to his neck.

For a split second he seemed almost entranced by the touch, but then he snapped his hand out and grabbed the vine, yanking it away from him before it could fully encircle his throat.

More and more vines edged in their direction. The quicker Phoenix moved, the faster they closed in. Slowly, her heart pounding with the effort, she edged closer to Ethan, never once taking her eyes off the green mass. "What do you think will happen if we make a run for it?" she asked under her breath.

Ethan's response was cut off as another shriek filled the air, closer this time. In a flash the ropes of ivy retracted, leaving only barren earth in their wake.

They looked at each other and back to the now empty space around them. When the creepy things fled, it was really time to go.

"Run!" Ethan grabbed her hand and pulled her behind him as he started to run.

They sprinted blindly through the ever-changing colours of the forest. Phoenix swung her head left and right, frantically seeking a break in the trees, or anything that might indicate they were near the edge of the forest. But the trees seemed to only close in tighter around them.

A third shrill cry sent chills skittering along her skin. She had no idea what could possibly be making the noise; she just knew that every instinct in her body commanded her to run. So when Ethan came to a jarring stop in front of her, she slammed straight into the broad expanse of his back.

"What the –" A sharp *click* froze the words in her throat.

Tension radiated from Ethan, and her mouth was dry as she moved her head an inch to the side to glimpse past him. What she saw was the gleaming tip of three arrows pointed straight at them.

The arrows were loaded into sleek, curved black crossbows, and at first glance Phoenix almost thought they were floating in the air. Then the three men holding them moved into a V formation, the movement breaking their camouflage from the surrounding foliage.

Each of the men had pale skin tinged with green. Long, green-blue hair was pulled back into braids entwined with twigs and leaves, showcasing the pointed tips of their ears. Steady yellow eyes fixed on her every movement, reminding her of the watchful gaze of a cat. A vine of ivy slid across the forest floor and wound itself around the foot of the lead fae. It crawled up his body and faded to form a faint shimmering pattern on his skin.

Ethan shifted his body to block their view of her and held up his hands, palms forward. "We're not looking for trouble."

One of the men let a humourless laugh. "What else could a wolf be looking for by coming to Faerie?"

Phoenix slid her body past Ethan, ignoring his frustrated glare. It wasn't that she didn't appreciate the show of chivalry, but he could get stuffed if he expected her to hide behind him like a scared little girl.

She squared her shoulders and with as much authority as she could muster, declared, "We've been sent by Morrigan. We wish to be brought to Lord Aodhán and Lady Clíodhna."

The ivy-covered fae in front sneered, his companions remaining stony-faced as they held the crossbows pointed unwaveringly at her heart. "You claim the great Goddess sent you here? And who might you be to demand an audience with our Lord and Lady?"

"I'm their granddaughter."

13

Home – 1 day gone

Abi chewed on the jagged edge of her thumbnail as she stared out the window to the sprawling expanse of the pack lands. The weather had taken a turn from clear blue skies and sunshine to an ominous blanket of grey clouds that perfectly matched her mood and the atmosphere in the house.

Six hours and thirteen minutes had passed since Phoenix and Ethan set off for Dunluce Castle. There'd been no news, and as time continued to tick on, her nerves were becoming even more frayed. Most likely they'd crossed over to Faerie by now, but would it really have killed them to send a quick text before they jumped ship to a magical land?

It wasn't getting to just her either; the whole house was on edge. As if the prophecy and Darius weren't enough, the pack had to deal with the shock of Sean's reappearance now too. The strain was painfully visible on

Cormac's and Fia's normally composed features as they talked quietly to Nate on the far side of the living room. The shifter's fingers danced over the keys of his laptop as he concentrated on the screen, giving the occasional nod or grim shake of his head.

Sasha sat quietly beside Abi on the sofa, her playful humour noticeably missing as she stared at the ashes in the unlit fire. More than once Abi had opened her mouth intending to say something reassuring, anything to take the look of pain from those brown eyes, but every time she'd closed it again before ever speaking a word. What could she say? She was only human; she knew nothing.

The rhythmic tapping of Nate's fingers on his keyboard ceased as he blew out a frustrated breath and leaned back into the sofa, scrubbing his hands over his face. "Unless we've missed something on the CCTV cameras around the Dublin clan's lair, Darius hasn't been back there in months. It stands to reason he's hiding out somewhere connected to the clan, but they've more than twenty businesses to their name. And they have an indirect or minority interest in dozens more."

Cormac let a low growl. "We need more information. If we go in gung-ho and start attacking the clan's businesses, it'll just make Darius go deeper underground and we'll never find him."

"So, what, we just sit around and do nothing?" Sasha's composure finally broke and she jumped up from the sofa and started pacing, fists clenched at her side.

Fia moved to put a hand on her daughter's shoulder, but Sasha shrugged her off and sat back down, seeming to deflate. Abi's heart ached for the wolf and she reached out to give Sasha's hand a gentle squeeze.

"That's not what I'm saying." Cormac's eyes were fierce, determined. "We need to be smart about it if we're going to get Sean back. And we *are* going to get him back."

"He'll be okay," Abi quietly reassured Sasha as the wolf gripped her hand. "Sean's survived this long; he can hang on a little bit longer."

Even as she said the words, she wondered if they were true. She could still remember every second of her time as Darius's guest, and it terrified her to even imagine what Sean must be going through. She'd only just managed to survive a few hours with him. How did someone endure years of that torture and still remain sane?

The door to the living room opened, and they all turned as Lucas and Shade strode into the room. At Cormac's questioning look, Lucas shook his head. "I'll keep asking around."

Of all of them, Lucas was the best connected within the vampire networks of the Lore. His clan was well respected, and from what she'd heard, Darius had even been a member of it once upon a time. He'd gone to Lucas seeking a new clan after his own Sire had died and subsequently ended up meeting Marcus, Phoenix's father. It had been a long shot to hope Lucas might be able to track Darius through his connections, but it seemed their avenues were few and far between at the moment and it had been worth a try.

A heavy silence fell over the room, only to be broken by a shrill ringtone.

They all reached for their pockets instinctively, but it was Cormac who pulled out his mobile and sighed. "It's William again."

The wolf head of the Council had been calling incessantly for days. Cormac had been avoiding his cousin, but he'd only be able to do that for so long before the Council lost their patience and decided to stop playing nice.

Once again Cormac moved to decline the call, but Fia put a hand on his arm to stop him. "Maybe you should talk to him? Darius was one of their Witnesses. If they can help us find Sean …"

He hesitated, a muscle twitching in his jaw as he glared at the phone. He gritted his teeth and nodded, slowly bringing it to his ear as he hit the button to answer the call.

Abi didn't need supernatural hearing to catch William's furious tirade on the other end of the phone.

"Where the hell have you been? I've been trying to reach you for days. You know it's an offence to ignore contact from the Council."

Cormac waited until his cousin had paused for breath before asking, "Did you want something?"

Abi watched his expression closely as the conversation settled into a more civilised tone – if Cormac's grunted responses could be considered civilised, or even conversation. His expression remained stony and unchanging, but at some point since getting involved in this crazy world she'd become attuned to the more subtle signs that gave away a person's mood. The darkening of his eyes worried her the most.

"We'll be there," Cormac said after a long silence, and hung up the phone without a goodbye. He looked around the room at the impatient expressions. "We're going to meet the Council."

White-hot rage filled Darius as Erik brought him up to date on the morning's events. He leaned back in his office chair, knuckles whitening when his grip tightened on the crystal tumbler in his hand.

"We've been unable to trace the hybrid," his head of security summed up, expression carefully neutral. "Last known location was Dunluce Castle, then the tracking spell we had on her just stopped working. Our sources confirm there is a gateway to Faerie on the castle grounds. Given our inability to track her, it would seem likely she's crossed over."

Darius took a slow, deliberate sip of his whiskey. He stood, and with a roar flung the tumbler at the window overlooking the heaving dance floor below. The tumbler shattered and golden liquid ran down the glass in rivulets to soak into the plush carpet. Erik waited silently.

"What about the witch who was sent after the hybrid?"

"He's been dealt with."

"Gather the remainder of the coven. It's time they understand the price of their failures." Too often now he'd overlooked the coven's mistakes. Mistakes that could cost him everything he'd worked for. Well, no more.

Erik gave a sharp nod and left to see to the arrangements. Darius waited until the door clicked closed, then made his way to the mahogany desk and pulled open the top drawer. Faded red velvet lined its interior and a scroll rested inside. Carefully, he lifted it out.

The scroll was ancient, made of vellum that had long ago been preserved by magic. The flowing words were as clear now as the day they were written, and he soaked them in as he unrolled the scroll.

Terror, destruction, death to man.
The fires of hell o'ertake the land.
So long as she alone shall stand,
Shall the Horsemen walk the land.

These words were his destiny. These words had shown him the way to restore the Lore to its former glory. He would do what his Sire had not been able to; he wouldn't succumb to weakness and death.

An icy calm settled over him as he rolled the scroll back up and returned it to its resting place. A thin haze of red clouded his vision as he strode from the office and made his way down to the lowest level.

Seven witches remained in the Dublin coven, and Erik had them all lined up and waiting by the time Darius reached the laboratory. Vampires stood on either side of them, and a heavy silence filled the room. The tension tasted bitter on his tongue and he noted more than one finger or eye twitch from the instinctive need to draw

98

magic. It wouldn't matter though – their magic wouldn't save them now.

He assessed the witches one at a time. A mere three of the seven were brave enough to look him in the eye, and only one of those managed to maintain a stony composure while doing so.

"One of your witches has put me in a very difficult position." He kept his tone conversational as he addressed them. "Because of him, a key element of our plan is now out of my reach, putting everything we've worked for at risk. I'm sure you'll agree, that is simply not acceptable. Now …" He paused to steeple his fingers as he paced. "I will give you each a chance to rectify this unfortunate situation. The one who provides me with a solution gets to live. The rest of you die." His smile was cold as he looked at them expectantly.

"But – but – You need us," a tall man in the middle stammered. His face was a mask of shock and beads of sweat dotted his forehead.

Darius regarded him for a moment, then, in a blur of movement tore his throat out with his razor-sharp fangs. He pulled a handkerchief from his pocket and dabbed delicately at the blood running down his chin before turning to address the remaining witches.

"Make no mistake in believing you're indispensable. Your coven has grown weak. I've kept you here out of convenience to me, but I grow tired of your incompetence. There is another coven is already lined up to take your place, and if you wish to be alive to join them, I suggest you get creative."

The next to open their mouth was a female witch. She lost her life when his fist ripped her heart from her chest cavity. The stammering terror of another two witches pissed him off enough that he didn't even give them a chance to speak before he tore them to shreds. One of the three remaining witches was foolish enough to draw on his magic and was buried under a pile of vampire guards in a feeding frenzy.

Two remained: a cocky-looking man that reminded him of a lawyer, and the stony-faced witch, a woman barely five feet tall.

The man opened his mouth to speak but broke off in a choked gurgle. The woman at his side quirked a lip and raised an eyebrow at Darius. Her magic skittered over his skin even as the man at her side turned a worrying shade of purple and fell to his knees.

The guards moved to subdue the female witch, but Darius held up his hand, halting their movement. "Someone with initiative. I like that."

"I don't plan on dying for other people's incompetence."

"Well then, let's hope you have an acceptable solution for me."

The witch considered him, no trace of fear in her steely gaze. "I can't give you the hybrid. If the rumours are true and she has passed over to Faerie, no witch can; that magic is beyond our reach and any who tell you otherwise are lying to you. But I can offer you a possible alternative to the prophecy."

Darius waited for her to continue, his curiosity peaked.

"The Horsemen need the fabric to fall completely in order to cross into our world in corporeal form, but their essence does not. If the prophecy was to fail – say, for example, due to a particular child being born – there will be a pivotal moment during which our world and theirs collide. If we can time this precisely, I can use the point of collision to draw their essence into this world. All I need is a vessel."

"A vessel? Someone to hold the Horsemen within them?"

The witch nodded. "The vessel would not hold indefinitely; the Horsemen's power is too immense and would destroy the body before long. But it would buy us time."

"Time for what?"

"Time to reverse the original spell and free them back into this world. With or without the prophecy."

Darius pivoted on his heel and paced the length of the laboratory, stepping over the fallen body of one of the witches. A solution that didn't require reliance on the prophecy was awfully tempting, but when something seemed too good to be true it usually was.

"I see one very large flaw in your suggestion." The witch raised an eyebrow and waited. "The timing of the child's birth is impossible to predict."

The witch gave him a satisfied smile. "Not if we decide the timing ourselves. With the right ingredients, I can create an elixir that will speed the progress of the hybrid's pregnancy and induce labour."

"And how do you propose that we get her to take such an elixir, given she's currently out of our reach?"

"A powerful man such as yourself must have some connections who are open to a more ... enlightened way of thinking. It would be a simple matter of getting some assistance."

He considered this. The fae were notoriously difficult to deal with, and his influence with them was a lot more limited than some of the other species – like the witches. However, he now conveniently had the head of the CLO at his disposal, and Vicktor had become infinitely more agreeable following his demonic upgrade. It stood to reason that the CLO rep would have some connections that could be of use to them. Darius knew enough about the power structure of Faerie to know that many of the high-ranking fae were not above temptation.

"If it's as simple as convincing someone in Faerie to assist us in giving Phoenix an elixir, why then would we not just give her one to end the pregnancy?"

The witch shrugged. "It could be done if you wished, though I would have thought you were more forward thinking than that."

Darius grew deathly still. The vampires in the room shifted nervously, but the witch continued, unphased by the obvious threat of death that was but a hair's breadth from her.

"If you force a termination of the pregnancy, it will indeed remove the current obstacle to the prophecy. But what of the next obstacle, and the one after that? There is still a significant amount of time to pass before the prophecy reaches its conclusion. Why wait, when you can control the outcome once and for all?"

14

Faerie – day 1

Phoenix followed the fae guards in silence, Ethan sticking close to her side. Her father's sword was a comforting weight across her back, though the fact they'd allowed her to keep a weapon was concerning.

There were no more terrifying shrieks as they walked, and the forest was suspiciously quiet. She scanned her surroundings warily, not fooled by the sudden calm. The path out of the trees was so straightforward that she was convinced the landscape had to be shifting to accommodate them. A ridiculous thought, really, but given Faerie was an unknown entity to them, it was entirely possible.

They emerged from the trees to stop in front of a towering stone wall. It ran as far as her eye could see in both directions, and guards patrolled the battlements at the top. Many sported a more traditional bow and arrow than the crossbows carried by the three fae surrounding her, and others carried what appeared to be long, coiled whips. Each looked more than capable of dealing with a potential intruder, though she had to imagine that the wall itself acted as sufficient deterrent to most.

Just as she was wondering how far they'd need to trek to find an opening in said wall, the lead guard stepped forward and placed his hand against the stone. He bowed his head and spoke so quietly that even with her enhanced hearing, she couldn't make out his words. A section of the wall dissolved, and an archway formed. A cobblestone path led into the distance, bordered on either side by rolling lawns of green and gold.

"Don't stray from the path," the guard with the ivy skin warned, giving them an accusing glare before leading them through the arch.

Phoenix exchanged an uneasy look with Ethan but followed without a word.

A large building loomed in the distance, its opulence so apparent even from afar that it could only be considered a castle. Beautifully ornate turrets framed huge panes of glass that glistened like crystal in the sun. Oak trees larger than any she'd ever seen before bookended the building on either side and seemed to meld into the walls. Thick branches snaked out from the trees and reached towards each other, making it look as if the castle had sprouted up from the centre of one giant tree.

Despite the knot of apprehension that was twisting in her gut, Phoenix couldn't help but stare in awe. *So, this is Faerie?*

Of course, it was easier to focus on the unusual scenery than the fact they really were in another world now. Alone and away from their family and friends. She took a shaky breath and forced the thought away as they drew closer to the castle.

Stone steps led up to two large oak doors that opened, seemingly of their own accord, at the group's approach. A long hallway led from the entrance, boasting a plush cream carpet that was so spotless Phoenix could only assume the fae were capable of hovering. Vines of ivy wound along the walls and across the ceiling, giving the effect of a long green tunnel.

She hesitated at the top of the steps for a moment before following the others across the threshold. The doors slammed shut behind her and she jumped, heart ricocheting in her chest.

Ethan put a hand on her back, his brown eyes searching her face for confirmation that she was okay. She gave him a small smile which might have been more of a grimace, then followed the fae guards, grateful for the comfort of his touch.

A gentle breeze blew through the interior, and Phoenix could have sworn she heard the chirping of birds. She eyed the vines of ivy, expecting them to close around her at any moment, as the ones in the forest had. When another pair of wooden doors came into view at the end of the hall, she hurried her steps with relief.

These doors didn't open in welcome as the first ones had. Instead, two sentinels dressed entirely in black stood on either side of the doors, hands clasped behind their backs, steely gazes focused ahead. The ivy guard broke from their group and stepped forward to speak with the one on the right.

The sentinel's silver eyes locked on Phoenix as he listened, his face blank. She wondered if he was going to simply stare at her, but after some consideration, he turned and slipped between the doors.

"Now what?" She clasped her hands together in an attempt to stop from fidgeting.

"Now you wait," the ivy fae answered coolly.

Minutes passed, each one feeling like an hour. Finally, the sentinel returned, his expression no friendlier. He held open one of the doors and indicated for them to enter. "Lord Aodhán and Lady Clíodhna will speak with you."

Phoenix's palms were sweaty as she stepped into a cavernous room with Ethan close by her side. Butterfly arches drew her gaze upwards to a ceiling that sparkled as if encrusted with diamonds. The cream carpet from the hallway continued down a long aisle, bordered on either side with rows of empty chairs. It came to a stop at a raised platform that boasted two large thrones carved into the ashen bark of a tree that rose upwards and disappeared from sight. Both thrones were occupied.

On the right, a slender woman with strawberry-blonde hair sat with her hands folded primly in the lap of her flowing green dress. Her expression was one of cold calculation, but there were enough similarities to her mother that Phoenix instantly recognised her grandmother, Clíodhna.

The other throne was occupied by a man with shoulder-length grey hair and a face that seemed experienced rather than old. His gaze was piercing, and from his assured posture and broad shoulders alone she could see he had an imposing presence. So, this was her grandfather.

A strange numbness wrapped itself around her as she stepped forward to address them both. "My name is Phoenix. My mother was Aria McGrath."

Silence.

"Was?" Aodhán asked eventually, his expression giving no indication of his thoughts.

Phoenix froze as a chilling realisation hit her: they didn't know her mother was dead.

"She … I mean …" Her throat constricted and the words refused to leave her lips.

Ethan stepped forward. He lowered his head respectfully but didn't take his eyes from Aodhán. "We regret to inform you that your daughter, Aria, has met her final death. She died nobly and saved many lives, including her daughter's and my own."

Phoenix cast her eyes down, but not before she caught her grandfather's flinch. She didn't want to see her grandparents' reaction; whether she was afraid of witnessing their pain or a lack of grief, she wasn't quite sure. But the very fact she had to question it made her angry in a way that she had no words for. Aria had been their child, and she didn't even know if they cared.

"And who might you be?" Clíodhna demanded, her voice betraying no reaction to the news of their daughter as she addressed Ethan.

"I am Ethan Ryan, son of the Donegal Alpha, and friend to your grandchild."

"Our grandchild." Clíodhna sounded the word out slowly as if it was difficult to say. "This is what you claim to be," she said, turning her cool gaze on Phoenix. "But how do we know you speak true?"

Phoenix forced herself to look up, taking in the paleness of her grandmother's skin, and pinched lips. "Why would we risk our safety to come here and lie to you? My mother was fae. She was your flesh and blood. My father was the vampire you banished her for loving."

"You know nothing of the choices we made." Clíodhna's eyes flashed with anger – her first real show of emotion.

Aodhán, who had been quiet since the news of his daughter's passing, placed a hand on her arm for a moment and stood. His tone was reserved when he spoke, but the tension in his body was clear. "We fae are bound to speak only the truth, but that is not the case for others, so you must forgive our scepticism. Though it's true your signature is different than any I've ever encountered, never in the history of the Lore has there been a vampire offspring, let alone a mixed species as you claim to be. Do you have any proof of what you speak?"

She'd expected this, of course, but still Phoenix had to swallow back the bitterness that burned her throat like bile. Reaching under the collar of her top, she pulled out her mother's pendant, ever close to her heart. "My mother's medallion, engraved with our family emblem."

Clíodhna arched a single, unimpressed eyebrow.

Not waiting for the dismissal of evidence she knew would come, Phoenix reached over her shoulder and grasped the hilt of her father's sword. Slowly, so as to appear as non-threatening as possible, she slid the blade from its scabbard and held it flat across her open palms.

"And I believe you may recognise Claíomh Solais."

Clíodhna gasped, leaning forward in her throne even as her hands gripped the armrests. Aodhán became deathly still, gaze riveted on the blade in her hands. Phoenix held her breath and made a conscious effort not to move.

Disbelief and shock passed over her grandfather's face as he stepped down from the raised platform and walked towards her. He stopped just out of reach of the sword, but he was close enough for her to see the pain darkening his violet eyes.

"I gave this to Aria when she reached her immortality," he said quietly. "She ... Your mother gave it to you?"

"She gave it to my father as a symbol of her love and commitment. It was his prized possession."

"You lie," Clíodhna declared, her icy tone cutting. "That is a fae weapon, passed down from the Tuatha Dé Danann themselves. It would never have allowed itself to be possessed by another species."

Anger twisted once more inside Phoenix. "Perhaps the sword doesn't hold the same prejudices you do."

"Enough." Aodhán's didn't raise his voice but the command in his tone was clear. "My lady does not mean any offence. She is speaking the truth as we understand it. If your father owned this sword as you say, then my daughter's love for him must truly have been something of magic." He paused, seeming to deflate. "You have her eyes."

Phoenix swallowed and clung tightly to the anger; it was preferable to the confused mix of emotions cloying for her attention. A heavy silence hung in the air for a moment. Then Aodhán cleared his throat and straightened, composing himself.

"What brings you to Faerie, my child?"

Phoenix hesitated. Morrigan had warned them about revealing her pregnancy, but what about the prophecy? Would her family also decide that killing her was the best way to prevent it? Her blood ran cold with fear, and when she glanced at Ethan, she could see the same concern shadowing his face.

"My parents were betrayed by someone they believed to be their friend," she said eventually. "Because of him, they were forced to sacrifice themselves to save us. This man now wants me, and will stop at nothing until he gets what he wants. Morrigan promised me I'd be safe here." She'd promised no such thing of course, only that it was the lesser of the evils. "Will you, my family, refuse us sanctuary in our time of need?"

Her grandfather gave a subtle jerk at the accusation in her tone, and Ethan sucked in a breath beside her. Too far? Well, tough shit. These people may be related to her by blood, but they had yet to give her any reason to forgive them for what they had done to her mother.

"You will have your sanctuary," Clíodhna's cool voice came from where she remained seated in her throne. "We would not turn away a child of our blood for the sins of the mother."

Ethan's hand grasped Phoenix's arm and squeezed gently in warning. She bit down on her tongue and focused on the stinging pain as she inclined her head in acknowledgement of her grandmother's words.

Her grandfather watched her closely, his shrewd gaze seeming to peer straight through to her soul. It was clear from his guarded expression that he believed she was holding something back, but he too nodded. "I would like to learn more about my grandchild." His eyes darkened, turning a stormy black. "And I would like to know more about the man responsible for my daughter's death."

A shiver ran through Phoenix at the calm tone that held more threat than any degree of anger would have. A part of her relished the thought of sending this powerful fae leader to deal with Darius, but some small voice in the back of her head warned that, as powerful as he may be, he wouldn't survive.

She was saved from responding when the door behind them opened and a woman with vibrant orange hair strode into the room, her face obscured by the clipboard she carried. "Mother, the convoy from Darkhaven have sent another message requesting an audience –"

The woman came to an abrupt halt as she looked up and realised there were others present in the room. "I'm sorry, I didn't mean to interrupt."

Phoenix took in the woman's face and her knees buckled. She crumpled to the floor, hands cupped around her mouth to hold in a breathless cry as she stared at a face that haunted her dreams. The face of her mother.

15

Faerie – day 1

Phoenix couldn't take her eyes from her mother's twin as she and Ethan followed Aoife out of the room, leaving her grandparents behind. She'd known Aria had a sister, of course, but the stark resemblance still came as a shock. A deep ache filled her chest and settled in the gaping hole that had been left in her heart with her parents' death.

There were differences between the sisters once you looked closer than a cursory glance. Aoife's eyes were green like her mother's had been, but less vibrant somehow, as if the mischievous sparkle was missing. And though her face was the same shape as Aria's, there was a sharpness to Aoife's features that made her seem older. She also showcased her pointed ears proudly, something Phoenix had rarely seen her mother do, even in the privacy of their own home.

"You'll have to forgive my mother for such an abrupt dismissal." Aoife looked back over her shoulder with a smile. "The court demands a lot of her attention. At times it can make her seem unapproachable."

"I can't really say she gave me the warm and fuzzies," Phoenix muttered, eliciting a laugh from her aunt.

"No, she's certainly not known for that."

"What role does your family play in the fae courts?" Ethan asked as they came to a large foyer with marble floors and a sweeping staircase.

He'd been quiet through much of Phoenix's conversation with her grandparents, careful not to encroach on her authority within the situation. But she'd been grateful to have him at her side – even more so after the shock of meeting Aoife.

"Many believe the Faerie courts can be viewed simply as Seelie and Unseelie, light and dark. But that's far from the case. Seven courts make up our political structure, and each play a role in maintaining the tenuous balance of rule. Our family …" She paused and looked at Phoenix somewhat wistfully. "We are direct descendants of the Tuatha Dé Danann. We preside over a significant portion of the fae, and as such, my parents have the pleasure of babysitting the other rulers who would happily tear each other's throats out. It's a rather thankless job."

Unimpressed by the strains of her grandparents' positions, Phoenix followed Aoife up the stairs and down several winding corridors. Stained-glass windows lined one wall, turning the path into a kaleidoscope of colours. At random intervals Aoife pointed out rooms and areas of note: the kitchen and family dining area, a large library

113

filled with ancient tomes, and her grandparents' private quarters, should she ever wish to speak with them.

At the end of one long corridor, Aoife came to a stop in front of a mahogany door. "I hope you'll find the room comfortable," she said, opening the door to reveal a spacious bedroom filled with a four-poster bed covered in the plushest cushions Phoenix had ever seen. "My mother has arranged a dinner for us all this evening, if you would both honour us with your presence."

Phoenix nodded, hoping her face didn't show just how unappealing the invitation sounded. She moved to go into the room, but Aoife placed a hand gently on her arm, stopping her.

"Did she have a happy life?"

Phoenix looked at her aunt, momentarily puzzled by the question.

Aoife pulled her hand back and cast her eyes to the floor. "Aria and I weren't close the way you'd imagine twins to be. In truth, I spent a lot of our childhood jealous of her. She had a special bond with our father; his golden girl who never seemed to do any wrong. While I on the other hand …" She gave a small smile. "Well, let's just say it came as a surprise to us all when she was the one standing before them for punishment. I always wondered what became of her after … I hoped she was happy."

"My father made sure she was." Phoenix swallowed, unable to say anything more than that. The resemblance to her mother made it impossible for her to cause her aunt pain, but it just wasn't in her at that moment to soothe her family's guilt. Even if Aoife hadn't been the one to banish Aria from their family, she'd stood by and allowed it to happen.

"You will join us for dinner?" Aoife asked softly as Phoenix slipped past her into the room.

Phoenix swallowed again and nodded, a throbbing headache starting to form behind her eyes.

Ethan made to follow her into the room but her aunt looked at him with a smile, seeming to compose herself once more. "Your room is down the next hallway. Come, I'll show you the way."

Ethan took a large gulp from his crystal goblet as he cast another surreptitious glance towards the entranceway to the dining room. Where the hell was Phoenix? A guard had summoned him from his room when it was time for dinner, as he assumed one had for her. But when he'd arrived at the family dining hall, he found only Aodhán, Clíodhna, and Aoife waiting. He'd been making polite small talk for nearly fifteen minutes and was running out of safe topics to discuss.

Much of the room was filled by a magnificent oak table surrounded with six high-back chairs covered in soft, green velvet. The table looked as if it had been carved straight from the heart of a tree and highlighted the intricate patterns of the wood grain beautifully. A masterpiece of a flower arrangement had been placed at the centre of the table. The flower petals sparkled like diamonds under the lights and the blooms moved in a way that made them seem alive. He had to give it the fae – they really knew how to make their décor magical.

"So, what brings a wolf to my grandchild's side, and to Faerie?" Aodhán's shrewd gaze assessed him as he took a drink from his own goblet.

Ethan met his gaze, letting the man see the truth of his words. "Phoenix has been a loyal friend and ally. Her safety is important to me."

"In what matters have you required her allegiance?" Clíodhna's cool tone made no attempt to disguise the suspicion that had tinged her every question since he'd sat down.

"She –"

"Sorry I'm late." Phoenix stumbled into the dining room, out of breath and a little flustered. "I got lost."

The filthy clothes she'd been wearing previously had been replaced by a flowing emerald-green dress which accented her eyes, and she looked as uncomfortable in it as Ethan felt in the tunic that had been brought to his room.

He stood and pulled a chair out for her, noticing the slightly green tinge to her pallor, and the dark shadows under her eyes. She gave a grateful smile but avoided his concerned look as she sat down.

"I hope I haven't missed anything important?"

"I was just getting to know your acquaintance," her grandfather responded, with a pointed look at Ethan. "It seems you've managed to make some powerful friends."

"Now, father," Aoife interjected with a frown. "I'm sure the last thing Phoenix and Ethan need is the third degree from you after the day they've had. Let us enjoy

116

our meal and celebrate the discovery of new family and friends." She raised her goblet in salute.

Ethan followed her lead and took a sip of his own drink, the heady spices and rich aroma titillating his senses. He generally preferred beer, but this wine was unlike any he had ever tasted before.

Beside him Phoenix raised her goblet as well, but placed it back down on the table without taking a drink. Her left hand rested on her lap and he noticed the twitch of her fingers as they seemed to be drawn to touch her stomach. He couldn't even imagine how unnatural it must feel for her to have to conceal something as huge as the child growing inside her.

Two fae males and two females bustled into the dining room laden with trays bearing every food imaginable. They were all silent as the lushest fruits and most succulent meats were laid out before them. The mouth-watering aroma of freshly baked bread filled the room even before the loaves came into sight. Ethan's stomach growled and he suddenly realised he hadn't eaten since they left Donegal.

Aoife gave him a bright smile. "Help yourself," she said before proceeding to fill her own plate.

He reached over to pick up a silver platter filled with juicy chicken legs and was about to offer it to Phoenix when he saw her complexion turn a worrying shade of green. Swiftly changing course, he grabbed a basket of bread rolls instead and placed one on her plate. She gave him a smile that was close to being a grimace and accepted some plump strawberries from him too before a subtle shake of her head warned she was at her limit.

His own plate full, he turned to Clíodhna with his most charming smile. "This all looks amazing. You honour us with your hospitality."

She arched an eyebrow. "Did you think we'd do otherwise?" Her eagle-eyed gaze zeroed in on Phoenix, who was picking forlornly at her bread roll but not eating. "You need not fear, child. We aren't trying to trap you here by feeding you the fruits of Faerie."

Phoenix's cheeks flushed. "Oh, no, I —"

"Or is blood more to your liking?"

"My Lord." Ethan turned to Aodhán before Phoenix could respond. "I'm curious about something you mentioned today. You said it was your understanding that a fae weapon could only be wielded by a fae. Forgive my ignorance, but as a child I heard of many great battles fought and won using fae weapons, often in the hands of other species. Are those stories little more than myths?"

The question had bothered him all day. Not because it shattered any childhood illusions he might have had, but if what Aodhán had said was true, what did it mean for their search for the spear?

Phoenix already possessed the sword, so it was possible her part-fae blood would be sufficient to wield the spear. But the sword had also belonged to Marcus, so maybe it held to different rules? He'd like to believe Morrigan wouldn't have set them a task they had no hope of completing, but then what did he actually know about the goddess?

"Some are myths, though many were borne from true events," Aodhán answered. "I assume you're familiar with the story of the Horsemen's banishment from the human realm?"

Ethan fought to keep the surprise from his face as he nodded.

"The four treasures of the Tuatha Dé Danann were used as part of the banishment ritual. In fact," Aodhán looked at Phoenix, "the sword you now carry is the very same blade that was used all those millennia ago. That is the last time, to our knowledge, that a fae weapon has allowed itself to be possessed and wielded by another species. And I think you'll find that's when the stories ended too."

"So, what happened?" Phoenix asked, perking up in her curiosity.

Aodhán's violet eyes darkened. "One of the treasures was stolen from us. After the ritual was complete, it was discovered that the cauldron of Dagda was missing. All were questioned – some even tortured – but it was never found. Maab was the Council head of the fae at the time and was not known for her benevolence. She saw the situation as a betrayal and crafted a curse that would prevent fae weapons from ever again coming to the aid of a non-fae."

Phoenix frowned, her brow furrowing. "Obviously something must have changed if my mother was able to pass the sword on to my father?"

"Perhaps, though I know not what. The cauldron has never been recovered, and though Maab is no longer the head of the fae, the magic she used to fuel the curse is ancient and formidable."

Maybe the magic knows something we don't. Ethan mulled over this new information as he took a sip of his wine. Morrigan had told them the cauldron was safe and that it would be returned when the time came. Had she always known where it was? If so, that would mean she kept it from the fae intentionally, and he wondered at her reasons.

The table lapsed into silence as each of them indulged in their fill of food – Phoenix's fill being little more than a cursory nibble or two so as not to draw further attention to herself. When they finished, Aoife gave them a kind smile. "I expect you'll want to get an early night so that you're well rested for the gala tomorrow."

Ethan glanced at Phoenix in question, but she just gave a confused shrug in answer. So he asked Aoife, "What gala?"

It was Clíodhna that responded in her clipped tone. "The gala to present Phoenix to the fae gentry, of course."

Phoenix froze, doing a remarkable impression of a deer caught in headlights.

He cleared his throat, attempting to keep his tone polite and reasonable. "We've had to pack rather lightly for our journey to Faerie. I'm afraid we wouldn't have anything suitable to wear to such an event."

Clíodhna pinned him with a steely gaze. "Our tailors have already been provided with your sizes." She indicated pointedly to the fresh clothes he and Phoenix wore. "It's all been arranged."

16

Home – 2 days gone

"Tell me again why we're entertaining this shit show," Shade muttered as his eyes skirted the cliff edge where he waited with Lucas and Cormac. The Atlantic Ocean crashed against the rock face below them, vicious and unrelenting. At this height the air was cutting, and the longer they had to stand around waiting, the more pissed off he got.

It had taken less than half an hour to drive the winding roads from the pack lands to the top of the cliff where they now stood in the middle of a wide stone circle. The area was one of many dotted around the country that was considered neutral territory by the Lore. The circle had long ago been warded with powerful magics to ensure no blood could be spilled within its boundaries. But magic or no magic, he felt as if they had glaring targets on their backs. And hey, words could hurt too.

"We can't face Darius alone." Lucas scanned the darkness with equal wariness. "We need the Council's help if we're to have any chance of getting Sean back."

"And we're meant to just believe their sudden change of heart?"

When Cormac had agreed to meet with the Council, they'd all felt that keeping close to the pack's territory was the best option – it wouldn't look good for the Council to attack them here when the local pack Alpha was meeting in good faith.

But considering the Council had tried to wipe out the pack once before, Shade had trouble reining in his usual scepticism.

Before Lucas could answer, the air in front of them shimmered and two figures materialised. The power that emanated from them was almost suffocating, and Shade sneered as he took in the red robes of the Council. William and Kam stepped forward into the moonlight, hoods down so that their faces were clearly visible. There was a tense silence as the wolf and shifter heads of the Council stepped across the boundary of the circle.

"Cousin." William greeted Cormac before nodding to Shade and Lucas in acknowledgement. "We had hoped the hybrid might join us for tonight's meeting."

Of course you did. Shade bit back the words but kept his scowl firmly in place as he watched the two men closely.

"I'm afraid *Phoenix* isn't available right now." The pointed emphasis Cormac placed on "the hybrid's" name didn't go unnoticed, and William bristled at the correction.

122

Kam placed a hand on William's arm in warning. "I believe William has explained to you that our position regarding Phoenix has been reviewed. We mean her no harm. In fact, we are here to offer her our protection."

"Bit fucking late for that." This time Shade couldn't keep the words to himself, and when Lucas gave him a censoring look, he glared right back.

Cormac, who had been quiet since their arrival at the meeting point, didn't look too impressed with the declaration either. He raised an eyebrow and crossed his arms over his chest, causing his biceps to bulge. "So kind of you to quell your bloodlust. Might we enquire as to what led to this change of heart?"

"We know about the baby." William's words caused them all to freeze, and the air became charged as they all regarded each other evenly.

"We sent a messenger to explain the situation and extend our offer of protection," Kam explained, his soft voice cutting through the tense silence. "When we realised he didn't make it to you, we began trying to contact you ourselves. We would have done so in person, but we were concerned it would mistakenly be seen as an act of aggression, given recent events."

Shade's disbelief expressed itself as a derisive snort. "So, you're done trying to kill us and now you want to be best buddies?"

"Hardly." William gave him a patronising look and Shade barely resisted the urge to give him the middle finger.

Lucas spread his arms wide in a placating gesture. "I think it's understandable why we wouldn't be willing to reveal Phoenix's location to you." His tone, though polite, held an edge of steel that brokered no room for negotiation on the matter. "We do, however, have a common enemy, and it would be in all our interests to work together."

"What enemy is it you speak of?" Kam assessed the vampire with a thoughtful look.

"One of your Witnesses has been working hard to ensure this prophecy comes to pass."

"He's taken someone of mine," Cormac interjected. "I want him back."

William and Kam glanced at each other, their blank expressions giving nothing away. But Kam's voice was low and deadly when he asked, "What Witness?"

"His name is Darius," Lucas answered. "Long ago he was a member of my clan and is now the head of the Dublin vampire clan. He was sired by one of your predecessors on the Council – Il Maestro."

A low growl rumbled from William's throat and Cormac met his cousin's eyes, jaw set in a tense line. "He has my Omega, William."

The wolf head of the Council froze, and pain flashed behind his eyes. Shade had never quite understood the structure of a werewolf pack – the thought of being so tightly bound to others made his skin crawl – but he'd seen how much Cormac cared for the wolves under his charge. And if the role of Omega was as important as he'd been led to believe, only a heartless wolf could feel indifferent to Cormac's predicament.

There was another tense silence as William digested the news. Something ancient and terrifying swirled in

Kam's dark eyes despite his otherwise outward calm, and it was he who finally spoke.

"Darius has come to our attention recently for a reason more personal to the Council. We too would like to speak with him, but ... Well, we've been unable to locate him. Our enquiries with the Dublin vampire clan indicate that he's no longer in charge there, and they claim to have no knowledge of his whereabouts."

"Bullshit!" All eyes swung to Shade and he shrugged. "Well, it is. There's no way he'd just walk away from the clan and give up all that power."

Kam inclined his head. "Eloquently put. Yes, we believe this is unlikely also. But the Council is bound to act within the confines of our laws, and without proof that Darius is still involved in the clan, we've been limited in the steps we can take against them. If what you say is true about Darius's role in the prophecy, we may have grounds to take emergency measures that enable us to conduct a more in-depth investigation into the clan's affairs."

"What about Sean?" Cormac interrupted. "Darius has been holding him against his will. We need to get him out. Now."

"It would seem that the best way to help your Omega might be to determine Darius's location. As I said, we've had no luck doing that to date. We are, however, willing to work together to resolve this situation as quickly as possible."

Shade could tell from the subtle drop of Cormac's shoulders that the Alpha had been hoping for something more concrete than a game of Where's Wally. It didn't bode well that the Council hadn't been able to track Darius, but then again, they'd been oblivious to everything he'd been doing thus far. Maybe they just needed stronger motivation.

"There's something else you should know," Lucas said, voice sombre. "We believe Darius is actively arranging the demonic possession of Supes."

And there it was.

Kam's eyes darkened. A wave of power rolled off him that seemed to suck the oxygen from the circle. The wards flared a bright white for a split second before fading. His voice was carefully even when he asked, "What makes you think this?"

"They sent one for Phoenix. A wolf with red eyes and a strangely tainted signature. He was stronger than a normal Supe. If it wasn't for some outside assistance, things might have gone very badly."

William's nostrils flared at the mention of the wolf and his frown etched deep lines into his face. Kam appeared troubled, though Shade couldn't have said exactly what it was that made him think that since the shifter's expression never changed.

"That is concerning indeed," Kam said finally. "Reports of demon activity have been increasing on a weekly basis, but it is early days yet in the prophecy timeline. The barrier should still be strong enough that only minor demons are crossing over. We didn't expect to be dealing with possession of our own for a number of months yet."

Shade thought back to Darius's previous attempts at manipulating the timeline. It was unlikely the vampire had become any more patient with his recent failures. "How bad can this thing get?" he asked.

There was a weariness that defied age in Kam's eyes when the shifter met his gaze. "When the Horsemen last walked this world, it took all of our strongest people working together to stop them. Not all of them survived, and some might have been better if they hadn't. Our Seer believes that the child can prevent this, but if it doesn't …"

"Then we're back to you trying to kill Phoenix."

"It would be the only way."

"What if we recreate the ritual that banished the Horsemen? Reinstate the barrier?" Lucas asked.

"Until the Horsemen cross over into this plane of existence, the ritual would simply buy us time by reinforcing the barrier. It would not stop the prophecy. Besides, I'm afraid we no longer have the means to recreate the ritual. Four key artefacts are required for the spell, one of which was long ago stolen. Your hybrid freed the only man who may have been able to tell us where it is."

Shade frowned, thinking back to what Morrigan had said about the artefacts. According to her, Phoenix had the sword, the stone was somewhere here in Ireland, and Phoenix and Ethan were to bring the spear back from Faerie. That only left the cauldron, and Morrigan had said she had that under control. So, who was Kam talking about?

He looked at the shifter, light dawning. "The Mists."

Kam nodded solemnly. "The ritual requires power from all the species. The Mists assisted us in banishing the Horsemen, but afterwards, Shayan, the youngest of the three, betrayed us by taking Dagda's Cauldron. We've never been able to ascertain why, nor has the threat of ultimate death persuaded him to divulge its location."

"You forced his family into centuries of slavery because he wouldn't tell you." It wasn't a question, and Cormac shook his head in disgust, turning away from the two Council members before either could answer or justify.

Kam didn't flinch or show any signs of remorse at the accusation, but William shifted slightly, looking away uneasily.

Diplomatic to the end, Lucas forced the attention back to the problem at hand. "Let's assume we can get the cauldron, and the assistance of the Mists. Will you aid us in completing the ritual if it's needed?"

"You don't believe the child will be born in time?" Kam asked.

"I don't believe in relying on chance. Will you stand with us or not?"

17

Home – 5 days gone

Darius stared through magically reinforced glass into the small white chamber. A single occupant crouched in the centre of the room, bonds of silver chain glistening where they were bolted to the floor. Blood coated wiry muscle and dirt matted shaggy white hair. The Omega was deathly still.

"Has there been any change?" Darius turned to Erik, who stood beside him, hands clasped behind his back.

"None. He still has moments of lucidity despite the strength of the demon possessing him. Last night he managed to partially shift and almost clawed his own face off before we could tranq him."

When Darius looked through the viewing glass again, red eyes stared at him through the hair that obscured Sean's face. There was no emotion in them, only the chilling calculation of the demon. But he'd seen the footage for himself; some part of the Omega remained inside the shell and fought back against the possession. It was unprecedented in all their trials to date.

"How did he manage to shift with the silver shackling him?"

"We don't know. He shouldn't have been able to. Tests confirm that silver is still as detrimental to him as it was before the possession. It's possible the regeneration ability of his demon element is mitigating the damage in some way."

"Interesting." Darius gave one final glance into the white room before turning to walk down the sterile white corridor, Erik keeping step with him. "Keep him under control however you need to. He may still be of use to us yet, and I don't want him finding a way to kill himself before I've decided what to do with him."

They made their way through the pharmaceutical complex to the front lobby, an odd mix of disinfectant, bleach, and herbs drifting to them from the various laboratories. Men and women in white lab coats nodded at them as they passed, barely looking up from their clipboards.

The humans who worked in the complex were well aware of the supernatural presence that surrounded them. He had to admire their arrogance; the only time they batted an eyelid to the situation was when a test subject ended up underneath their microscope.

He'd purchased the floundering pharmaceutical company under an alias twenty-five years earlier when it had become clear that the time had come to make preparations. With a bit of financial backing and some … motivation, the company had quickly become one of the top players in the field of genetic engineering. Some of the less savoury trials he'd kept off site until recently, but the facility offered the perfect space he needed to house his growing army.

"We have another problem." Erik handed him a letter with a familiar emblem in the top corner. "The Council have frozen the clan's assets. It seems that they have grounds for an investigation into the clan's affairs, whether or not we currently claim association with you. Our lawyers are dealing with it, but it's making business difficult to say the least."

Darius clenched his teeth. He wasn't afraid of the Council, or their so-called influence, but he had too much to do right now to humour such interference. He considered his options as he watched a sleek black Mercedes pull up in front of the glass doors of the building.

"Perhaps the Council need something better to do with their time than bothering hard-working members of the Lore," he mused. "We still have the more unruly transfer subjects contained, correct?" At last count Darius was aware of close to fifty subjects who had survived the demon transfer but proved too difficult to be controlled to add to the ranks of their army. The worst of these had been detained in a secure part of the facility until he was ready to make a decision on their fate.

Erik nodded.

"Release them. I want them sent to Brussels. I've heard the neighbourhoods around the Council headquarters are some of the safest areas to live in the world. Let's see if we can rectify that, shall we?"

Erik's lips twitched, but his expression remained serious. "If you do this, you know it'll show your hand? They will double their efforts to find you; it will only be a matter of time before they come."

"And when they do, we'll be ready for them."

With that, Darius strode outside to the cool night and waiting car. He opened the rear door and slid into the leather seat beside Vicktor.

"Well?"

Vicktor's smile was as smarmy as it had always been, but there was a cunning calculation in his red eyes that belied the new intelligence behind them. "I believe we've found a member of the fae gentry sympathetic to our cause. They are aware of the hybrid's presence in Faerie and have agreed to monitor her on our behalf while the witch makes the necessary preparations."

"Very good." Things were finally starting to go right. Darius leaned back in the seat with a satisfied smile. "Take us to the club," he ordered the driver.

18

Faerie – day 2

Phoenix stared at her reflection in the floor-length mirror. But no matter how long she stared, she hardly recognised the image looking back at her. The silver gown that had been brought to her room earlier that morning fit as well as her own skin did. The material was light and delicate despite the sparkling crystals covering every inch of it; she'd never seen anything like it before. A male and female had come to her room an hour previous to attend to her hair and make-up, and the results convinced her that they must have used some kind of fae magic on her.

She turned sideways and ran her hand over the soft swell of her abdomen. The flowing material of her dress managed to make the bump unnoticeable, but still she could have sworn that it had grown overnight. If time moved differently here in Faerie, how would it affect her pregnancy? It was all well and good keeping her secret so long as her body didn't give her away.

A soft flutter tickled her belly just beneath her hand and she smiled sadly. "Hey, munchkin. I'm sorry I have to keep you hidden. I'm sorry that I'll be bringing you into a world that's so full of hatred for things people don't understand."

A knock sounded and she jerked her head up, yanking her hand away from her stomach. The closed door mocked her paranoia and she shook her head, mentally berating herself for being an idiot. She took a deep breath, smoothed down her dress, and went to answer it.

Ethan stood in the hallway looking awkwardly handsome in a traditional fae tunic, embroidered with gold thread that brought out the hint of his wolf's yellow eyes hidden beneath the surface. His normally unruly hair was slicked back, and though rough stubble covered his jawline, the contrast only accentuated the raw masculine energy that oozed from him. His eyes widened in surprise as he took her in.

"I see they got to you too," she said with a wry smile, fighting the urge to fidget self-consciously.

He laughed and moved to run a hand through his hair before stopping himself with a grimace. "I guess they're hoping it might help me blend in a bit. You look stunning." He offered her his arm with a wide grin.

Blend in? Fat chance of that. She closed the door behind her and slipped her arm through his, allowing him to lead her down the hallway.

Two guards waited for them in the large foyer, tasked with escorting the so-called guests of honour to the gala. Phoenix raised her eyebrows, but neither she or Ethan commented as they were led to a balcony that overlooked the open courtyard at the centre of the castle.

She'd caught a brief glimpse of the courtyard through the window when Aoife had shown them to their rooms the previous day. It was even more beautiful now.

Flaming torches lined the walls, complementing the dimming light from the dusky pink sky. At the centre of the courtyard, azure-blue water cascaded over a marble fountain that had been carved into the naked form of a couple entwined in a loving embrace. Four trees that looked like weeping willows marked the compass points, and small fluttering balls of light moved in an intricate dance between the hanging branches. It was breathtaking.

Fae mingled in the courtyard with drinks in hand, few bothering with the glamours Phoenix was used to seeing back home. They proudly showcased the subtle points of their ears, and many made a conscious effort in their outfit or make-up to highlight the trademark features that marked their respective heritages: pale green skin faintly patterned with leaves identified the earth elementals, while Phoenix spotted more than one fae with the orange and red flame-like hair that marked sun elementals like her. The water nymphs were nearly impossible to miss thanks to their oozing sensuality, and the accompanying harem of males and females hanging on their every word.

The guard beside her cleared his throat impatiently and ushered them forward to the top of a stone staircase. Curious gazes swept in their direction, and she was struck with a vivid image of falling on her face as she descended the steps. She clung tighter to Ethan's arm.

"Should we go find my grandparents?" She cringed at the low murmuring of the crowd as hundreds of eyes observed their descent. No one had explained the etiquette for the gala so she had no idea if she was supposed to present herself or slip quietly into the shadows, which was her preference.

"Let's get a drink first."

As if summoned by Ethan's words, a waitress appeared at his side with a tray in hand and a seductive smile on her face as she gave him a blatant once-over. He accepted two champagne flutes with a polite smile and handed one to Phoenix.

"You don't have to drink it," he assured her when she eyed the purple liquid suspiciously. "It's like armour. Holding a glass is a requirement for surviving awkward social engagements."

"He's not wrong, you know." Aoife appeared beside Ethan, a champagne flute in her own hand, and gave Phoenix a conspiratorial smile. The turquoise dress she wore made her green eyes sparkle, and she looked even more like Aria in that moment. "Mother and Father have been waylaid; they send their apologies. Let me introduce you around."

Driving hot pokers through her eyes sounded more appealing to Phoenix, but she dutifully followed Aoife and Ethan, smiling when expected to, and keeping to polite, mundane conversation where possible. Of course, polite seemed to be a relative term given that the fae's sense of personal boundaries varied wildly from any she'd ever encountered before.

"You don't *feel* right. What are you?"

"Are you sure you're fae? Your ears are awfully round."

"Oh, you live in the human realm? How very quaint."

The comments were delivered with such open curiosity and bluntness that in most cases she sensed no real malice behind them. Just ignorance.

Ethan stuck close to her side the whole time, and she felt him tense at more than one inappropriate comment about her tainted genetics. Aoife, for her part, moved the conversation on with the ease and relaxed air of someone well versed in managing the political minefield of Faerie.

Oddly, the fae seemed less disturbed at having a werewolf with absolutely no fae blood among them than they did by her half-fae status. In fact, many of the fae – males and females alike – flirted shamelessly with Ethan. He engaged in playful banter in return, his cheeky smile and suggestive comments enough to make even the water nymphs blush. Phoenix knew he wasn't seriously considering their advances, but a small part of her sulked as she watched them preen and flutter their eyelashes at him.

"Aoife, where have you been hiding this beauty?" A tall man with silver hair stepped into Phoenix's view. His grey eyes sparkled as he took her hand and raised it to his lips. "Please, let me introduce myself. I'm Eoghan, high lord of Eldridge."

Startled, Phoenix looked to Aoife, noting that her aunt's smile didn't quite reach her eyes.

"Eoghan, this is my niece, Phoenix. You might want to return her hand now."

"Oh, but it is such a lovely hand." He gave a cheeky wink, but did as asked.

Heat flared in Phoenix's cheeks and she fought the urge to fan herself with a girly giggle.

What the hell? Is he using a glamour on me? She straightened up and frowned at him. The smile he gave her in return didn't look the least bit apologetic.

"Forgive me. I couldn't resist."

The urge to giggle disappeared in an instant and she glared at him. "Don't do that again, or you'll find no amount of glamour will make up for the damage I do to your manhood." She gave a pointed look at the bulk that was nicely highlighted by the tight fit of his trousers – and no doubt also accented by magical means.

The fae lord bowed his head, attempting to look suitably chastised, but amusement and something else she couldn't put her finger on danced behind his grey eyes. "Will you be staying long with us here in Faerie?"

"Just a few days," Aoife answered coolly before Phoenix could respond.

She looked at her aunt in surprise. Though Aoife appeared relaxed, and even friendly, her green eyes had a hard edge that piqued her interest. If Eoghan noticed the chilly response, however, he didn't show it.

"I do hope you'll give me a chance to show you some of the delights Faerie has to offer," he said, his attention and smile still firmly fixed on her.

A collective gasp rose from the crowd, smothering her polite decline. She turned, looking around in confusion to see what had caught everyone's attention. And froze.

Her grandparents stood at the top of the stone staircase. Clothed in fine silks of purple and silver, they were every inch the regal image as they looked down upon the rapt audience. A woman with vibrant red hair cascading in loose waves over one shoulder stood between them. Her sultry red lips were held in a delicate pout and the pale skin of her thighs flashed teasingly from between the slits of a shimmering gold dress that clung like water to her body. It was this woman whom all eyes were fixed on, a sense of reverential awe oozing from the crowd.

"Who's that?" Phoenix whispered. A shiver of trepidation ran through her.

Eoghan's eyes were riveted on the stairs as he answered. "That's Méabh. Leader of the fae."

19

Faerie – day 2

Phoenix's head spun as Eoghan's words sank in. Leader of the fae? That meant Council. Her eyes met Ethan's as she tried to keep the fear from showing on her face. The tight set to his jaw did little to reassure her, and she could see the same thoughts racing through his mind – the Council had agreed to leave them alone, to give them time to find a solution. What had changed?

She could almost see Ethan's muscles twitching as he fought against his instincts to get her the hell out of there. But they both knew leaving wasn't an option, and the slightest movement from either of them would likely draw the attention of everyone present.

As if the whole courtyard was suddenly released from a trance, Méabh began a steady descent down the stairs and low murmurs of wonder filled the air. Clíodhna and Aodhán followed in her wake, Phoenix's grandfather holding himself proud as he looked over the crowd, while her grandmother's stoic expression told little of her thoughts.

Everything moved in painfully slow motion as Méabh glided along a clear path towards Phoenix. The fae she passed watched her with a mix of reverence and awe. A few wore poorly disguised looks of envy that suggested a well-placed dagger in the back wouldn't have been unexpected. Méabh for her part seemed unconcerned by the attention, her shrewd green eyes focused solely on her target.

When the procession finally came to a stop before Phoenix, Aodhán stepped forward, meeting her gaze for a second before turning to formally address Méabh. "If I may, I'd like to introduce you to our granddaughter, Phoenix."

The weight of all eyes in the courtyard fell on them. Phoenix cringed, sinking into herself in a futile attempt to escape their scrutiny. Her throat was barren, and she gripped the champagne flute tightly in her hand as if it really was the shield Ethan had promised.

"Leave us," Méabh ordered with a flick of a hand tipped with lethal red-enamelled nails. "I wish to speak with Phoenix and the wolf alone."

Looks of surprise were quickly masked by bows of obedience, and suddenly Phoenix found herself standing alone with Méabh and Ethan at the centre of the courtyard. Around them, music and conversations resumed, but everything seemed muted, far away, as if they'd been encased in some sort of bubble.

As soon as the area cleared, Ethan growled. "The Council agreed to leave Phoenix alone."

141

Méabh's green eyes traced a slow path down his body, and she ran her tongue over her bottom lip. "Down, boy. I have no intention of breaching any agreements here tonight. I simply wished to verify some interesting new information for myself."

"What new information?"

All traces of flirtation were forgotten and Méabh's expression turned thoughtful as she shifted her attention to Phoenix. "You're not what I expected."

Phoenix bit back the urge to tell her to go fuck herself, and instead said, "Sorry to disappoint."

The smile she got in return held no trace of humour. Méabh looked down at Phoenix's stomach. "Cassandra may be right, but it appears there's a long way to go before any saviour might be born of your union. Time passes very differently back home than it does here in Faerie. It remains to be seen what, if anything, is left to save even if the vision proves true."

Ice ran through Phoenix's veins and all thoughts fled her mind except one: *she knows.*

The terror must have shown on her face because the leader of the fae laughed, cold and harsh. "Oh, do calm down. I'm not here to harm you or the child. I simply wished to see for myself."

"You've seen, and now you should leave," Ethan said, the muscle at the side of his jaw jumping, even as a deadly stillness held him in place.

Méabh purred low in her throat and placed a hand on his chest. "You have so much pent-up aggression. Is she not helping you to work it off?"

She pulled her hand away with a wink, all business once more. "When Cassandra informed us of her vision, the Council voted to offer you assistance. A messenger was sent, but it seems they never reached you. Perhaps that's for the best. I, for one, am not yet convinced you're worthy of that assistance. I guess time will tell."

A loud buzzing rang through Phoenix's head. The Council knew. Who was Cassandra? What did Méabh mean that there might not be anything worth saving? A strange numbness settled over her as she asked, "Will you tell them? My grandparents?"

The fae woman waved a hand, looking suddenly bored. "I have more pressing matters that require my attention right now. I have no interest in being dragged into any family drama. I will keep your secret. For now."

Clearly deciding the matter was settled, Méabh plucked the full champagne glass from Ethan's hand and swallowed the purple liquid. She ran a nail across her lip to clear some imaginary droplets and handed the glass back with a seductive smile.

Phoenix's tongue felt strange and swollen in her mouth, but still she managed to form one last question. "The vision … Will we have enough time? Will the baby …"

Stormy shadows passed behind Méabh's eyes. "Let us hope so."

The drinks continued to flow and there was no break in the hypnotic music that had revellers dancing with

143

abandon around the courtyard. Ethan leaned against the wall of the castle, sipping his drink as he watched Phoenix dance with Eoghan. He made a conscious effort to keep the scowl from his face.

The fae male hadn't been shy in expressing his interest in Phoenix since Aoife had introduced them earlier that evening. Phoenix, for her part, had kept the conversation polite and humoured him with the occasional dance when pushed. Ethan knew the attraction wasn't reciprocated, but it took more restraint than he cared to admit to stop himself from marking his territory.

As the music shifted tempo, she pulled away from Eoghan's grasp and excused herself. She slipped from the crowd and headed for a quiet corner of the courtyard, moving out of sight. Noting the subtle slump of her shoulders now that she thought no one was looking, he followed her.

She stopped under what looked like a cherry blossom tree except for the fact the small blooms continuously shifted colour, and sat on the stone bench beneath it. Even in the dim light he could see the shadows under her eyes and the sharpened edges of her cheek bones. When had he last seen her eat properly?

She gave him a tired smile as he approached and shifted over to make space for him. "Hey."

He sat down next to her and gave her a gentle nudge with his elbow. "How you holding up?"

"I just needed a break. It's been a long night."

It had been a long few days, never mind a long night. The fact she'd had to flee to Faerie before she'd even had a chance to recover from Darius's attack – because he

144

couldn't quite bring himself to think of it as Sean's doing – still bothered him. The stress couldn't be good for her, never mind the baby. He'd kept the thought to himself so as not to worry her further, but he couldn't stop watching her for even the slightest sign that something may not be right.

"At least Méabh didn't stick around for long," she said with a sigh.

"Do you think she'll say anything to your grandparents?"

She shook her head. "The fae can twist words, but they can't lie. The 'for now' part will only cover us so long as it suits her, but I don't think we need to worry about it right now. It's the other part that bothers me."

"That we might not have enough time?"

Phoenix stared at her hands in her lap, eyes tight with tension. She didn't answer, instead chewing on her bottom lip.

"We can't think like that," he told her firmly, pushing back his own sense of unease. "All we can do is focus on the things we can control. Méabh said the same thing Morrigan did, that time passes differently here. We need to find the spear, and sooner rather than later. How the hell we're meant to do it, though, I've no idea."

Phoenix's brow furrowed. "It has to be here, or somewhere close by at least. Otherwise, what was the point in Morrigan telling us to find it while we were here? If the four treasures call to each other like she said, then I guess we bring the sword on a treasure hunt and hope it lights up like a Vegas casino with big flashing arrows."

She sat back against the bench and closed her eyes. "I'm exhausted. You think anyone will notice if I slip off to bed?"

He looked back at the courtyard and the party that was still in full swing. "I think you've served your time in the zoo." He stood and offered her his arm. "I'll walk you up."

She rose and linked her arm through his without a word. Nobody intercepted them as they made their way back into the castle, keeping to the shadows. Inside, they followed the winding corridors until eventually the music of the gala was little more than an echo on the wind.

"So, other than tired, how are you feeling?" he asked when he was sure they were alone. "You haven't been eating much."

She grimaced. "Apparently even lands filled with ancient magics can't defeat morning sickness. I could really do with your mam's special tea right now." They came to a stop outside her bedroom and she turned to look up at him. "It's hard. Having to hide …"

His chest ached at the sorrow that darkened her eyes. Hesitantly, he reached out to touch her cheek. He'd had to fight the urge to touch her so many times since they'd arrived in Faerie that he took a moment to relish the softness of her skin beneath his fingers. A smile tugged at one corner of her mouth as she covered his hand with her own and rested against his palm.

He moved closer to her.

His eyes fixated on her mouth as he ran his thumb over the soft swell of her bottom lip. Her scent wrapped around him, warm and inviting, drawing him further in.

"Oh, there you are."

Phoenix jerked away from him as if she'd gotten an electric shock. He dropped his hand, heart pounding as he turned towards Aoife's approaching form.

"You caught us," he said with what he hoped was a relaxed grin. "We were both a bit worn out from all the excitement, so we slipped away when no one was looking."

Aoife's friendly smile never faltered, but something unreadable passed behind her eyes for the briefest of moments.

Before she could say anything more, he stepped away from Phoenix's door. "If you'll excuse me, I shall bid you fair ladies a good night." He swept a low, theatrical bow and turned on his heel, careful to keep his pace relaxed as he headed for his room.

20

Faerie – day 3

Phoenix groaned as she rolled over somewhat clumsily in the bed and struggled up to sitting. Sleep clung with determination to her eyes and she blinked at the sunlight streaming in through the window. Surely it couldn't be morning? She'd only just fallen asleep.

She'd been exhausted when they'd left the gala, but as soon as her head had hit the pillow, the internal monologue had begun. Thoughts of exactly what Méabh's words might mean for them and the prophecy alternated with memories of Ethan's gentle touch. All of it, combined with her body's inability to get comfortable, had plotted against her quest for sleep. It would be a miracle if she could keep her eyes open for the day, but they had a spear to find so she'd just have to pull on her big girl pants.

Indulging herself with a martyred sigh, she set about making herself look somewhat presentable. She eyed the swell of her abdomen critically in the mirror and grabbed a loose-fitting tunic from the wardrobe before strapping Claíomh Solais across her back. It was becoming clearer to her that they should have pressed Morrigan for details on just how long they were likely to be here.

She left the room and made her way to the place she knew she was most likely to find Ethan: the dining room. Sure enough, she found him at the large oak table, the remnants of what looked to be a hearty breakfast on the silver platter in front of him.

He gave her a sheepish grin. "I can see where the myths about accepting fae food came from. I'm not sure I want to leave now that I've tasted it either."

Laughter came from behind her, and Phoenix turned to see Aoife approach, her eyes sparkling.

"Oh, don't be fooled. Not all of the stories are myths, and there are plenty of foods here in Faerie that have undesirable effects for the unaware. But fear not," she said, gliding into the room and plucking a luscious red apple from a bowl on the table, "we simply like showing off the fruits of our land. So, what have you two got planned for the day?"

"We were hoping to explore the grounds a bit more." Ethan pushed back from the table with a contented sigh and stood. "We haven't really had a proper chance to look around since we got here."

Aoife smiled widely. "Why don't I come with you? I can show you the rest of the castle and introduce you to some of the fae who tend the lands."

Phoenix opened her mouth to politely decline, but Ethan caught her eye and gave a subtle shake of his head.

Taking his hint, she pasted a smile onto her own face. "If you're sure we wouldn't be taking you away from your duties?"

Aoife laughed. "I'd be more than happy for the excuse, believe me."

"Did many of the gentry remain in the castle after the gala?" Ethan asked, sweeping his arm out in an invitation for her to lead the way.

"A few."

A troubled look passed over her aunt's face, gone so quickly that Phoenix wasn't sure if she imagined it. She followed Aoife out of the dining room, casting a questioning glance at Ethan to see if he too had noticed it. His face remained impassive, but his eyes were watchful and alert.

They skipped the parts of the castle Aoife had shown them when they first arrived in Faerie, and instead made their way through the farthest reaches that extended away from the family's living quarters. As they walked, Aoife supplied intriguing explanations and facts about the castle's history. On the uppermost levels, the glass walls allowed for stunning views of the land surrounding them, and the high wall that bordered it. Thick branches snaked across the exterior of the glass from the trees on either side of the building, turning the image into a patchwork of artistry.

"What's beyond the wall?" Phoenix thought back to the creepy forest that had been their first introduction to Faerie and shuddered.

Her aunt's face darkened. "Death," Aoife answered softly, before beckoning them on with smile.

Phoenix gaped after her, and Ethan's eyes widened in surprise. They hurried to catch up with her, neither really sure how to respond.

With each floor they explored, Phoenix was painfully aware of the sword hanging silently across her back. She didn't know what exactly it was meant to do if it came close to the spear, but as it was their only guiding point, even the slightest shift of it against her spine made her breath catch. It got to the point that, at times, she even imagined it was vibrating.

"How are the trees so interwoven with the building?" Ethan asked when they passed yet another hallway of glass windows displaying a spider web of branches on the exterior.

Aoife placed her hand against the glass and the branches writhed, seeming to respond to her touch. "Everything in Faerie is derived from nature in some form. The environment is malleable and changes as requirements demand it. This castle wasn't always here, and may not always be. Nature responded to the need of our people."

"Do many people live here?" Phoenix watched as small forms moved about the land in the distance. Aside from the gala, she hadn't yet encountered too many fae during her time in the castle.

"More than you may realise. Some live here in other quarters. Some have their own dwellings on the land. There's no obligation for them to stay within our boundaries, but much of Faerie is wild and unforgiving for the less-powerful fae, and they choose to stay where it's safest."

Phoenix chewed her lip, wondering what it had been like for her mother growing up here. Had she been sheltered from whatever horrors lay beyond the wall? Knowing her mother's fierce spirit, Phoenix doubted it.

Back on the ground level of the castle, they came to a long, dark corridor which led towards the west wing. Aoife paid it little heed, turning to head back to the main foyer, but an odd tugging sensation stopped Phoenix in her tracks. The shadows seemed to almost beckon her forward.

"What's down there?" she asked, her voice little more than a whisper.

Her aunt looked at the corridor in surprise, as if only just remembering it was there. "Oh, there? Nothing as far as I know. It used to lead to old escape tunnels that ran under the castle, but it's a dead end now. I guess the building decided the tunnels weren't necessary anymore." She shrugged as if the suggestion was perfectly natural, then turned back towards the main part of the castle. "Let me show you the grounds outside. We have the most magnificent stables."

Ethan gave her a quizzical look, and Phoenix discreetly placed a hand on the leather strap that crossed her body. She wasn't sure if it was the sword drawing her towards that corridor or something else; she just knew she'd be coming back later.

As with every day since they'd arrived in Faerie, the sky was a cloudless blue when they made their way outside. If Phoenix hadn't already known that magic filled this place, the constant sun would have proved it to her; no place could have weather this perfect all the time.

The estate was larger than it had appeared from the castle, housing hundreds of residences that blended seamlessly into the landscape. Aoife stopped at regular intervals to introduce them to the fae who were tending the grounds. They all greeted her with warm welcome, and Phoenix was pleasantly surprised by her aunt's friendly ease with those whom some might have considered beneath her.

As they drew close to the stables, Aoife deep in conversation with Ethan about the unique herbs they grew in the medicinal gardens, a male came riding over the horizon on a magnificent white steed. Phoenix recognised the silver hair immediately, and the scowl that settled on Ethan's face told her that he too had spotted the rider. Eoghan waved and headed in their direction.

It was only as he neared that Phoenix realised he was riding bareback. Even she had to admit that he looked terribly regal sitting astride the beautiful beast, his hair glistening in the light of the sun. His dismount from the steed was equally impressive, and she rolled her eyes with a smile as he bent to kiss her hand in greeting.

"Well now," he said. "I believe my morning has just brightened considerably."

Ethan's scowl deepened.

"To what do we owe the honour, Eoghan?" Aoife asked, something slightly off with her polite expression. "I thought you were returning to Eldridge this morning?"

"I decided to stay a little longer. The views are much more interesting here." He gave Aoife a wink while still somehow managing to keep his attention firmly on Phoenix.

Squirming uncomfortably at the intense focus being aimed her way, Phoenix grasped for a way to redirect it. "That's a beautiful horse. Is it yours?"

"Yes, his name's Jack. Would you like to meet him?"

She choked in surprise. "Jack?"

"Well, I couldn't make his name too impressive. He's already far too spectacular. If I gave him an impressive name, the ladies would surely think I'm trying to compensate for something."

She laughed despite herself and shook her head.

Aoife turned towards the horizon, where another rider was heading towards them on a steed the colour of rich chestnut. "I didn't realise you were riding with my father."

"We had some business matters to discuss. It seemed a shame not to make the most of this wondrous morning as we concluded them."

Aoife's eyes narrowed on the fae lord, but before she could say anything further, Aodhán brought his horse to a stop next to them. Phoenix noticed with interest that he avoided his daughter's questioning gaze as he greeted them.

"What a pleasant surprise." He dismounted with an ease even more impressive than Eoghan's and patted the horse's back. "Are you going riding?"

"Actually," Eoghan jumped in, "I was just about to ask your granddaughter's assistance in getting Jack here settled after our ride."

Phoenix moved to protest, but her grandfather nodded approvingly and turned to Ethan. "Perhaps I could interest you in some sparring then? It's been a long time since I've had a chance to test my reflexes against an opponent of another species."

Ethan didn't even glance her way to acknowledge the plea in her eyes before he inclined his head and said, "I'd be honoured."

That settled, her grandfather passed his horse over to the stable hand who had rushed to assist him. Phoenix tried once again to politely suggest alternative plans, but somehow she found herself standing alone with Eoghan as Ethan followed her grandfather to the training fields, and Aoife distractedly muttered an excuse about needing to speak with her mother.

Ethan eyed the impressively stacked weapons rack and wondered exactly what kind of sparring Aodhán had in mind. For some reason, he didn't think Phoenix would appreciate him slicing her grandfather to shreds with the wickedly sharp blades of the twin daggers or bludgeoning him to death with a mace.

Though their search for the fae weapon would never be that easy, he scanned his eyes over the rack for any sign of a spear. Oddly enough, it was one of the only weapons not represented in the vast selection.

"Many of these weapons were passed down to me by my father," Aodhán said, coming to stand beside him. "Claíomh Solais I kept in my own personal collection, of course. At least until I passed it down to Aria. She was impressive with the blade, even at a young age."

Ethan thought back to the battle in Darius's underground chamber, the images still etched in his mind. "I fought at her side once. She was a magnificent fighter. Phoenix is too, despite her lack of training."

Aodhán frowned. "Her parents never taught her to fight?"

Ethan hesitated. Phoenix's story wasn't his to tell, and yet some part of him wanted it to be known, wanted the man before him to understand just what she had lost, and how strong she was.

"They trained her as much as they could, but they disappeared when she was quite young. The man who hunts her held them prisoner for ten years until we found them. She was left alone, without any family to train her or help her understand her powers. She feared who and what she is because that's all our world ever taught her to do." He stopped, clamping down on the anger that welled inside him on her behalf.

Her grandfather stood deathly still beside him, his expression unchanged except for the storm swirling in his dark eyes. For a minute he was quiet.

"When you live a long time, you make many decisions that haunt you," he said eventually. "It's clear that you care for my granddaughter a great deal. I would hate for you to have to understand firsthand what it's like to make a decision like that."

Ethan met his gaze silently. There was a warning in those words, he knew that much. But he also knew it changed nothing. He straightened and gestured to the training area. "Shall we spar?"

21

Home – 10 days gone

Abi watched over Nate's shoulder as rows and rows of code filled the black computer screen. Not so long ago the words and numbers would have meant less than nothing to her, but Nate had been a patient teacher. In the week and a half since Phoenix had left, Abi had found the art of hacking to be an exciting distraction from her racing thoughts. Of course, it probably didn't count as hacking since the Council had voluntarily handed over their data this time.

From all accounts, the meeting with the Council had yielded an uneasy acknowledgement that they needed to work together to stop Darius. True to their word, the Council had set about making life very difficult for the Dublin vampire clan by freezing their assets pending investigation.

Coincidentally – or not, as the case might be – they began seeing a surge in suspicious and violent attacks in the communities surrounding them shortly after that, with all information suggesting crazed demon-Supe hybrids were to blame.

Despite the incentive to find him, the Council's best trackers had failed to pinpoint Darius's location, and so William had shocked them all by willingly providing Nate with access to the Council databases. She felt it was gracious of Cormac not to point out just how easily the shifter had gained access to their security systems in the past, and was only a little disappointed that she didn't get to properly test her new-found hacking skills.

"What exactly is it we're looking for?" She scanned the data, waiting for something to magically jump out at her.

They'd already run checks on all businesses even remotely connected to the Dublin vampire clan. She'd reviewed their financials for any odd changes in recent months, and Nate had trawled through countless hours of security footage in and around the businesses. Everyone was acutely aware of how much time was passing and what it might mean for Sean.

Nate leaned closer to the screen, squinting in concentration. "I was up all night trying to figure out how we might approach things from a different angle. We've already covered Darius and any of his known aliases, but I remembered that when we first discovered his link with the prophecy, he was going by his Sire's name, not his own."

"Il Maestro." Abi shuddered as she thought back to the fevered light that had burned in Darius's eyes when he'd talked about his Sire. "He told me that Il Maestro was the one who gave him the scroll."

"That would make sense. Il Maestro served on the Council when Cassandra proclaimed the prophecy. No doubt it was written down to preserve the wording; he'd have been in a prime position to take it or make his own copy …"

He trailed off as an icon flashed in the bottom corner of the screen, notifying him of a new email. He moved to click on it but suddenly the lines of code halted their scrolling, and there was a sharp beep as one of the lines flashed green.

"Bingo!" Nate slapped a hand on the table and pushed back from the computer with a triumphant smile, email notification forgotten.

Abi leaned closer and scrunched her brow in confusion. "Who's Alessandro Rossi?"

"*That* is the birth name of Darius's Sire. And it's our answer to finding Darius." Nate slid his chair back towards the desk and tapped the keyboard in a blur of movement. "Look." He pointed to a list of three names with dates beside them. "These are all the companies that Alessandro Rossi acquired in the past twenty-five years. Quite a feat for a man who's been dead for centuries."

She scanned the list, the letters thankfully forming words that made sense to her now. "A law firm, a pharmaceutical company, and a night club. A bit of a strange combination. So, how do we find out which one he's hiding in?"

Nate was quiet for a few moments as he flicked between various screens and websites. He chewed on his lip, eyes darkening as he digested the information quicker than she could follow.

"It's the club. It has to be. I can't find any record of it in normal channels, and from the limited information I can find on the Dark Web, it seems to cater to the" – he grimaced – "less savoury of our kind. A psychopath like Darius would be in his element in a place like that."

Butterflies skittered around in Abi's stomach. Was this it? Had they finally found him? "What do we do now?"

Nate gave her the most genuine grin she'd seen from him in months. "Now we call in reinforcements."

He tapped a few more buttons to transfer information over to his mobile phone, then pushed away from the table and beckoned her to follow him. They made a beeline for the kitchen where they found Cormac sitting at the table, deep in discussion with Lucas. Shade leaned against the counter with a mug of blood in hand. All three looked up at their approach, and Abi felt a pang of sympathy at the wary hopefulness on Cormac's face.

Nate placed his phone face-up in the centre of the table and grinned at the Alpha. "Call the Council and tell them we're going to need backup at this address, and distractions at these two."

"You found him."

"I think so." Nate turned to Abi, his grin widening. "How do you feel about going back to Dublin?"

22

Faerie – day 3

Phoenix had never been the type of person who became drained by interacting with others. Though she loved having time to herself to recharge, she was well used to making polite small talk with customers in the pub and generally managed to keep up her side of a conversation without too much effort. But conversation with Eoghan? That was a different story altogether.

The fae lord's definition of talking with another person involved him spewing a never-ending monologue about his formidable achievements, with not-so-subtle hints as to how that might translate to his prowess in the bedroom. At first she'd listened with some interest, figuring it might be an opportunity to learn more about Faerie. However, it didn't take long to deduce that she'd be better off finding an alternative source of information. She wasn't even lying when she pleaded the start of a headache and excused herself.

She checked Ethan's room first to see if he had returned from sparring with her grandfather, but when she found no sign of him there, she made her way to the family dining room. That too was empty except for a kindly fae female who worked in the kitchen.

The female offered to make her some honey tea and Phoenix accepted with an embarrassing rumble of her stomach and a gracious smile. She was surprised to find hunger gnawing at her as she sipped the warming liquid and was warily contemplating trying actual food when Ethan strolled in.

He gave her a teasing grin as he shoved his damp hair out of his face. "Where's his Lordship Smarmy Pants?"

She glared at him, crossing her arms. "I can't believe you just abandoned me like that. Do you know how much he likes to talk about himself?"

He snorted and grabbed a bread roll from a basket of fresh-baked bread on the table. "I can imagine. Anyway, I wasn't really given a choice. It seems your grandfather had a few things he wanted to get off his chest so he decided to do it while kicking my arse. He's pretty spry for an old guy."

"Get what things off his chest?" she asked, the subtle tension underlying his tone making her forget her irritation.

"Nothing important." He dismissed the issue with a wave of his hand and bit a chunk out of the bread roll. "He did mention having an important meeting this afternoon. I got the impression your grandmother and Aoife would be involved too, so it might be a good opportunity to go back and check out that corridor."

He didn't have to ask her twice. She hopped to her feet and grabbed Claíomh Solais from where it rested against her chair. "Let's go."

Phoenix tried to look casual as they made their way through the castle back to the corridor they'd passed earlier that day with Aoife. Her palms were sweating and she was convinced that she had guilty written all over her face. What if she'd only imagined the strange pull? She'd been so focused on finding any clue to the spear's whereabouts that she wouldn't be surprised at all if it turned out to be little more than wishful thinking. But as they drew closer to the dim corridor, the tugging sensation came again. The inexplicable pull beckoned her forward as if the darkness itself were calling her. She kept walking, only dimly aware of the logical voice in the back of her mind that warned her to be careful.

Tension radiated from Ethan as he kept close to her side, but he stayed quiet and let her lead the way. The light was almost non-existent as they moved deeper into the corridor. So much so that even with her enhanced sight she had to strain her eyes. She didn't need to see, however; not when the sword, and her gut, were telling her exactly where she needed to go.

Eventually they reached the end of the corridor and came face-to-face with a blank wall. Just as Aoife had said, it appeared to be a dead end. Ethan let out a low curse that mirrored her own sentiments. The pull had turned into a vibration, and it was thrumming though her now, insisting that she go forward. But there was no forward.

Frowning, she reached out and placed her hands on the wall and ran them methodically over the smooth surface. A hidden doorway seemed awfully cliché, but it wouldn't be the first time they'd found one.

Ethan followed her lead, concentrating as he searched with her. After a minute, he shook his head.

"Maybe there's a password or something?" She stepped back with a huff of frustration to assess the wall. As she did, her heel got caught on an uneven stone, and before she could regain her balance, she landed unceremoniously on the ground with a thud.

Ethan was at her side in an instant, checking for injuries. "Are you okay?"

"I'm fine. I'm fine." She brushed him off and twisted around to see what she'd stumbled over. Nothing obvious caught her eye so she rolled onto her knees and ran her hands over the floor. A ridge ran across the cool stone, barely noticeable. "Look."

Ethan bent down to examine the spot where she indicated. His eyes flashed yellow for a second before huge claws extended from both his hands. He gripped the ridge and pried the floor upwards. A cloud of dust preceded the musty smell of earth as he revealed a decrepit wooden staircase. Thick mud and spindly roots surrounded the opening, and Phoenix could only see a few steps down before complete darkness consumed everything. Were these the escape tunnels Aoife had mentioned?

Ethan pulled a small torch from his pocket. "I'm game if you are?"

When she nodded, he lowered himself into the narrow space. The stairs creaked with each step he took, but held firm. Carefully she manoeuvred herself into the hole after him and he reached back to steady her. The air was heavy and stale and she had to fight the urge to hold her breath.

At the bottom, a tunnel led deeper into the earth. It was narrow enough that they had to walk single file, so Phoenix let Ethan lead the way with the torch while she kept one hand on his shoulder and the other firmly gripped to her scabbard's leather strap. The light of the torch threw shadows around them and lent an eerie feel to the darkness.

After a few minutes, the tunnel widened and she was able to move to Ethan's side. The earth beneath their feet was smoother now, and she noticed that the dirt walls also seemed smoother, more intentionally carved. Thick roots ran through the walls like veins, and she guessed they must be moving towards the tree that braced the west side of the castle.

The vibration that thrummed from the sword rattled through her with every step forward she took. When the passage suddenly branched into three separate directions, she took the far left one, without hesitation. Muck turned into a stone walkway, and a light breeze caressed her skin. The fragrance drifting through the air was so unexpected that she stopped and looked at Ethan in surprise.

"Is that …"

"Roses," he confirmed, looking every bit as puzzled as she felt.

Though the air seemed fresher in this tunnel, there had been no let-up to the darkness, suggesting there was no opening to the outside world nearby. So where was the smell coming from?

Her question was quickly answered as the passage veered around a bend and they found themselves in front of the most magnificent sight. The walls were no longer coated in mud, but instead thick green stems covered every inch of the walls and ceiling. Deep-purple roses bloomed from the ends of the stems, their perfume subtle yet pleasing. Finger-length thorns protruded from the shadows and Phoenix shivered as she took in their vicious tips.

A single wooden door stood at the end of the passage, as if waiting just for them. There was no sign of a lock or even a handle, but her head buzzed with the surety that what they sought was behind it. She took a step forward, but Ethan grabbed her, halting her motion.

"Let me go first."

She opened her mouth to argue and stopped. The stubborn set of his jaw was far too familiar by now, so she just sighed and waved a hand for him to proceed. He'd gone less than two feet before she followed.

About halfway to the door, the plants around them came to life.

The thick stems covering the walls writhed and the blanket of green seemed to undulate. A couple of particularly large stems lazily slithered down the wall and along the floor, making their way towards her and Ethan. The light of the torch glistened off the blade-like edge of the thorns.

She swallowed and looked back the way they'd come, debating whether retreat was necessary. But instead of the open entrance that they'd stepped through, there was now just a tangled web of thorns and roses.

"Ethan," she whispered, tugged on his arm with barely restrained urgency.

A vine darted out from the wall and before she could even yelp her surprise, it latched on to her right wrist. She froze, afraid to even breathe.

Ethan turned, paling when he took in her newly acquired restraint and the blocked exit. His eyes glowed an eerie yellow in the torchlight. "Don't move. I'll cut it with my claws."

She shook her head, eyes riveted on another vine creeping closer on her left, this one sporting a terrifying thorn. "I think that will just piss it off."

"Shit." He growled.

"I have an idea." She tried to keep the tremble from her voice but failed. Tentatively, she reached out towards the approaching vine with her free hand. She scrunched her eyes closed as she inched closer to the thorn.

"What are you –"

A burn of pain caused her to hiss, cutting off Ethan's protest. She opened her eyes and watched as a single bead of blood ran along her palm and dripped onto the plant. The blood absorbed into the fibrous skin of the plant's stem, and an instant later the grip on her right wrist released, the vine sliding back to its spot on the wall.

She blew out a shaky breath. "Come on," she said, her attention once again focused on the wooden door as she started forward.

A strangled cry halted her mid-stride.

23

Faerie – day 3

Horror clutched Phoenix in its claws as she turned and saw the thick vine wrapped around Ethan's throat. The muscles in his forearms bulged in his attempts to pry it away, but he might as well have been tickling the plant for all the good it was doing. She cursed as panic threatened to choke her. Whatever spell protected this place either didn't like his werewolf blood, or was keyed to her family line only.

"Okay, don't struggle," she said in a calm, soothing voice, as if that might stop the vine from squeezing the life out of him.

She inched towards him, hands held out as if to assure the roses she was coming in peace. But even as she moved, more vines snaked their way towards Ethan. Their blooms looked full, and dare she say it, hungry.

He gave her a pained look, but did as she asked and calmed his attempts to remove the fibrous rope that was a mere contraction away from strangling him. His hands remained firmly in place, however, in case the vine took the opportunity to tighten further.

It felt like an eternity before she reached his side. Slowly, so as not to spook the plant, she placed her still-bloodied palm on the vine and held her breath. Nothing happened.

"Looks like there's no option for a plus one," Ethan said wryly.

The vibration of the sword on her back was so strong now that between it and her fear, she couldn't think straight. She looked from the vine around his throat to the wooden door and back again. They were so close, she could feel it. Maybe she could grab the spear and then find a way to free him? The vine hadn't tightened enough to cut off his oxygen; maybe it just wanted to restrain him.

Even as the thought crossed her mind, another thick rope of green latched on to Ethan's right foot. This one was barbed with an entire row of small thorns and he hissed as they pierced his skin.

"Go. I'll be fine."

Another wince of pain belied his words, and she hesitated.

"Go!"

She sucked in a breath and with a final look at the noose around his neck, she turned and sprinted down the short passage. A muffled grunt behind her sent her heart ricocheting in her chest, but she kept her focus firmly on the door. *It's not like the thorns are made of silver,* she reminded herself. *He'll be okay.*

She skidded to a stop and immediately began searching the door for a handle or catch of some sort. The wood was rough beneath her hands, but she could find no mechanism to open it. She cursed and kicked the door in frustration. It didn't even shudder in response.

"Phoenix," Ethan called, his voice sounding strained. "Any chance you can hurry it along?"

She turned to look back and a sharp cry escaped her lips as she took in the vines that had latched themselves on to his arms and legs. Blood seeped from a multitude of cuts made by the thorny edges, and thick purple blooms caressed him almost lovingly.

Forgetting all about the door she ran back to him, drawing Claíomh Solais from the scabbard on her back as she did. New vines reached out from the wall and tried to pull the blade from her hands, but she cleaved clean through them and kept moving.

Once she was within reaching distance, she swung the sword at the ropes binding Ethan. They fell to the ground, but others replaced them before he barely had a chance to move. She bit back a scream of frustration.

Gritting her teeth, she hacked at the plant over and over again, hoping that if she just kept cutting it would slow its ability to regenerate. A black, tar-like substance oozed from the severed limbs, and by the time she managed to get Ethan's arms and legs free long enough for him to move, she was covered in it.

He extended his claws and sliced clean through the remaining vine around his neck. Still more came for him. He snatched her free hand and pulled her towards the mouth of the passage, writhing vines and razor-like thorns clutching at them from all sides. Neither his claws nor her sword ceased slashing for a moment.

Attempts to hack through the wall of roses that blocked their exit made little impression, and sweat mixed with the black tar covering Phoenix's skin as she tried in vain to create an opening.

A shudder ran through the ground and she stumbled. She reached out to steady herself and let out a cry of pain as a thorn pierced her palm. The wound burned with an intensity that caused her vision to swim.

"Phoenix." Ethan grabbed her elbow as another tremor rippled beneath them. He hissed as he looked at the damage to her hand and back to the barrier that kept them trapped. "Can you call the sun?"

This far underground? And with her power as glitchy as it had been recently? Doubt niggled at her, but she forced herself to take a slow breath and focus on the exit. "Get behind me," she ordered, hoping like hell she would be able to control the power enough not to incinerate him.

With her bloody hand she gripped her mother's medallion hanging warm against her chest. *Please let this work, please let this work.* The heat came slower than normal, but it came. It stuttered, and her chest tightened in panic for a split second before she regained her focus. Inhale. Exhale.

As the warmth built, she let it flow from her chest down her arm and into the sword gripped tightly in her hand. She raised the sword towards the exit and unleashed her power.

A blinding flash of light seared her retinas and in the moment of silence that followed, her heart stopped. Only when she heard Ethan groan behind her and felt his hand grip her arm did it start beating again.

Where once an impenetrable wall of roses stood before them, a large, charred hole now opened into the dark passage beyond. Her legs went weak, but the relief lasted no time at all. The ground began to shake under their feet and dirt rained down from the ceiling above them. She looked at Ethan with wide eyes.

"Move," he commanded, pushing her through the opening.

Her feet caught on vines and she fell to her knees on the far side of the tunnel. Ethan's hand disappeared from her back and she heard a strangled cry behind her. She turned in time to see him yanked backwards by a thorn-filled vine that had locked itself around his throat.

"Ethan!"

An ear-splitting roar filled the air and the ceiling collapsed around her.

24

Home – 2 weeks gone

A slow smile spread over Darius's face as he observed the writhing bodies on the dance floor below his office. The vampires not rostered to work that night had been warned to make themselves scarce, but that still left plenty of bodies to act as an obstacle for the coming fun.

"How many?" he asked, turning to Erik.

"Twenty-five from the south, another thirty or so from the north. The wolves and their companions seem to be heading for a point between the two. Presumably a rendezvous point."

The Council had sent little more than fifty of their security team? *Hmm.* They either highly underestimated him, or the present he'd sent them the week prior was still keeping their resources tied up back in Brussels.

It didn't matter; they could have sent double the number and it wouldn't make a difference to the outcome of tonight's events. The Donegal pack might think they had strong allies on their side, but he would show them just how wrong they were.

"And everything's in place?"

"The wolf was transferred earlier today," Erik confirmed, a wicked gleam in his eye.

"Good. Leave guards on the main doors of the club and clear out the rest of our people. Get the car started out back, I'll be down in a moment."

Erik left without a word. Darius sat down at his mahogany desk and pulled out a cream sheet of paper and a gold pen. He composed a brief note and folded the page, leaving it resting in plain sight. Pity he wouldn't be able to greet its recipients in person, but he had work to do.

Shade shoved his way through a sea of sweaty bodies and flailing limbs. The Club of Night was in chaos. Humans ran in panicked circles like headless chickens as they scrambled towards anything that even remotely resembled a door, while the Supe patrons had chosen to vent their anger at a ruined night by turning the dancefloor into a scene from *Battle Royale*.

Strobe lights flashed to a now-silent beat, allowing him glimpses of the Council security team that was busy securing the exits. He'd been surprised that the Council had come through on their promise of backup, but sure enough, they'd found the best part of fifty Supes waiting for them at the agreed rendezvous point, each carrying enough weapons that they looked like they were ready to go to war.

Cormac had taken five of his wolves and made a beeline for the upper floor of the club, where the offices were likely to be. Another ten wolves were busy rounding up the staff while the Council team corralled the less-helpful patrons. For his part, Shade had his sights set on an auspicious set of double doors at the back of the club, and anyone who got in his way was going to get hurt.

A beefy shifter with beer stains down his torn shirt clearly hadn't gotten the memo, however, and lumbered into his path with a sneer. Shade didn't even slow as he lashed out with a well-placed strike to the windpipe that left the man gasping in a heap on the floor. Two more vamps tried their hand at him before he made it to his target on the far side of the dancefloor. One ended up with a penknife in the eye for good measure, while the other would likely need to drink his blood through a straw for the foreseeable future.

Lucas reached the double doors at the same time as he did. The wary look on the vamp's face told Shade he wasn't the only one suspicious about the obvious lack of security; nothing was ever that easy. They each moved to either side of the doors. Lucas mouthed a silent countdown to him, and they yanked them open.

Shade held his breath waiting for a flood of vampires or an explosion, or hell, anything. But no nasty surprises greeted them.

They slipped through the doors and made their way soundlessly through the darkened corridors that wound along the back of the club. At each turn he expected to be faced with some form of attack, and at each turn they were met with silence. Rather than allowing him to relax, it only made him warier.

On the second floor below ground level they reached a corridor with a row of nondescript black doors lining both sides of the hallway. A shiver ran through him as he eyed the doors; something told him he didn't want to know what was behind them.

Lucas moved ahead, indicating for Shade to take the doors on the left while he took the ones on the right. Shade grimaced but nodded in acknowledgement before moving to the first door.

He shoved it open and was hit with a stench of decay so strong it sent his head spinning. Whatever had been in that room was no longer alive enough to be a problem, so he made a swift retreat before he was tempted to empty his stomach contents in a very undignified manner on the floor.

The second room was oddly sterile, a complete dichotomy to the previous one. A single metal table sat in the middle of the room and a tray was laid out on a rolling stand beside it. No amount of bleach could hide the metallic tang of blood, and no stretch of imagination could convince him that the instruments spread out on the tray had been used in enjoyable endeavours. The space was thankfully empty.

The third room was not.

The girl who hung limply from chains in the centre of this room looked to be barely eighteen – an impression only heightened by the schoolgirl outfit and pigtails. Her head lolled to one side, eyes glassy and unfocused as a vampire knelt before her, trousers around his ankles while he ravaged her femoral artery.

Red haze filled Shade's vision.

Before the vamp could turn from his helpless prey, Shade pulled his penknife out and rammed it into the side of the vamp's throat.

The vampire roared and stumbled backwards, tripping over the trousers tangled around his feet. The sight was so pathetic that Shade couldn't even bring himself to make the man's suffering last; he snapped the vamp's neck in one swift movement and retrieved his penknife in disgust.

He turned to walk from the room but stopped before he could reach the door. Unable to stop himself, he looked back at the girl's limp body.

There was no helping her, he knew that. Either she'd come here voluntarily, in which case she'd do it again, or she'd been stupid enough to be tricked into coming. If so, it wouldn't be long before some other predator would scent her out for the easy prey that she was. Whichever way he looked at it, it was only a matter of time before she was dead. And yet, he couldn't bring himself to leave her in her current state.

"Fucking idiot," he muttered to himself.

He unhooked her from the chains as quickly as he could and lowered her to the ground. There was no hint of awareness from her as he did, and he didn't make any attempt to get a response either. He simply tore the end of his T-shirt off and tightened it around the wound on her upper thigh. Whether it would be enough to keep her alive, he had no idea. He left the room, his head pounding in rage and the scent of the girl's blood clinging to his nostrils.

The remaining rooms were each different variations of depraved. Lucas's features were as strained as his own when they had finally cleared them all.

Grateful to be away from the black doors, they continued down the corridor until they reached a dead end and an elevator. Metal doors stood open, beckoning them into the empty interior. A retina scanner to the left of the lift glowed green.

Shade looked at Lucas.

The older vamp pressed a small earpiece in his left ear that allowed them to communicate with the others outside the club. "Nate, did you hack the elevator security on this level?"

Shade couldn't hear Nate's response in his own earpiece, but Lucas frowned and shook his head. "This wasn't Nate. Which means someone is expecting us."

Footsteps could be heard in the distance, and they both tensed until Cormac's signature reached them. The wolves came into view seconds later, their expressions grim.

"Darius is gone." Cormac's eyes blazed in the dim light and blood spatter dotted his cheeks. "We found this in the main office." He held out a piece of white paper, crumpled and smeared with blood.

Lucas took it from him, and Shade read the words over his shoulder: "He's my pet now." He sucked in a breath and risked a glance at Cormac. The tightening of the wolf's jaw was subtle, but there was a calmness to the

Alpha that was more terrifying than any show of anger could be.

Lucas indicated to the waiting lift. "It appears he may have been expecting us."

Cormac's answering smile was terrifying. "We wouldn't want to be rude then, would we?"

25

Home – 2 weeks gone

It was a tight fit, but the two vampires and six wolves squeezed into the small tin container. *Now would be a perfect time for someone to cut the cables,* Shade thought as Cormac pressed the single button and the lift doors closed.

The descent took seconds, and they all spaced out around the sides in preparation for the attack that was surely waiting. The doors opened to silence.

Warily, they edged out of the lift one at a time. The room appeared to be a laboratory of sorts. Complicated-looking gadgets lined metal tables running along one side of the room, while the faded remnants of a chalk circle could be seen on the other. A large window allowed visibility into an empty white chamber on the left.

The fragrance of herbs mingled with the burnt aftertaste of chemicals and the odour was so potent it choked him. Yet none of it hid the coppery tang of blood, or the rot of days-old faeces. He shuddered as his mind offered him possibilities for what the lab and chambers had been used for.

A man in a stiff grey suit stepped through a shadowed doorway at the back of the room. "Oh, there you are. I was wondering when you might join us."

The man's posture was relaxed and open, and his smile made Shade want to punch him in the face. Even from a distance the swirling red of his eyes was apparent, and his signature, although familiar enough to be recognised as a shifter, felt tainted in a way that made Shade want to scrub his skin raw. Low growls rumbled from the wolves, but they all held still, awaiting Cormac's orders.

The newcomer moved further into the room, completely unphased by their reaction. "Please, let me introduce myself. I'm Vicktor, head of the Council Liaison Office. Darius asked me to make sure his guests were properly welcomed. Can I get anyone a drink?" Vicktor's smile widened and he folded his hands in front of him.

Cormac stepped forward, his eyes flashing yellow in warning. "Where's Sean?"

"Oh, do forgive me." Vicktor clicked his fingers and called, "Can someone please bring out the mutt?"

A man and woman appeared from the shadows behind the CLO rep, dragging a limp form between them. Blood and dirt caked the body, and shredded rags hung loosely from emaciated limbs. The man and woman took no care as they dumped their package on the ground and stepped back, flashing grotesque grins which failed to hide the chilling calculation in their red eyes.

A deathly silence fell over the room. Shade could just about make out the faint beat of the Omega's heart so he knew Sean was alive, but there was no hiding the fact that he had been tortured to within an inch of his life.

Vicktor shrugged. "I guess some people just can't handle the pressure."

Without warning, Cormac lunged for him. Vicktor sidestepped the attack even as the other wolves followed their Alpha's lead and swarmed towards him. That left the other two demon-Supe hybrids to Shade and Lucas.

Shade faced off with the male – a vampire with a signature muddied enough to make him question whether there was truly any Supe left in the man – while Lucas turned his focus to the female. Shade allowed himself a moment to remember the young girl hanging from the chains while her vitality was slowly sucked dry from her. He let all the rage he'd felt in that moment to take him over now; he was going to make this hurt.

The room turned to chaos as bodies crashed into metal tables, smashing glass bottles and knocking equipment to the floor. Darius's abominations were outnumbered almost three to one and they shouldn't have stood a chance. But Shade was dimly aware of Vicktor's maniacal laughter in the background as each of his strikes missed by a fraction of a second; his opponent was just too fucking fast.

A fist connected with Shade's jaw, spinning him a full three-sixty and causing his vision to blur for a second. He groaned.

The vampire opened his mouth in what was probably supposed to be a cocky grin, and the stench of rotten flesh smacked Shade in the face. He fought against the urge to gag as he took in the blackened maw crawling with maggots. Yellow fangs lunged for him.

A loud rumble sounded and a tremor ran through the floor. The vamp was thrown off balance mid-lunge, and Shade used the reprieve to slip behind him and slice a clean line across his throat with his penknife.

Another shudder ran through the ground, and he had to reach for the wall to maintain his footing.

"Shade!" Lucas yelled from the far side of the room.

Shade turned to see the older vampire driven back by a blur of flashing claws that were attached to one scary-ass female. Despite Lucas's fighting skill, he seemed unable to get through the strikes to launch his own attack, or even disable the woman.

"Dammit." Shade launched himself over one of the metal tables that had been shoved into the middle of the room. He was dimly aware that the wolves had managed to surround Sean in a protective circle as he moved to help Lucas. Cormac was holding his own against Vicktor, but the CLO rep showed no signs of real damage.

An explosion sounded from the back of the room and suddenly the lab swarmed with a hoard of red-eyed Supes. Everything went to hell.

Shade lost sight of Lucas and found himself face-to-face with something from his nightmares. He could hear Cormac's roars as he tried to protect Sean and howls of pain from the wolves as they were attacked.

Another rumble tore through the earth and the ground beneath his feet split apart. A groan of metal was the last thing he heard before the ceiling caved in on top of them.

The world shook around Abi as she stumbled her way down the fire escape of the abandoned building across the road from the Club of Night. Only Sasha's grip on her arm stopped her from falling down the metal steps when the next tremor hit. Her head was pounding and a thin stream of blood ran from her forehead, obscuring her vision.

"Get to the street," Fia ordered from behind them as she helped Nate haul what little of their comms equipment remained intact.

The first tremor had taken them all by surprise. Earthquakes were unheard of in Ireland, so Abi's first thought had been a bomb explosion.

When the next shockwave hit and the road between their building and the club had split in two, she realised what was happening just in time to get brained by a falling plank of wood that had moments before served as a rooftop billboard.

On the far side of the road, bodies streamed out of the club. The Council security team had obviously unblocked the exits when the building had begun to crumble around them. As she raced down the final flight of steps, Abi scanned the crowd for any sign of a familiar face. Where were the others? They couldn't stay in there; the building was going to collapse.

Behind her, Nate muttered curses under his breath as he tried without luck to get the comms to connect. "I'm just getting static. Either the signal's down or …"

"Okay," Fia said with a calm she couldn't possibly feel as they reached the chaos of the street. "We need to go in after them. Sasha, come with me. Nate, get Abi clear in case the building falls."

Abi opened her mouth to protest – she was pretty sure a collapsing building was just as dangerous for a Supe as it was for her – but the two wolves took off at a run before she could speak. They leapt over a huge crevice that bisected the road and disappeared into the wreckage of Darius's club.

"Dammit, now would have been a good time for that backup to arrive," Nate muttered.

She gave him a questioning glance, but he ignored it and beckoned her to follow. "Come on. We need to secure the back of the building."

Her legs were shaky, but she managed to keep pace with him without breaking an ankle on any of the spiderweb cracks that had created an obstacle of concrete ahead of them. Sirens echoed in the distance, and the sound seemed to spur the club's patrons to clear the vicinity at record speed. Only a few of the more badly wounded men and women stumbled about in a daze and if Abi had to guess, she'd say they were the human customers.

Miraculously, the worst of the damage appeared to be at the front of the club. The tight knot of dread eased just a little in her chest as she took in the remaining people fleeing through the emergency exits. Most were covered in dust and appeared a little worse for wear, but if they were alive she had no reason to believe their friends weren't too.

Nate pulled her back into the shadows, his eyes darting between the doors and the cracked screen of his phone. His phone did little more than flicker on and off as he pressed the power button repeatedly, and she could sense his irritation growing with each futile attempt. It had to be killing him to be stuck out here babysitting her while his friends were trapped inside. Guilt gnawed at her and she stared at the doors, willing a familiar face to appear.

Minutes ticked by.

Finally, a woman Abi vaguely recognised as being part of the Council's security team emerged from the club. She moved with a limp, carrying a lifeless body over each shoulder. The woman didn't stop for a breath as she dumped the bodies on the ground and disappeared back inside.

Not waiting for Nate's permission, Abi hurried across the street to the lifeless forms. She couldn't help the uneasy sense of relief that struck her when she realised neither face was familiar, and she didn't even have the capacity to feel bad about it.

More of the Council's team emerged from the club hauling injured men and women. Nate grabbed one of them. "Have you seen –"

The door slammed open, and Cormac's bloodied form appeared carrying an equally bloody body over his shoulder. He stumbled out into the street and his knees

186

buckled beneath him. Nate grabbed his shoulders and eased him to the ground.

"No." Cormac gritted his teeth and pushed back to standing. "We have to move. They're coming."

The door swung open once more, bringing with it the sound of fighting and a loud crash. Fia pushed Sasha through the exit and, without stopping, wrapped her arm around Cormac's waist, urging him to move. "Shade and Lucas are trying to hold them back. We don't have long."

Abi had no chance to ask who it was they were running from before Nate lifted her off her feet and took off at a speed that sent her already-pounding head spinning. He didn't slow down until they reached a quiet street a few blocks over, at which point her stomach retched in protest and deposited its contents on the ground.

The others reached their side a moment later. Breathing hard, Cormac lay the body he was carrying down on the ground. He pushed the blood-caked hair back from an almost skeletal face. "Sean? Sean, can you hear me? Come on, Omega, your Alpha is talking to you, give me something, dammit."

Fia knelt opposite him and quickly ran her hands over the unconscious wolf, assessing his injuries. Her features tightened as she uncovered vicious slashes that exposed muscle and sent Abi's stomach reeling again. Charred bands surrounded the wolf's ankles and wrists, and now that he was lying down, Abi noticed that more than one limb was bent at an unnatural angle.

She bit back tears and bile rose up in her throat. What had they done to him?

A light breeze skimmed her face and she almost jumped out of her skin as Shade and Lucas appeared beside her. Cormac looked up from his position on the ground in question.

"They don't seem to be following us," Lucas told him, grey eyes darkening as he took in Sean's injured form. "We held them back until the emergency vehicles and human authorities arrived. After that, none of them seemed inclined to follow us out of the club."

Fia frowned, looking off in the distance to where the sounds of sirens could still be heard. "Darius clearly isn't ready to show off his new toys to everyone just yet."

Shade grimaced. "We're fucked when he is. The bastards were strong. Fast too. If that roof hadn't collapsed and trapped half of them …"

They all fell silent, no one wanting to consider just how tenuous their victory tonight had been. Abi wrapped her arms around herself as a chill that had nothing to do with the cool night air settled into her bones.

"How is he doing?" Lucas asked, crouching down beside Cormac.

"Alive, but –"

Everyone froze. As one, the Supes all whipped their heads around to face the end of the street, tension radiating from each of them.

Abi's breath caught in her throat and she swallowed hard to hold back the whimper that tried to escape. She stared into the dark, waiting. As silent as the night, Sasha moved to her side, vicious claws elongating from her hands.

Seven shadowy figures came into view from around a corner. They walked in sync with each other, staying side by side so that they spanned the width of the street.

"Witches," Sasha whispered, her eyes flashing yellow.

The seven figures stopped about fifty feet from their group and a slender girl with long, fair hair stepped forward. If Abi had to guess she'd say they girl was little more than sixteen, but the witch showed no sign of fear as she faced them with her shoulders squared.

"We're going to need you to give us the Omega." Her voice rang clear in the silence, no hint of threat in her tone, but also no room for doubt.

Cormac and Fia stood, placing themselves as a barrier in front of Sean. Sasha moved to their side. Low growls rumbled from the wolves as three pairs of yellow eyes glowed in the darkness.

"We don't have time for this," the girl said firmly.

The wolves all tensed to attack, but Nate pushed past them, his hands held forward in a gesture of peace. "Izzie?"

Abi felt as much as saw the others around her flinch with the same confusion she felt. Nate knew this girl?

"It is Izzie, isn't it? I got your email. I'm the one who sent the message from Annabelle's account. We're on the same side."

Abi struggled to follow exactly what was happening. Who the hell was Izzie, and why was Nate messaging a witch from a dead girl's account? Was this the backup he'd mentioned earlier?

"You need to step away from the wolf," the girl repeated, eyes firmly fixed on the wolves.

Abi glanced down at Sean and gasped when she saw his body twitch. Instinctively, she moved to crouch at his side.

"No!" Izzie yelled.

She stretched out her hand and a blast of blue light shot from her palm. It wrapped around Sean just as his body jerked up from the ground, eyes wide and crazed. He froze mid-movement.

The wolves roared and moved to attack her, but Lucas shot in front of them, arms wide to halt their momentum. "Wait. Look." He pointed back at Sean, who seemed to be held in some kind of stasis by the blue light that shone like a bubble around him.

Abi's heart pounded in her throat as she too looked at the Omega. Sean's wolf fangs were fully extended, saliva dripping from them, and his eyes ... his eyes were flooded crimson red. "Is he ..."

The witch walked to their side, expression sombre. "Possessed."

26

Faerie – day 3

"What exactly did you think you were doing in the tunnels? Access was blocked off a long time ago, and for a very good reason."

Ethan could feel the weight of Aoife's hardened stare boring into him, but he couldn't take his eyes off Phoenix's still form. The crisp white sheets of her bed only accentuated the deathly pale of her skin, and her hand was cold as it rested in his. Every second that ticked by was torture. Every minute that she remained unconscious only increased the roaring in his head until he was convinced that he'd go crazy.

He ignored Aoife's question, just like he had every other time she'd asked, instead repeating, "We need to get her to a doctor."

Aoife huffed out a frustrated breath. "The healer has already checked her. Her vitals are strong, her body just needs time to heal."

"You don't understand." He clenched the bed sheets with his free hand to stop the scream of frustration from freeing itself from his throat. It had been hours. She should have woken up by now.

Every time he closed his eyes he could see the avalanche of earth swallow her whole. He'd watched, trapped and helpless as the tunnels collapsed on top of her. He'd fought with every last breath in his body to free himself of the vines so he could go to her. His only thought as the world turned black had been of Phoenix and their baby.

When he'd come to in the glaring light of day, he thought for a moment that he'd passed to the other side. The stories always tell of that magical white place where good people go when they die. He had been a good person, hadn't he?

But then the pain had kicked in and he knew he was still alive.

Aoife had come to him soon after he'd awoken. How she'd known where to find them he still wasn't sure, but either the cave-in, or whatever ward controlled the roses, had alerted her to their presence in the tunnels. Initially, her only concern had been getting them both to safety and ensuring they were unharmed. But when he'd refused to stay in bed – ignoring her frustrated protests to stumble weakly to Phoenix's side – anger had overtaken her concern, and she'd deemed him fit for an ear lashing.

"So, tell me," she snapped. "What is it I don't understand?"

When he didn't immediately answer, she threw her hands up in the air and resumed pacing. Her hair was in disarray and her clothes were still covered in dirt from when she had dug Phoenix free of the earth that had buried her. He knew she'd kept a vigilant watch at her niece's side for the brief time that he'd been unconscious himself, and something vaguely like guilt settled in the pit of his stomach.

"I know you and Phoenix have been keeping secrets, and I won't force you to confide in me. But I don't understand what it is I've done to earn your mistrust."

He let out a growl of frustration, looking once more at Phoenix's still form. The swell of her abdomen was more noticeable than it had been when they'd left home. How much longer before it would become difficult to hide? If they had to stay here, it was only a matter of time before their secret was revealed, and he needed to know that the baby was safe.

"She's pregnant."

Aoife's pacing abruptly ceased. A tense silence fell over the room and Ethan held his breath.

"Is it yours?"

He nodded.

Aoife exhaled, long and slow. "Thank you for being honest with me. You have nothing to worry about. The baby is fine."

He looked up in surprise. "You knew?"

She gave him a sad smile. "The healer discovered it when she was examining Phoenix. She is sworn to secrecy, but I needed to know whether or not you would tell me the truth."

The soft murmur of voices reached through the fog to Phoenix as a warm heat radiated through her. Her eyes were so heavy, the simple effort of peeling them open was enough to exhaust her and make her want to sink back into blissful oblivion. A kind face peered down at her before giving a satisfied nod and disappearing. Harsh, unforgiving daylight assaulted her eyes and she scrunched them closed with a wince.

"Phoenix. Phoenix, can you hear me?"

There was a barely contained urgency in Ethan's voice as his calloused hand gripped hers. His musky scent filled her senses, and that along with his touch became her focal point to centre herself.

Where was she? She blinked her eyes gingerly.

It was Ethan's worried face which filled her vision this time as he leaned over and smoothed her brow with his thumb.

"Hey." The word came out more of a croak than she'd intended it to.

A slender hand held a small shell of water to her lips so that she could drink. Phoenix flicked her eyes up as she took a grateful sip and was surprised to find that the hand belonged to her aunt.

The familiar surroundings of her bedroom came into focus, and she struggled to think through the murkiness that clouded her head. She was cocooned by the soft cushions on her bed, and Ethan and her aunt were both here with her in the room. But how had she gotten here? And why were they looking so worried?

A thunderous roar filled her head. An overwhelming sense of suffocation washed over her, replacing the warm feeling she'd had only moments before. The smell of earth assaulted her. The heavy weight crushed her.

She bolted upright in the bed.

Ethan grabbed her shoulder, stopping her before she could move any further. "Shh. It's okay. Everything's okay now." He eased her back to the pillow, all the while murmuring quiet reassurances and telling her again and again that it was okay.

But how could it be? The memory of the cave in hit her in full Technicolor. It had happened so fast she hadn't had a chance to be afraid, but even in that fraction of a second, she'd known it was going to be anything but okay.

"The healer said you might have a bit of a concussion, but your body is doing what it needs to in order to repair itself," Ethan said gently, propping pillows up behind her so that she could sit up a little. "You just need to rest and let your body do its thing."

She looked at him with wide eyes, trying desperately to convey without words the panic that was racing through her.

"The baby's fine," he confirmed.

She jerked, her eyes darting towards Aoife.

He gave her a wry smile. "She knows. The healer discovered it when she was examining you."

Phoenix's breath caught for a whole different reason this time as she looked from Ethan to her aunt. Neither of their expressions gave any indication of how the news had been received and nausea twisted in her gut.

"How ... how long have I been out? What happened?"

"A few hours. From what we can tell, there seems to have been an earthquake of some kind that rippled through Faerie. It caused the cave-in."

An earthquake? A few hours? How badly had she been hurt? She reached for her abdomen, seeking comfort from the small flutter of life beneath her hand.

"I haven't shared your secret with my parents," Aoife said finally. "But I'm going to need you both to start being honest with me. What were you doing in the tunnels?"

Ethan gave a slight shake of his head to indicate he hadn't told her aunt anything else. Phoenix gave sighed and met her aunt's shrewd gaze, resigned.

"When Morrigan sent us here, she also wanted us to find something. A spear."

Aoife's manicured eyebrows shot up. "The Spear of Lugh?"

Phoenix bit her lip and nodded.

"Why would Morrigan send you to retrieve the spear?"

It was Ethan who answered when Phoenix struggled for the right thing to say. "She believes it may be needed again – to banish the Horsemen."

Aoife's already pale skin turned ashen. "The Horsemen were banished a millennia ago. They can't return."

And that was the problem. How could they explain it all without revealing the prophecy? How could Phoenix admit it was her fault that there was now even a possibility of the Horsemen's return without it being seen as proof her parents' love really was wrong?

"The fabric is growing weak," Ethan said in answer. "Demons are managing to cross over again, and human possessions are happening at an increasing frequency. They've only been minor demons so far, but it's clear from the pattern that the problem is progressing and it's only a matter of time before the barrier fails."

Aoife digested his words, her brow creasing with worry as she did. She was quiet for a moment before nodding, seeming to come to some internal decision.

"As I'm sure you've guessed by now, the spear is here in the castle. The tunnels, while once used as a secure escape route, also lead to some underground chambers that have been used over the centuries to protect important fae artefacts held by our family."

"The roses ..." Ethan shivered.

"One of many wards set to protect the chambers. The artefacts used in the original banishment were created by the Tuatha De Danann themselves, and as such were passed down through our family. The sword was Aria's birthright and was passed to her when she came of age and reached her immortality. The spear is mine."

Phoenix's heart stuttered. The spear belonged to her aunt? She could help them. If they could just make her understand.

She sat up, ignoring Ethan's protests, and reached out a beseeching hand to the woman who looked so much like her mother and yet was not. "I know you have no reason to trust us —"

"It is not I who has the issue with trust."

She bowed her head, unable to refute the accusation in her aunt's words. Quietly she said, "We came here because we have been betrayed, more than once, by people we trusted. The man I looked up to as an uncle my entire life was the very same monster responsible for my parents' death." Her breath hitched, but she swallowed and forced herself to continue. "You know our secret. Surely you must understand why we would be afraid to confide in you?"

A deep sadness softened Aoife's hard expression and she inclined her head. "Be that as it may, if you had come to me with the truth from the beginning, we would be having this conversation from a place of greater understanding now. You seek the spear, and you now know the only way to acquire it is with my help, or through my death. I'm not quite sure what to do with this information."

A numb sense of disbelief settled over Phoenix. Did her aunt honestly believe they would challenge her for the spear if she chose not to help them? How had they gotten to a place where it was even fathomable for family to turn on each other like that?

Aoife sighed and straightened. "As with all children of the Lore, I grew up hearing stories of the Horsemen and the horrors that followed in their wake, so I'm well aware of what it would mean for both our lands if what you say is true. However, we have heard no mention here in Faerie of the fabric failing, nor can I see of any reason

198

why it would after all these millennia. Unless there is more that you can tell me, I don't know if I can help you."

"It's my fault," Phoenix blurted out. "It's my fault that the fabric is failing." She looked at her hands and let the words hang heavy in the air.

When the barrage of disgust and condemnation wasn't immediately forthcoming, Phoenix risked a quick peek up from under her lashes. Aoife simply waited, looking at her in patient expectation. So she took a deep, shuddery breath and explained it all. She told her aunt about Darius, and her parents' abduction, about the prophecy she'd unknowingly triggered, the people who were trying to stop it. And about the baby, who was their greatest hope.

When she finished, her aunt smiled. The haunted look remained in those green eyes, but for that moment, there was something different in Aoife's expression that reminded Phoenix of her mother.

Aoife stood from her chair by the bed. "You need to get some rest, and I need to think on what you've told me. I will keep your secret for now, and I advise you to do the same. But I fear there will come a time when we'll all have to face our own personal demons. The Horsemen were not banished by weapons alone. It took all species of the Lore working together to defeat them. I'm not quite sure if that capacity exists within us anymore."

27

Home – 2.5 weeks gone

Abi curled her legs closer to her body as she sat on the sofa and sought warmth from the mug of tea clasped in her hands. The sun had begun its descent beyond the city skyline as she stared out the panoramic window that ran the length of Ethan's apartment, and the sky had gone from a clear blue to streaks of red and orange. Almost a week after their arrival, and it was still strange to be back in Dublin. To be so close to her beloved pub knowing that it still sat in ruins after the witch fire.

They'd all agreed that it wasn't a good idea to move Sean far; the witches' stasis spell was limited by distance, and until they could find a way to help him, they couldn't risk releasing him from it. She'd agreed to stay behind with Nate and Sasha to watch over him, though how much her bedside vigil really helped she had no idea.

It had devastated Cormac and Fia to leave their Omega. The group had barely made it back to Ethan's apartment after the earthquake when word came from Donegal that wildfires were spreading across the pack lands and destroying homes. The whole country, in fact, seemed to have been hit with a series of freak natural disasters, and instinct warned Abi that it was not a good omen.

God, she still couldn't believe that Darius had turned Sean into one of his demon hybrids. For him to survive so long only for it to come to this ... She clutched the mug tighter to her as if it alone might push away the chill that settled in her heart.

The sharp buzz of the apartment bell sounded, and low voices drifted towards her from the hallway. She unfurled herself from the soft cushions and stood as Nate came into the open plan living area with Izzie close behind him.

Izzie shook her head when Nate offered her a drink and settled herself on a stool at the island in the centre of the kitchen. Her expression was grim, and Abi was struck once more by just how young the girl looked.

Nate had told her that Izzie had been a friend of Annabelle's – Lily's younger sister who had died before Abi had had a chance to meet her. When they'd learned that the Council head of the witches was dead, Nate had tried to reach out to Izzie through Annabelle's email account. They'd need a witch to aid them with the banishment spell if it came to it, and with the Dublin coven at Darius's beck and call, it was hard to know who they could trust. What better option than a witch whom that very coven had tried to sacrifice?

Abi pulled up a stool beside Izzie, and unable to stop herself, she reached out and placed a hand on the girl's forearm. "Are you okay?"

Izzie gave her a weak smile. "An eighty-year-old lady tried to claw my eyes out earlier, and I'm not even sure she was possessed. Things are getting a bit weird out there." She blew out a breath and seemed to pull herself together. "Anyway, that's not why I'm here."

"Did you get what you need?" Nate asked.

Izzie regarded him with a serious expression. "We did. But I'm advising you again not to go through with this."

Abi's heart sped up its pace. The witches hadn't been very confident about their chances of freeing Sean from the demon. The level of demon Darius was pulling across was far beyond anything Phoenix had managed to trap in Lily's amulets, but they'd promised to try. They had to try.

"We can't leave him like that." Abi cringed at the desperation in her voice as she beseeched the young witch to understand. He had held on so long; they couldn't let him down now.

This time it was Izzie who reached over to give her hand a comforting squeeze. "Ethan saved my life. So if you ask me to do this, I will. But you need to understand this is bigger than anything I or any of the other witches have faced. We don't have the power of a coven behind us. We might not be strong enough."

Abi's brow furrowed in confusion. "I don't understand. You all work together. Does that not make you a coven?"

She didn't know much about the group of witches who'd turned up just in time to save them as Sean regained consciousness. Nate had told her they were fugitives from their various covens – witches who had rejected the use of dark magic. From what she understood, that made them weaker than witches who chose the dark magic path, but surely it didn't make them completely powerless?

"No," Izzie said, a hint of bitterness tinging her tone. "We are all still bound to our old covens, even if we don't agree to their practices. That kind of bond is unique, meant only to be forged once. It's impossible to create another with it in place."

"So find a way to sever it," Nate said simply. "Your coven tried to kill you; surely that's an acceptable loophole? You said it yourself, Ethan saved your life. You owe him this."

"Can … Would you do it?" Abi asked, searching the girl's face.

Izzie contemplated his words as painful memories warred behind her eyes. Eventually, she nodded slowly. "If the others agree, there may be a way we can sever the bonds so that we're free to form a new one. It will take a few days."

"We'll wait," Nate said, even as something in Abi rebelled at the thought of leaving Sean in his frozen hell for a moment longer.

"There's one more thing you should know. If we do manage to separate Sean from the demon, I can't promise you he'll still be whole. We don't know what damage has been done to him, but it's possible he may never recover from this. You need to decide if that's a chance you're willing to take."

Abi met Nate's amber eyes, unease twisting in her stomach. Is this what Sean would want? She didn't know the Omega, had no way of knowing what he might want for himself.

Footsteps sounded and Sasha came into the kitchen, her eyes appearing tired but her expression determined. She put the book she'd been reading to Sean down on the marble top of the island. "We'll take the chance."

"My dad's ready to blow a gasket," Sasha said as she dropped into the leather recliner across from Abi with a sigh.

Nate had gone to his room to do some more research on the history of demon possessions once Izzie had left, and Abi had found it impossible to sleep as worries for Phoenix and Sean both competed for attention in her head. She'd given up trying a little after midnight and decided to make some warm milk like her mother used to do for her when she was small. It didn't surprise her that her friend was still awake and looking wired. She'd heard the murmur of Sasha's voice down the hall as she'd spoken on the phone with Cormac. Even without being able to hear the words, it had been clear to Abi that things weren't going well.

"Did the fires do much damage?"

Sasha waved a hand, looking distracted. "Some, but the pack will rebuild any of the homes that need it."

"So what has him so wound up?"

"The Council. William called and thanked him for his assistance at the club, but now that we have Sean back, our part in things is done." Sasha looked up, her brown eyes hard. "Apparently, the situation is too dangerous for 'civilians' to be involved, and they will 'deal' with it from here."

Abi grimaced, imagining all too well the reaction that call had gotten from Cormac. Hell, even she thought it was insulting, given the Council probably still wouldn't have a clue what Darius was up to if not for their help.

"What's your dad going to do?"

Another sigh, this one telling her just how much the recent weeks had taken their toll on the wolf despite her joking and sarcasm. "Damned if I know. It's his job to protect us, to protect the pack. Every part of him will be screaming for revenge for what Darius did to Sean, but with everything going on at the moment, and worrying about Ethan …"

"You think it's better letting the Council deal with it?"

"Hell no! The Council can't get their own shit together, never mind deal with Darius, but I worry that if he gets into another situation like the one at the club and his head's not fully in it … Well, you saw for yourself. It was only luck that got them out of there last time." Sasha fell quiet as she remembered whatever horrors she'd seen in the club that night.

Abi took in her friend's creased brow and the subtle tightness around her jaw. She wished there was something she could do to ease the worry they were all feeling, to make a real difference to the situation rather than hanging around the sidelines and trying not to be a liability. If Phoenix was here she could talk to her best friend about it, admit just how inadequate she felt. Phoenix might be a Supe, but she understood — she'd spent most of her life believing she wasn't good enough to be part of the Lore.

But Phoenix wasn't here, and there wasn't anything Abi could say. So she stayed quiet, and they sat together, each lost in their own worries of what was to come.

28

Home – almost 3 weeks gone

Darius leaned on the metal rail of the platform and assessed the mass of bodies below. Men and women stood with lethal readiness, their crisp black uniforms a stark contrast to the sterile white walls of the pharmaceutical complex's centre chamber. All species were accounted for except two: the Mists and the fae.

A shiver of anticipation ran through him as he finally beheld the fruits of his labour. Years of testing and failed experiments had to be endured before they'd perfected the process that allowed him to first break the subjects to his will. Hundreds of wasted test subjects. But now, here they were. His army.

Ideally, he'd have liked to manage a full house, a demon match for every species. But recent centuries had seen the Mists become so rare that many forgot they were even a species of the Lore, and something about the ancient nature of fae magic meant the few transfers he'd attempted on them had failed drastically. It wouldn't matter though, because the time had come to move forward.

Erik appeared at his side, his head of security's movements even more silent and deadly since his own transfer had been completed days before.

"They're quite impressive," Erik noted, following Darius's gaze to the army that awaited their orders.

"The final behavioural issues seem to have been resolved."

He'd waited as long as possible before placing his head of security into the transfer chamber. A strong army needed a strong commander to keep them in line, and he needed the barrier as weak as possible to have a chance of pulling through an acolyte of the Horsemen. The recent spate of natural disasters was enough to assure him that the balance was finally shifting in their favour, and it seemed his faith had been rewarded.

Erik's wide smile showcased razor-sharp fangs and caused his red eyes to gleam. "They just needed a firm hand. It was nice of the Council to give us a chance to test them in the field. Though I'm a bit disappointed that their security teams didn't provide a better challenge."

Indeed, it had been depressingly predictable when the Council followed up their raid on the Club of Night with further raids on his other businesses, the pharmaceutical complex included. Their security teams didn't get far, though he'd made sure his army left some alive to send a message back to the Council.

"How many of the rejects are left?" he asked, turning his thoughts to the subjects who had completed the transformation, but whose level of control hadn't made the cut. They could still be useful to him. He turned from the platform, Erik moving with him as he made his way down the long corridor that led back to the private laboratories.

"Thirteen are left after the last group were sent to entertain the Council. Ready to be released when you say."

"Have them prepared, we may need them as a distraction. You managed to get hold of Vicktor?"

"He's waiting in your office."

"Good. It's time he makes up for his failure at the club."

Darius stopped in front of a metal door with a retina scanner and dismissed Erik with a wave. The scanner moved across his eyes and the door opened with a hiss to reveal a small white room that was as sterile and nondescript as the rest of the building. The heady aroma of herbs drifted to him from a glass vial of green liquid resting above an unlit Bunsen burner.

The witch didn't bother to look up as he approached, her attention focused on a half-torn piece of parchment lying on the metal table to the left of the burner. Her lips moved soundlessly as she scanned the faded words, a scowl firmly fixed on her face.

"Have you found anything?"

She made no attempt to mask her irritation as she raised her head, one eyebrow arched. "Your Sire kept some interesting records, but I've found nothing to suggest that he knew the cauldron's location."

Darius had expected that answer. He'd gone through Il Maestro's records many times over the centuries; if there had been anything to find, he was confident he would have already.

"We will proceed regardless."

The surprise that widened her eyes disappeared as quickly as it came. "Without the artefacts, the vessel —"

"Yes, yes, I know." He waved a hand dismissively. "We have the ingredients we need to proceed, do we not?"

"Yes," she answered warily.

"Then it is decided. We move forward with the transfer. Once I hold the power of the Horsemen within me, it will be a simple matter to find the artefacts; no one will dare stand in my way." He turned and strode back to the door. "Come. We need to send word to Faerie. It's time for the hybrid to return."

The witch's expression screamed her disapproval, but she wisely kept her mouth shut. She walked to the Bunsen burner and removed the glass vial resting above it, plugging the top with a small cork. Without a word, she followed him from the lab and down to his office on the ground floor.

Vicktor was already seated when they arrived, his red eyes fixed firmly ahead. There was no sign remaining of the damage he'd sustained when the earthquake had hit the Club of Night, or of the punishment he'd received afterwards for his failure. It seemed the shifter's natural healing ability was significantly accelerated by the presence of the demon within him, a fortunate coincidence or he might not be alive now to make up for his shortcomings.

"Vicktor, it's time you made yourself useful." Darius leaned against the mahogany desk as the witch stood by the door watching the two men closely. "We are ready to proceed to the next stage of our plan."

"What do you need me to do?"

"Send word to our friend in Faerie." He waved for the witch to hand over the vial. "They need to ensure the hybrid drinks this just before she returns to our world."

Vicktor took the glass vial and slipped it into a pocket on the inside of his suit jacket. He was about to speak when a sharp rap sounded, and Erik stepped into the office.

"Sire, we have guests."

Darius raised an eyebrow at the glint in the vampire's eye.

"The Council are here. They are in the lobby and are demanding to speak with you."

Vicktor straightened in his chair. "As head of the Council Liaison Office, please let me kindly escort them from the premises for you?"

He moved to stand, but Darius stopped him with a hand on the shoulder. "You have a more important job to see to." He turned to Erik and the witch, both standing alert by the door, and smiled. "I think we will go greet the Council personally."

29

Home – almost 3 weeks gone

Abi still found the sound of her voice strange in the quiet of the bedroom. She'd first started reading to Sean while he'd been unconscious, held in a magical stasis by the witches. His being in a magic-induced coma hadn't stopped her from feeling self-conscious, but she'd kept going in the hope that some part of him could hear her and would appreciate the sound of a friendly voice. Now that the stasis had been lifted, the gentle flow of his breathing accompanied her words, and occasionally his eyelids would twitch as if he might be dreaming.

She sometimes wondered whether his dreams were pleasant. Did he have a safe haven he could retreat to in his sleeping hours that allowed him to escape the horror of his waking reality? Or did those horrors follow him even to the depths of his unconsciousness?

Izzie had warned them the spell to separate Sean from the demon would take a lot out of him and that it might be a while before he woke, even with the stasis now lifted.

There had been a grey tinge to the witch's skin as she said this, and it had taken an obvious effort for her to remain standing, the spell having taken everything she and her newly formed coven could give. And even after all that, they still had no guarantees. The waiting was torture.

Cormac and the others had returned from Donegal to be there when their Omega woke. While they had more right to be by his side than she could ever claim, Abi found herself reluctant to leave him. So, she stayed and read to him, just like she had in the days before the separation.

The others didn't question her presence as they took turns to check on him, and she took that as an excuse not to delve too deeply into her own motivations.

She flipped to the next page of the book and told the sleeping wolf with a smile, "This is my favourite part. Rachel goes to –"

A bang of a door and shouting somewhere in the apartment froze the words in her mouth. The book fell to the floor as she scrambled to her feet. Heart pounding, she crept to the door of the bedroom and peered out.

Cormac stood at the open front door, a look of shock on his face as a large bloody man stumbled through, nearly collapsing before Cormac caught him. A smaller Asian man followed, helping a red-haired woman through with him. Both were as battered as the first man, with vicious cuts visible even from Abi's vantage point down the hall.

She could hear Fia issuing orders to get first aid supplies as she slipped out of the bedroom, book forgotten, and hurried to join the others in the living area.

"What happened?" she asked Sasha as she grabbed the first aid box from the cupboard in the kitchen and handed it to the wolf. So much blood, god there was so much blood.

"Council" was the only response she got before Sasha hurried off to help Fia, who looked like she was about to tackle the red-haired woman to the ground if she didn't shut up and agree to have her wounds checked.

An almost hysterical giggle caught in Abi's throat as she noticed the woman's eerie likeness to Jessica Rabbit. With all the blood covering her, it looked like she belonged in a horror movie, but the resemblance was there, nonetheless.

On the far side of the room, Cormac was arguing with the large man he'd hauled into the apartment, barely able to stand. Only the Asian man seemed willing to cooperate as he quietly allowed Lucas to clean up the worst of his injuries. Abi stood in the middle of it all, unsure exactly what to do.

"Dammit, William," Cormac growled, throwing the first aid box at the bloodied man. He stalked to the drinks cabinet, poured a large glass of whiskey, and slammed it down on the table in front of him. "What the hell were you thinking going after Darius without backup?"

William just glared back, his eyes blazing. But there was something else other than anger behind those eyes; there was fear too.

It was the Asian man who answered softly. "We had no choice other than to step in. In the days since the raid on the Club of Night, we have sent three teams to the locations linked with Darius's alias to retrieve him so that he might be punished for his actions. All but one of those teams failed to return, and the one that did … Well, his message was very clear. The Council had to confront him."

"He was expecting us," William said through gritted teeth. "It shouldn't have mattered – no one person is stronger than the Council combined. But those things he's created, they're stronger and faster than all of us."

"Wait," Shade cut in, pushing away from the window where he'd been observing the chaos with a scowl on his face. "If all the remaining Council confronted Darius, where is the head of the vampires?"

The red-haired woman's expression went blank, but the look in her eyes chilled Abi to her very core. "Vlad chose to make himself scarce when it was clear things weren't going how we expected."

"He ran away?" Lucas's eyebrows shot skywards.

The three Council members stayed quiet, but their silence was answer enough.

"So why come to us now?" Cormac pushed, no sign of the anger on his face letting up. "After the club, you made it clear our help wasn't required anymore. You could have gone anywhere to sort these injuries. Why are you here?"

A tense silence fell over the room as Cormac and William stared at each other, neither blinking or looking away.

215

The anger drained from William's face to be replaced by pure exhaustion. "We underestimated him. Whatever Darius is planning, we need to stop it now before he gets any stronger than he already is."

"What do you propose?" Nate asked, a curious glint in his amber eyes.

Abi jumped; she hadn't noticed that the shifter had moved to her side.

"We need to cut off his access to the demons," the Asian man said quietly. "We can't stop the prophecy without killing the hybrid –"

"Still an option," the red-haired woman interjected brightly. Everyone in the room glared at her, but she simply shrugged.

"As I was saying," the Asian man continued with a pointed stare at her. "We can't stop it without the hybrid's death or the birth of her child, but it might be time we consider trying to repair the barrier to buy us time."

"I don't understand." The words came out without thinking, and Abi blushed as all eyes turned to her. "I mean, I get that demons are tough to fight, but I thought the barrier needed to be almost entirely gone before the really bad guys could get through?" She looked at Nate and he nodded in confirmation. "So how is Darius getting hold of demons strong enough to possess Supes, not to mention defeat the Council?"

An uneasy silence fell in the room. Eventually William shook his head. "We don't know."

"I do."

Everyone turned in surprise to the softspoken voice. Sean leaned against the entryway to the kitchen, his face

216

gaunt and body looking like it was struggling to keep him upright. His shaggy white hair hung in stringy clumps around his face, partially obscuring his sunken blue eyes.

"Sean." Cormac was on his feet and at the Omega's side in an instant. He wrapped his arm around the other wolf and half-supported, half-carried him to the sofa opposite William.

Abi couldn't take her eyes off them. Though Sean appeared remarkably lucid, the haunted look shadowing his eyes was unmistakable. That same look had stared back at her from the mirror on more than one occasion, and her heart constricted in pained recognition.

The wolf lifted his head and met her gaze. A ghost of a smile tugged at the corner of his mouth, and then it was gone as the room turned into a buzz of eager questions.

Sean answered as best he could, explaining exactly how it was that Darius was pulling through major-level demons. His voice faltered more than once, and Abi felt an unexplainable urge to yell at them all. Could they not see how hard this was for him? He needed to rest. But she knew they didn't have that luxury. As hard as it was watching him relive what was done to him and the other Supes, they needed any information that Sean could give them.

It wasn't just Abi who was on edge by the time the questioning finished. The tension simmered at near-boiling point in the room, and she had the uncomfortable sense that it would take only the barest spark for it to explode.

Cormac's head rested in his hands, his knuckles white as he took a moment to deal with whatever emotions he felt at hearing his Omega's story. When he finally looked up, his face was an unreadable mask, and his eyes were calm and calculating. "What's involved in strengthening the barrier?"

"The ritual that was used to banish the Horsemen should work with a few tweaks, but it takes a significant amount of power." William picked up the untouched glass of whiskey and knocked it back in one. "If we do this and shit keeps going south, we'll have severely weakened our ability to fight."

"But if we don't, Darius keeps getting access to more and more power. He'll be unstoppable."

"*If* we do it," the Asian man said, "we must get it right the first time. There will be no second chances."

"Which means we have to make sure we can stop the prophecy. Otherwise the fabric will just begin unravelling again." The red-haired woman examined her red-tipped nails, seeming unconcerned with the possibility.

Abi snorted in disbelief. "Phoenix can't exactly click her fingers and speed up the pregnancy so that it coincides with the ritual."

The room fell quiet and everyone averted their eyes from her except the woman, who gave her a pitying look that made it clear she thought Abi to be stupid.

Nate placed an awkward hand on Abi's shoulder. "Morrigan said time moves differently in Faerie than it does here. Maybe enough time has passed …"

This time it was the red-haired woman that snorted.

Realisation punched Abi in the gut, knocking the wind out of her. "You don't think the baby will be enough." She looked around the room, beseeching them all to deny it.

Lucas's grey eyes were sympathetic when he finally met her challenging gaze. "We want to, Abi, but the Horsemen aren't our only problem now. Even if the baby comes in time to stop the prophecy, the longer we have to wait, the more time Darius has to amass his power. He may not need the Horsemen to destroy us all."

She shrugged off Nate's hand still resting uselessly on her shoulder and shook her head vehemently. "You're not killing Phoenix." She would fight them all with every breath in her body if that was what it took.

Lucas held up his hands. "No one is suggesting that."

She looked at William, who had remained silent throughout her outburst, and at the quiet Asian man who met her anger with calm understanding. The red-haired woman simply raised an eyebrow in amusement. "You are though, aren't you?" she challenged them. "The Council will kill her if there's no other way."

Silence was as good an answer as any.

Sean stood from the sofa, brushing off Cormac's protest. His legs were unsteady as he made his way to her and took her hand in his. "I will help you protect her. I give you my word."

There were exclamations of agreement from everyone in the room except the Council, but it was the steady assurance in those blue eyes that calmed her and allowed the tightness to ease marginally in her chest.

"What do we need to enact the ritual?" Fia asked, her voice sombre as she watched the interaction between Abi and Sean with a glint of curiosity.

"First off, we need the artefacts," William said.

"We can get them."

"Then we'll need a member of each species. The Council are short a witch at the moment, so we need to determine which of the covens can provide a trustworthy candidate."

"I'll speak to Izzie," Nate said. "She wants to end this as much as we do."

"And then there's the slight problem of the Mists."

Cormac nodded. "The Mists have sworn an oath to Phoenix; they will honour their vow." He turned to William. "I want your word that the Council will do them no harm. If they help us with this, it clears any debt they owe."

"Agreed."

Cormac's expression darkened and Abi shivered as she caught a glimpse of the predator lurking under the surface. "And let me be clear, if the Council do anything to hurt the mother of my grandchild, I will hold you all personally responsible."

"Let's hope it doesn't come to that."

The two wolves held each other's gazes for a long moment before seeming to come to a silent understanding. Cormac turned to Nate. "Get word to Morrigan. It's time to bring them home."

30

Faerie – day 4

Phoenix gritted her teeth as she yanked the brush through the knots and clumps of dirt that were still embedded in her hair. She'd made it out of bed and managed to get dressed without her body protesting too much. Now she just had to make it look like she hadn't been buried alive, and she'd be good to go.

A soft knock sounded on the bedroom door, and she sensed Ethan's signature even before he peeked his head inside. An argument about her being out of bed was inevitable and she tried her best not to laugh as she watched his expression turn from concern to exasperation almost in slow motion.

"What are you doing up?" His tone was careful as he stepped into the room and closed the door behind him, eyeing her like she might actually have gone crazy.

The temptation to wind him up was more than she could resist so she shrugged nonchalantly. "I was going to go for a run, but I'm not sure I'm dressed appropriately." She waved a hand over the loose tunic and trousers she'd chosen for convenience, the leather strap of her scabbard slung across her chest.

His face turned a worrying shade of red and muscles bulged in his arms as he folded them across his chest. "You can't be serious. You're meant to be in bed resting. What about —"

She burst out laughing, unable to hold it anymore. He glared at her.

"Oh, relax. I'm just going for a very tame stroll. I've been stuck in this room for the best part of twenty-four hours, I need fresh air." She smiled, feeling a little bad for winding him up when he was just worried about her and the baby.

She walked over and reached up to kiss him on the cheek. "The baby's fine," she assured him, taking his hand and placing it on her stomach.

He stared at his hand where it rested over the soft swell of her abdomen. A mix of emotions showed on his face all at once: fear and the all-consuming need to protect. He looked so lost and vulnerable that her heart ached. Her wolf.

"Will you walk with me?"

He gave a martyred sigh but offered his arm in defeat. "Your escort awaits, my lady."

It took longer than normal for them to make their way outside, with Ethan insisting that she move at a snail's pace. And though she resented being treated as an invalid, she had to admit that her body wasn't up to its full capabilities.

She breathed deeply as the light breeze tickled her skin and the warmth of the sun soaked into her cells, rejuvenating her body in a way nothing else other than blood could. There was something oddly peaceful about being here in Faerie, she realised.

Yes, they had to hide some of the most fundamental facts of their lives from her grandparents, but it was a relief to not be constantly looking over her shoulder, waiting for someone to try kill her, or for Darius to appear.

Now that she'd come clean to Aoife, it felt like a weight had been lifted. She'd confessed her sins to a member of her family, and she hadn't been rejected. It gave her a glimmer of hope that maybe, just maybe, history wouldn't have to repeat itself.

Thinking of her aunt turned her thoughts back to less cheery topics, however. "Has Aoife said any more about the earthquake that caused the cave-in?" she asked, shuddering as the smell of earth came to her as fresh as when she lay helpless beneath it.

Ethan gave her a sideways glance and hesitated, no doubt wondering if she was too fragile to have this discussion. "There's been word of similar earthquakes back home. She believes it might have something to do with the prophecy shifting the natural balance, and it's being mirrored here in Faerie." His expression tightened with the concerns he wouldn't voice.

Her mouth grew dry as she too thought of their friends back home and wondered where they'd been when the earthquake had hit.

"I'm sure they're all fine," she said as much for her own benefit as for his. "Morrigan would have sent for us if they were in trouble."

"Phoenix." Clíodhna's sharp voice stopped them in their tracks. "There you are."

Phoenix's breath caught in her throat. Aoife had promised not to say anything to her grandparents, but still her heart raced as she plastered a smile on her face and turned to see her grandmother striding towards them. Eoghan followed in Clíodhna's wake, and though his expression was carefully controlled, Phoenix got a strange sense that he was feeling particularly smug with himself. Beside her, Ethan bristled as he too spotted the fae lord.

Eoghan stopped before her and took her hand to place a soft kiss on the back of it. "Might I say, you are looking quite radiant this morning."

She squirmed uncomfortably under the intensity of his gaze and gave him a small smile.

"Indeed." Clíodhna's shrewd gaze assessed her. "Aoife mentioned that you were feeling unwell. Naturally we were concerned, given how few ailments afflict our kind. But perhaps it's just another quirk of your more ... unusual nature."

Phoenix fought to keep the smile in place. "I'm feeling much better, thank you, Grandmother." She extricated her hand from Eoghan's grip. "Eoghan, how lovely to see you again. I thought you'd be heading back to Eldridge by now?"

"Lord Eldridge has decided to remain in our court for a while longer," Clíodhna answered before he could speak. "He has declared his intentions to pursue you, and

I have given him my blessing." She smiled, but there was no warmth in her expression, only determination.

"He – you what?" Phoenix's ability to speak coherently failed her and she gaped at her grandmother, wondering if she'd missed the joke.

"With all due respect, my lady, surely Phoenix should be the one making that decision." To anyone that didn't know him, Ethan's words would have sounded polite, but Phoenix could see the danger that lurked in the lightening of his eyes and the tense set of his jaw.

Clíodhna's eyes flashed. "With all due respect to you, I do not expect a *werewolf* to understand our ways."

A low growl rumbled from Ethan's throat and Phoenix looked from him to her grandmother in panic. "Might I have a word with you in private, Grandmother?" she asked, moving her body ever so slightly as to place herself between them.

Of course, privacy was little more than an illusion in supernatural company, but nonetheless, Clíodhna humoured her by stepping aside, leaving the two men glaring at each other.

"While I appreciate the sentiment – and I am truly honoured – I didn't come here to find a mate," Phoenix said. "It would be unfair of me to lead Eoghan on."

If she hoped to find compassion beneath the steel of her grandmother's façade, she was sorely disappointed. Clíodhna shook her head, a mild look of disgust on her face. "Lord Eldridge is a very eligible match. You *should* be honoured. I will not have you disgracing this family further by denying him."

The look in her grandmother's eyes said everything her words did not. Phoenix might not be her mother, and Clíodhna might not realise just how much she'd followed in Aria's footsteps, but all she was to her grandmother was a reminder. She couldn't be punished for the sins of her mother, but she sure as hell wouldn't be allowed to forget them either.

Clíodhna turned from her and returned to the men, clearly deciding the matter was settled. Phoenix followed, a cold numbness settling through her as Eoghan offered her his hand.

Phoenix was physically and mentally exhausted by the time Eoghan finally took a breath from his incessant prattling and stopped walking. She looked up in surprise to find the huge wall that bordered her family's land in front of her. A shiver ran through her as she remembered Aoife's ominous comment about the lands beyond. She'd been so lost in her own thoughts that she hadn't even realised what direction they were walking in. Now, a creeping sense of unease made its way up her spine and she looked around, hoping to see someone who might question their presence. They were alone.

"What are we doing here?" she asked, hoping her voice sounded more curious than nervous.

The silver-haired fae lord gave her a conspiratorial wink. "I thought you might be up for a little adventure. It can't be much fun being stuck here in the castle all the time."

"We haven't exactly been prisoners."

"Ah, but have you had any adventures?"

If you only knew, she thought to herself.

She should have resisted more when Eoghan had led her away from Ethan and her grandmother. She'd been so afraid that Ethan's reaction to the lord would make Clíodhna suspicious that she'd hurriedly agreed to the walk and hadn't thought to insist they stay close to the castle.

Some naive part of her had even thought that maybe she could use the time to make him realise why a relationship between them would never work; but that had assumed she'd be able to get a word in edgeways to the very one-sided conversation.

Eoghan strode up to the wall, made an intricate gesture with his arms and said, "Open sesame." He gave her a cheeky grin. A wooden door appeared in the solid rock of the wall, and he opened it with a flourish.

"I don't think –"

"Nonsense." He waved away her protest. "We wouldn't want to waste this beautiful day. Let me show you some of Faerie's secrets. If nothing else, it will give us a break from your grandmother's interfering, well intentioned though it may be." He said this as though he hadn't been the very reason for Clíodhna's meddling, and Phoenix had to grit her teeth to stop herself from pointing it out.

She glanced behind her, hesitating, then stepped through the doorway after him. A solid line of trees faced her and she shivered again as she remembered the terrifying screeches that had sent her and Ethan running through the forest when they'd first arrived in Faerie.

She turned to step back through the door, suddenly convinced this was a really bad idea. But the door had disappeared, and she found herself looking at a solid wall of brick. Unconsciously, her hand reached for the leather strap that crossed her body. The weight of her father's sword was comforting and she focused on it, taking a shaky breath. It was fine; she was freaking herself out for nothing.

Eoghan beckoned her forward, clearly unphased by the shadowy recesses of the forest. He offered her his elbow. "Don't worry, I know this place like the back of my hand."

Not in the least bit reassured, she allowed him to lead her between the trees. The eerie silence of the forest seemed every bit as unnatural as the screeching had been. The scenery was still as weird and wonderful as she remembered, but it didn't hold the same appeal now that she understood just how quickly that beauty could turn ugly.

When they'd walked far enough that she was worried about finding her way back, the thick expanse of trees opened to a clearing. Perfect golden grass formed a blanket in the centre and a ring of daisies surrounded it. A decadent display was laid out before her: juicy berries of all colours, succulent legs of lamb, and glasses filled with a clear bubbly liquid that glinted like crystal.

Eoghan swept his arm out in a grand gesture. "I thought you might care for a picnic."

Her stomach rumbled – the traitor – and though she was starting to think that she should have listened to Ethan and stayed in bed, she gave him what she hoped was a grateful smile and settled herself down on the ground before the feast.

Eoghan fussed about for a moment before finally folding himself elegantly beside her. He offered her a glass with a delicate crystal stem. Her attempt to politely refuse fell on deaf ears, and she finally accepted the glass with a resigned sigh.

He picked up a second glass and raised it. "A toast. To strong women. And to strong kingdoms."

She clinked her glass against his and took a small sip of the fizzy liquid, as much to hide her grimace at the pretentious words as to mollify him. The drink tasted like summer exploding in her mouth, and she couldn't stop herself from taking another small sip before placing the glass back down.

The picnic he'd laid out was beautiful, and she should have been grateful for the effort he'd gone to, but her mood turned sombre as she realised that it wasn't so long ago she'd gone to meet Ethan for a similar picnic. It was going to be their very first date. Instead, here she was with a male she had no interest in while Ethan was back at the castle having to conceal his feelings at the fact.

"How have you enjoyed your time in Faerie?" Eoghan asked, watching her intently.

"It's a beautiful place. Though I do look forward to returning home soon." *And a long-distance relationship would be naturally doomed to fail.*

His face dropped in cartoon-like shock and disappointment. "Surely you can't wish to leave?"

"I have a life back home. I'm eager to return to it."
Get the hint!

"A life among humans?" His face twisted into a grimace of distaste before he smoothed out his expression to one of interest, the change so quick that she almost missed it. "I'd imagine it must be quite quaint."

Before she could reply, he offered her one of the plates laden with colourful berries. She plucked a few from the bunch with a half-arsed attempt at a smile.

"What of your father's people?" He popped a plump berry into his mouth, not waiting until he finished before asking, "Do you have much dealings with them?"

Wariness mingled with a vague sense of disgust at his eating manners. Where was he going with this? "I'd rather not speak about my family, if you don't mind."

"Ah, but the vampires are hardly your family, are they? It's not like their blood runs in your veins. Lucas is no more your grandfather than he was Marcus's father."

She froze. "How did you –"

"And Darius isn't really your uncle either, is he?"

Her blood turned to ice in her veins. The amicable look on the fae lord's face hadn't changed, but now she took a closer look, forced herself to really see him. There was steel behind his grey eyes. The playful sparkle that she'd been quick to dismiss as flirtation had been little more than a screen to distract from the cool calculation.

Pasting an apologetic smile onto her face, she rose unsteadily to her feet. "I'm very sorry, Lord Eldridge, I'm feeling a little unwell. Perhaps it would be better if we return to the castle."

A terrifying stillness came over the fae lord, and Phoenix's fingers twitched with the urge to reach for her sword. After a moment, he smiled widely and got to his feet as well.

"Of course. I know a shortcut back." He brushed some imaginary dirt from his clothes and offered her his arm again.

Her skin crawled as she rested her hand lightly on the crook of his elbow. Maybe there had been nothing behind the comment? Maybe his ego was just bruised because she'd been making it clear she wasn't interested in pursuing anything with him and he was looking for a reaction? But why use Darius's name? And how did he even know about Darius?

The questions raced through her head with a pounding beat that made her close her eyes in pain. When she opened them again, her surroundings were blurry and unfocused. Her feet suddenly felt leaden and each step she took was a monumental effort. Her tongue felt strange and fuzzy in her mouth as she tried to speak.

Her legs buckled beneath her and she sank to the ground, still clutching Eoghan's arm. He looked down at her with a chilling smile as the world swam to black.

31

Faerie – day 4

Ethan paced the length of the castle's family dining room. He had the completely irrational need to punch something – preferably Eoghan's face – and it was taking all his willpower to keep a leash on his wolf.

It wasn't that he thought Phoenix would ever be interested in the smug prick, but the idea of her having to humour her grandmother's blatant scheming when she should be in bed recovering was more than he could take. He was meant to be keeping her and their baby safe; that was the whole point of him being here. He'd done a damn shit job of it so far.

He stopped his pacing and gripped the back of one of the wooden chairs surrounding the table as he tried to get his frustration under control. There was a low groan and the wood splintered beneath his hands. He looked down at the chair in surprise.

"What's wrong? Did we run out of teabags?"

He turned to find Aoife standing in the doorway decked out in tight, black training gear with her hair pulled back from her face. She had one eyebrow quirked and was watching him with something approaching mild amusement. At least until she took in his expression.

"Is Phoenix okay?" All hint of teasing instantly disappeared and she stilled.

With effort, he unclenched his jaw and cracked his neck. "She's fine. Your mother just coerced her into going on a date with that insufferable twat."

"Insufferable –" Aoife froze, light dawning in her eyes. "Eoghan."

Ethan nodded. "She's still weak. She should be in bed resting, not having to entertain pretty-boy fae lords."

"Ethan. How long ago did they leave?"

There was an edge to Aoife's tone that made his wolf stand to attention. Her face was a mask of control, but her green eyes turned stormy. His pulse sped up. "What is it?"

"How long?" she repeated.

"An hour. Two, maybe. Aoife, what's going on?"

"It may be nothing, but I think we should go speak to my parents."

He hurried after her towards the large greeting room where he'd first met Phoenix's grandparents. He didn't even bother trying to rein in the tension that prickled along his skin and it took all his willpower to keep quiet, conscious of the curious glances they received from the fae they passed.

Two sentries stood before the closed doors of the greeting room, just like they had on that first day. Aoife paid them no heed, shoving her way through, her head high and eyes flashing in defiance. The guards recovered swiftly from their surprise and moved as if to block Ethan's passage, but he let the yellow of his wolf flash in his eyes and they stepped back, clearly deciding it was pointless to try and stop him.

Aodhán and Clíodhna's hushed conversation cut off abruptly as they looked up from where they sat in their thrones on the raised dais. They made no attempt to hide the annoyance at the sudden interruption, but Aoife stalked up to the dais, unperturbed, and stopped in front of her mother.

"What did he promise you?"

Clíodhna arched an eyebrow. "Is that any way to greet your mother?" She frowned slightly, looking in Ethan's direction.

"Eoghan. What did he say to you? What did he promise you to get you to agree to this?"

There was a pause before her mother answered, her tone conveying nonchalance even as her eyes hardened. "He simply expressed his interest in our darling granddaughter, and I gave him my blessing to pursue her."

Aodhán straightened, confusion evident in the frown lines that creased his forehead. "What did you do, Clíodhna?"

She shot him a withering glare. "I merely arranged for them to spend some time together. I really don't see why everyone is making such a fuss."

Aoife's mouth dropped open and she shook her head in disbelief. "You fool! You know he's been scheming and plotting against this court for years. What were you thinking?"

"How dare you speak to me like that?" Clíodhna stood from her throne, eyes blazing.

"How dare I? How dare you, Mother? It is because of *his* court that you were forced to banish your own daughter. And now you offer Phoenix up to him on a silver platter. How could you do this?"

Both Ethan and his wolf stilled at Aoife's words. Blood pounded in his ears, blocking out the argument that continued before him. A red haze filled his vision and his claws began to push through his skin. Eoghan's family was the reason for Aria's banishment? He would tear the fae lord into confetti and enjoy every moment of it.

No. He stopped himself, clamping down on the animalistic rage that bubbled inside him. Whatever role Eoghan or his family had in matters, they weren't the ones who ultimately made the decision to banish their daughter. The only thing that mattered now was ensuring Phoenix's safety; the rest could wait.

"Lord Eldridge can't be held accountable for his predecessor's actions," Clíodhna said, as if reading his thoughts. "It is a suitable match – one that will ensure history does not repeat itself." She lifted her chin with the stubborn determination of one who would never be swayed from her deep-seated prejudice.

"Don't be so damn naive." Aoife's voice shook with barely restrained anger. "Eoghan is a hundred times worse than his father ever was. And you sent my niece out there with him."

She gave her mother a disgusted look and turned to Ethan. "Wait here," she said and stalked from the room.

The door slammed behind her and a charged silence settled between the three Supes who remained. Clíodhna glared at Ethan with hate-filled eyes that almost dared him to attack her. He simply stared back, refusing to look away from her challenge. Aodhán ignored both of them, pain creasing the corners of his eyes as he looked into the distance, lost in his own thoughts.

Ethan knew he'd be wasting his breath trying to reason with Clíodhna, so he turned his attention to the fae lord. "Phoenix is pregnant."

He let the revelation hang in the air before turned back to Clíodhna, steel in his voice. "Because of your actions, your decisions, your daughter died without you even knowing. She had a whole life that you weren't part of. A child that you didn't get to see grow. I hope the guilt tears you up because you deserve every bit of it. My mate is out there alone with my unborn child, both of them likely in danger, all because you can't see past your stupid prejudice. So, I swear to you here and now, if anything happens to either of them, I will destroy you. You won't need to worry about the purity of your line, because there will be nothing left of it when I'm finished."

Clíodhna turned bone white. Flames flickered in her eyes, and she moved as if to lunge for him. Aodhán grabbed her arm, his expression a storm of emotion.

She reeled on him, pure venom in her voice as she hissed, "What do you think you're doing?"

"Enough! Ethan is right. I told myself all those centuries ago that the only way our people could be safe was if our court presented a united front. I told myself that even as I allowed my own child to be banished by my silence. But I won't stay silent anymore. Not while it puts our granddaughter at risk. Or our great-grandchild."

The double doors slammed open, and before Clíodhna could respond, Aoife strode back into the room and came to a stop beside Ethan. She carried a long, narrow object wrapped in black velvet and the look she gave her parents was of pure defiance before she turned to him.

"My mother is right. We need to ensure the mistakes of the past are not repeated."

Ethan jerked backwards as if slapped, but she continued. "I, too, watched my family bow to pressures from the other fae courts. They banished my sister for breaking an antiquated law created by bigots, and I stood by and said nothing while they turned their back on my kin. I won't do it again."

She raised the long package in her hand and unwrapped the velvet cloth to reveal a spearhead made of a metal so bright it almost appeared white. The shaft of the spear was weathered wood, its natural markings forming an intricate pattern which reminded Ethan of the Celtic symbols he'd seen on Claíomh Solais. Energy thrummed from it.

Clíodhna gasped. "How could you?"

Aoife didn't spare her mother a second glance; her attention remained fixed solely on him. "If Eoghan wishes Phoenix harm, he'll take her beyond our walls. Can you track her?"

237

Ethan nodded, his eyes riveted on the spear he could only assume to be the Spear of Lugh.

"Then let us go save my niece."

He didn't waste a moment arguing, just turned with her towards the large doors. Aodhán's quiet plea was the last thing he heard before the doors closed behind them.

"Find my granddaughter. Please."

32

Faerie – day 4

Two fae guards fell in beside Ethan and Aoife as they made their way from the castle. When Aoife didn't protest their presence, Ethan ignored them, his only thought and focus on finding Phoenix before something happened to her.

It didn't take him long to latch onto her trail once they crossed beyond the barrier of the wall. Even with the unfamiliar surroundings battering at his senses, her scent called to him. He stalked into the trees, unconcerned by the dangers that might be hidden within their depths. If anything was stupid enough to stand between him and his mate, it would find out what terrifying really was.

The group was silent as they cut a swift path through the forest. The guards and Aoife swept the terrain with watchful gazes. Somehow, he knew they weren't looking for Phoenix but whatever hidden threat had his instincts also on high alert.

After a couple of minutes, the trees parted to reveal a clearing. He inhaled deeply and Phoenix's scent caused his wolf to perk up. She'd been here recently.

His eyes scoured the abandoned picnic of berries and meats, delicate glasses toppled on their sides and left lying like fallen soldiers. There were flattened patches on the golden grass where people had clearly sat or trod, but other than that the clearing was empty.

It was ridiculous, but he couldn't help the sharp pang of jealousy at the sight of the picnic, or the thought of Phoenix here with Eoghan. He clenched his fists and forced himself to block out the feeling; emotion wasn't going to keep her safe.

As he stared at the wasted remains of the picnic, one of the guards checked the perimeter. The other guard moved forward to pick up the discarded glasses. He raised one to his nose and then the other, closing his eyes as he inhaled deeply. His mouth tightened and his eyes were dark when he opened them. Dropping one glass to the ground, he ran his finger around the rim of the other glass and held it up to examine it.

His expression was grim when he met Ethan's and Aoife's questioning gazes. "This one has been tainted."

A vicious growl ripped from Ethan's throat before he could stop it. His wolf shifted inside him, agitated, as he digested the words and what they might mean. "Do you know with what?"

The guard glanced at him with something that almost looked like sympathy and shook his head. "Something to incapacitate, if I had to guess. Whatever it was, it was strong. Most fae tinctures are nigh untraceable, but the stronger the formula, the more residue remains."

"He probably didn't want to take any chances on how a hybrid would metabolise it." Aoife spoke quietly, but her eyes blazed as she surveyed the scene.

Ethan didn't need to hear any more. He walked around the edge of the clearing until he found where the scents were strongest and beckoned the others forward.

They'd barely gone ten feet when a chilling cry rent the air. Ethan froze, power crackling like electricity around him, pricking at his skin. Another shriek followed the first, and a sense of déjà vu sent a burst of adrenaline shooting through his veins.

The guard closest to him pulled an arrow out of the quiver that hung across his back. He stared into the dense shadows of the trees and said quietly, "If you want to see your lady again, you better run."

Aoife grabbed his hand and they didn't look back.

Phoenix struggled to focus on her surroundings. The world tilted and shifted at odd angles, and colours flashed before her eyes only to disappear again. Her limbs were leaden, the ability to move them so far beyond her capacity that they didn't even feel like they belonged to her anymore. Yet somehow, she was moving. She could tell that much by the way the world blurred past; she just couldn't figure out how, or why.

There was a sudden jolt and she landed on the ground with a painful thud. She was grateful when the world stilled, even though her head continued to spin. The bright blues and greens that had filled her vision were replaced by a blurry face. She squinted.

There was something strangely familiar about the face, but the more she tried to concentrate, the more her head felt like it might explode. The image warped and twisted into a terrifying grin and a scream bubbled up in her throat, but no sound came out.

"It will be harder for you if you fight. Just accept your fate and I'll make the pain go away."

A gentle hand smoothed damp hair from her face and the need to scream was replaced with the inexplicable desire to giggle hysterically. The voice, it was so familiar. Why couldn't she place it?

Then the face was changing. The hard grey eyes staring down at her morphed into kind brown ones; the smooth jaw became bristled with stubble that matched the hair that had moments ago been silver and was now brown. *Ethan*. Her mind reached for him eagerly.

He placed a rough hand on her cheek and gave her a cheeky grin. She leaned into his touch and froze. Something wasn't right.

Through the murky fog that filled her head, her brain screamed a warning at her. She tried desperately to grasp at the meaning, but her thoughts were so jumbled that she couldn't make sense of it.

Ethan was here; he'd make it better. But he didn't *feel* right, and though she wanted to believe her eyes more than anything else in the world, some part of her knew. The realisation solidified in her mind and she jerked back from the touch. Her head struck something hard behind her, sending a lance of pain through her skull.

The smile disappeared from Ethan's face, and his expression twisted into a snarl that looked unnatural on the face of her wolf. She cringed, shrinking away from him.

The hand that had moments ago touched her cheek with tenderness shot out and closed around her throat in a bruising grip. "You filthy half-breed. You think you're too good for me? You're an abomination!"

The man wearing Ethan's face yanked her up by her throat so that his breath burned against her cheek. "I could have made this easier for you. We could have had a little fun before I handed you over to Darius." He flung her to the ground and stood.

Darius. Alarm bells shattered the fog holding her mind. *He can't be here, he can't be.* Panic threatened to drown her as she willed her body to move. A finger. A toe. Anything.

As she watched, the man's image morphed once more until familiar grey eyes stared down at her, full of disdain. Eoghan – she remembered his name now, could think clearly enough to remember – reached a hand into his tunic and pulled out a small vial of green liquid. He used his teeth to pull the cork out and bent down to her. An eerie calm settled over his features as he grabbed her jaw in a steel grip, forced the vial to her lips, and held her mouth closed until she had no choice other than to swallow. Hot tears ran down her cheeks as pure, undiluted fear gripped her.

"Not long now," Eoghan promised in a chilling voice. "Once I have the gateway open, you'll be his problem. Don't worry though, I'll make sure all the courts know who's responsible for destroying the natural balance of our world. All of these disasters that are damaging even our protected lands." He shook his head. "I'll make sure your family are suitably punished and –"

He paused, cocking his head, and smiled. "I do believe we have company."

33

Faerie – day 4

Ethan sensed more than heard the string of a bow being pulled taut. He dived for the trees to his left, knocking Aoife into the brush with him. An arrow whistled through the air, grazing his shoulder in a blaze of fire. He let the momentum of his fall continue into a roll and came up to a crouch, only to meet the smug smile of Lord Eldridge pointing a bow and arrow directly at him.

He growled; he was going to enjoy wiping that smile from the fae lord's face.

He launched from the ground just as another arrow struck the dirt where he'd been mere fractions of a second before. Aoife was hot on his heels as he closed the distance between himself and Eoghan, intent on shredding the male to pieces.

Eoghan stood watching them with that cocky fucking smile, right up to the moment when Ethan barrelled into him with claws extended. Then he disapp-eared.

Instead of hitting solid flesh like he'd expected, Ethan found himself tumbling through the air. His breath left him in a huff of pain as a tree halted his momentum. Eoghan's laughter floated on the wind, seeming to come from all corners of the forest at once. He snarled, looking around but unable to see the fae lord.

Aoife appeared on his right and offered him her hand. "Do not trust your sight alone. Eoghan is a master of illusion."

He nodded and closed his eyes. There was one thing he knew wouldn't lie to him no matter what tricks the fae lord had up his sleeve: Phoenix's scent. Warily he beckoned Aoife forward, every muscle in his body tensed in preparation for the attack that was sure to come. They made it ten feet before his instincts roared to life.

Aoife pushed him aside as a small blade spun through the air and lodged in the tree behind where he'd been standing. Two more blades followed in quick succession, forcing Ethan and Aoife to separate further apart from each other.

A blur of movement in the trees caught Ethan's attention and he lunged towards it. A pained groan froze him mid-motion.

Phoenix.

"Help her," Aoife ordered before reaching out with her free hand and flinging a ball of bright white light into the trees. She sprinted after it, disappearing out of sight.

He was torn. His wolf wanted blood – the fae lord's, to be precise – but another moan sounded from the

246

opposite direction and set his heart skittering. Bearing in mind what Aoife had said about Eoghan's skill with illusions, he closed his eyes again. Phoenix's signature came to him instantly, but it was weak, almost like it had been muted somehow. Still, he grasped that connection for all it was worth and followed it.

The flash of bright red hair was the first thing he saw when he opened his eyes and spotted her slumped against a tree. Her skin was pale and clammy, and her body was limp. All thoughts of going after Eoghan fled in an instant and he rushed to her side.

Claíomh Solais's scabbard was tangled around her, but the blade remained in its sheath, showing no sign that she'd attempted to use it in self-defence. The start of a bluish bruise was visible on her cheekbone, and it took all his effort to quell his fury long enough to check her for injuries.

When he was sure there was no obvious physical damage that needed attention, he cradled her face in his hands. "Phoenix. Phoenix, can you hear me?"

A low whimper escaped her lips, and though she didn't open her eyes, she flinched away from him. A single tear slid from her eye and burned a path down her cheek.

His chest ached with the need to help her, but he had no idea what to do, and in that moment he felt completely lost. Gently he lifted her body up from the hard ground and cradled her in his arms. He rested his forehead against hers, willing her to open her eyes as he whispered to her over and over. "Come back to me. Please. You're safe. I promise, I've got you."

He could feel her heart beating in her chest, could tell by her breathing that she was alive, but still the fear wouldn't loose its grip on him. Despite the lack of visible injury, every instinct he possessed told him that something was wrong, that she needed his help.

An agonised groan ripped from her throat, and her whole body clenched. His heart clenched too.

A rustle of leaves came from above and he tensed for an attack as he cursed himself for letting his guard down. A large black crow burst through the trees, and before it landed, the air shimmered and Morrigan appeared beside him. Her ethereal beauty was marred by worry as she looked down at Phoenix. She ran her fingertips over Phoenix's pale cheeks and when she looked up to meet Ethan's gaze, his stomach lurched at the troubled look in the goddess's eyes.

"I couldn't interfere," she said softly, pain evident in the tone of her voice. "I wanted to, but some things …" She shook her head. "You need to help her. We don't have much time left."

His throat constricted. "What can I do?"

"We need to slow down the effects from the potions Eoghan gave her. We need to dilute them in her blood so that her body might have a chance of clearing them out, or at the very least buy us time."

"How –" He cut off as realisation dawned.

She nodded in confirmation at the thought that was written across his face. He didn't hesitate. He extended a claw and slashed a thin line down the inside of his left arm. "Go, help Aoife. I've got this."

Red swelled from the wound and he pressed it against Phoenix's too cold lips. "Come on, Phoenix, drink for me. Please, baby."

Phoenix could hear Ethan's voice through the haze of pain clouding her mind, but she knew better than to believe the illusion this time. Something warm and wet pressed against her lips and she cringed away, shaking her head in helpless desperation. No more. She couldn't take any more.

A drop of blood hit her tongue and a jolt of electricity shot through her. Before she could stop them, her fangs elongated and latched onto the throbbing pulse of life. She sucked eagerly, and with each pull the fog lifted. The vile poison that tainted her blood lost its hold and somewhere between one swallow and the next, her awareness sharpened.

Don't leave me, Ethan's voice whispered in her mind, more real to her in that moment than she was even to herself.

Her eyes fluttered open, and she met a gaze so full of fear and love that she knew instantly no illusion could ever have replicated the pure honesty of it. The real Ethan smiled down at her and the chill that had permeated the very depths of her began to fade away.

His blood coursed through her, forming a connection at the most primal level as it rejuvenated her cells and repaired parts of her that until a moment ago had felt utterly broken. Even when her fangs retracted and he eased his wrist away, the connection remained. She clung to it like one might a life buoy when stranded in a never-ending ocean.

As everything came back into focus, fragmented memories tried to piece themselves together in her mind. Every muscle and ligament in her body ached as if they had been stretched to the point of tearing, and her head pounded to a beat that only she could hear.

Razorblades scoured her throat as she asked hoarsely, "Eoghan?"

Ethan's eyes flashed yellow, fury and violence burning like golden embers within them as he looked towards the trees. "Aoife –"

His words were cut off by the snap of a twig. His arms tensed around her as her breath froze in her chest. She snapped her head around towards the direction of the sound, but it wasn't Eoghan who stepped through the trees a moment later.

Her aunt was barely recognisable as Phoenix took in the fierce fire hardening Aoife's features beneath the bright red blood smeared across her cheek. She was favouring her right leg, a vicious gash visible on her thigh. The ancient spear she used to support her weight seemed oddly clean of blood, its almost-white tip glinting in the stray rays of sunlight that filtered through the trees.

Morrigan stood beside Aoife, looking as beautiful as the first time Phoenix had seen her. There was a hint of sorrow in the goddess's smile and a shiver of apprehension went through Phoenix. She placed a hand on her abdomen, seeking comfort in the movement of new life there.

"Eoghan?" Ethan asked, saving her the trouble of repeating her question.

Aoife's mouth tightened into a hard line, but there was no regret in her voice when she said, "The spear's aim was true."

The spear? Phoenix looked again at the weapon gripped in her aunt's hand. Surely it couldn't be the Spear of Lugh, could it? She jerked forward, suddenly reminded of her own artefact. Panic robbed her of breath as she scrambled on the ground, looking for her father's – her – sword.

Ethan grabbed her shoulder to halt her frantic movements and held a black scabbard out to her. "It's here, it's okay."

She pulled the scabbard in close to her, not caring if any of them thought her foolish for hugging a sword. Its power was like a gentle caress as it wrapped around her and soothed the terror that still balanced on a finely honed knife edge inside her.

"I wish I could give you more of a chance to recover," Morrigan said, "but I'm afraid time is against us."

Phoenix looked up at her guardian's grave expression, unease once more settling in her centre. "Is it time to go back?"

"We need to get you and the artefacts home, and we need to do it quickly," Morrigan said, her expression turning guarded. "Eoghan had prepared a gateway to return you. We'll have to take our chances with it."

"But why would Eoghan want to send Phoenix back?" Ethan's brow creased in confusion as he looked from Morrigan to her.

"Darius." Phoenix's answer was little more than a whisper, and even saying the name out loud sent a bolt of adrenaline through her. Much of the time since she'd agreed to the walk with Eoghan was now a foggy blur, but the one thing that stuck clearly in her mind was that name. Eoghan had known Darius's name.

The expected growl never came from Ethan and she was surprised enough to look up at him. His expression was one of deadly calm and surety, and it terrified her more than any anger could have. She knew without a doubt that he'd make Darius pay for hurting her. Even if it meant getting himself killed in the process.

"Yes, Eoghan was working for Darius," Morrigan confirmed.

"Which means using his gateway will lead us straight into danger." Ethan shook his head. "No. No way."

The goddess ignored his outburst, instead letting Phoenix see the solemn plea in her eyes. "Here in Faerie, my hands are tied. But back in the human world, they're not. I need you to trust me, Phoenix. Please."

Phoenix stared into those fathomless eyes, searching for an answer or something to tell her the right thing to do. Eventually, she nodded. At this point she was too tired and numb to feel fear at the thought of stepping into yet another of Darius's traps. And as a strange twisting sensation shot a bolt of pain through her lower abdomen, she couldn't help but think that Morrigan was right. Time was running out.

With difficulty, she secured Claíomh Solais across her back and indicated for Ethan to help her to standing. She hid a wince of pain as she got to her feet and turned to her aunt, who was watching them with obvious concern.

"I know you haven't had long to think on things," she said to Aoife, "but if Morrigan believes we need the artefacts back home, I'm inclined to believe her. Will you come with us?"

Aoife assessed her niece for a long moment. The thoughtful expression was so reminiscent of her mother that Phoenix's heart ached at the similarity that was both a reminder of her loss and a gift that allowed her to remember.

"No," Aoife said finally. "I can't go with you. I have a duty to my court to warn them about the prophecy and what might face us if it comes to pass."

Something inside Phoenix broke at her aunt's words, but she forced herself to nod in acceptance. They hadn't given her enough time. Blood or not, how could she expect the woman to trust her when she'd given her absolutely no reason to do so?

As if understanding the thoughts going through Phoenix's head, Aoife reached out and brushed a hand over her cheek with a regretful smile. Her aunt turned to Ethan, shifting her weight to her good leg before holding out the hand that held the spear.

"Ethan Ryan, before the Goddess Morrigan and all of those who stand here in witness, I willingly bequeath you the Spear of Lugh. So long as your quest remains honourable, so too will your aim."

Ethan's jaw dropped and he stared at her outstretched hand in disbelief. When he didn't move to take it, Aoife limped forward, lifted his hand and wrapped his fingers around the wooden shaft.

"I know now that you are the one who is meant to protect my niece. Show them you are worthy." Before Ethan could react, Aoife turned back to Phoenix, eyes glistening. "I'm so glad I got to meet you. You remind me so much of her."

She reached inside the neck of her tunic and pulled out a small, milky-pink crystal on a black silk cord. She placed the crystal in Phoenix's hand and closed her fingers over it. "I hope that the next time I see you, it'll be in happier circumstances. But if the worst should come to pass, use this crystal to call for me. The fae will come to you, I will make sure of it."

Tears stung Phoenix's eyes. There was so much she wanted to say to her aunt, so much she wished had been different. Before she could say any of that, however, a cramping pain unlike anything she'd ever felt twisted her insides. She was dimly aware of Ethan grabbing her, asking what was wrong, then Morrigan was at her side. There were whispered words she didn't understand, and the world fell away.

34

Home – 3 weeks gone

The corridor was quiet as Darius made his way along the lower levels of the Dublin vampire's lair. It was the first time he'd returned to the clan's main base of operations since that night all those months ago when he'd enacted the spell to expedite the prophecy. He may have failed on that occasion, but things were going to be very different this time.

Only a skeleton security crew remained dotted throughout the building now – enough to maintain the façade of an ambassador's residence that had kept the humans from prying for many decades. He'd relocated most of the clan to the pharmaceutical complex when the Council began their incessant meddling. Of course, the Council had since been deterred from their prying too, but the lair no longer suited his needs save for one last task.

Erik was waiting patiently for him when he reached his old quarters, seven floors below ground level. He'd briefed his head of security the day before, but still he asked, "Is everything in place?" as he stepped into the room he'd once used as an office.

Distracted, he realigned one of the priceless paintings on the wall and eyed the files and papers strewn across the floor. He had no doubt that the Council had been thorough in their search of the office and the lair, but they wouldn't have found anything. It was almost insulting that they believed him to be so amateur as to leave any evidence of his plans lying around for them to find.

"The gateway should open at the Cathedral soon. Vicktor has taken five soldiers with him to await the hybrid's return, and he'll notify us as soon as she crosses back to this world."

Darius absently gathered the papers covering the mahogany desk and arranged them into a neat pile – chaos and order didn't have to be mutually exclusive. "Vicktor knows she's not to be harmed under any circumstances?"

"He's been given strict instructions. The hybrid will be allowed to birth her offspring, then they will retrieve any artefacts in her possession. Everything will be in place by the time the transfer is complete."

A shiver of anticipation ran through Darius. *Soon*.

Assuming Phoenix returned with both the sword and the spear as they expected her to, they would only need to worry about finding the cauldron. It bothered him that this final piece continued to elude him, but he refused to allow the witch's warning to sway his decision; he was done waiting. Once he carried the essence of the Horsemen inside him, he would simply destroy anyone who got between him and the last artefact.

"And what of the witch?" Erik asked, calculating red eyes watching him closely.

Darius paused, considering the question. The ritual would place him completely at the witch's mercy should she wish to betray him. He had seen the ambition in her steely eyes and had no reason to doubt anything she'd done or said to date, but he hadn't gotten this far by being careless.

"If she so much as breathes wrong during the ritual, kill her."

35

Ethan was simultaneously light and heavy. Nothing felt real to him anymore except the spear clutched in his right hand and the warmth of Phoenix's hand in his left. The world around him ceased to exist and somewhere in the depths of his mind, Morrigan's voice whispered a warning: *be prepared.*

Everything came back into focus with a violent jolt. He had only a second to register the crumbling ruins of the Cathedral in the dim light of the moon before Phoenix's hand was jerked from his. Something struck him, sending him sideways. He scrambled to regain his footing, allowing the momentum to pivot him around to face his attacker.

The next blow came from overhead, and instinctively he brought the spear up to block it. He found himself staring into a snarling face that was hardly recognisable as human.

A woman stood before him, patches of grey fur covering her cheeks and forehead as if she'd gotten stuck midway through a shift. Her rabid fangs dripped yellow slime as they snapped at him, and the red of her eyes had bled from their pupils so that no white remained in their terrifying depths.

Ethan thrust out with his foot in an attempt to push away the weight bearing down on the shaft of the spear. She barely budged. With a feral grin, she stalked towards him, driving him back.

In his peripheral vision he caught a flash of blue light, followed by inhuman screeches of pain that told him this *thing* wasn't the only member of the welcoming party. Instinct roared at him to find Phoenix, to make sure she was safe, but he didn't dare take his eyes from his assailant for even a second.

The abomination before him reached out, dark shadows wrapping around her arms and seeming to slither from her clawed hands.

"Don't let her touch you," Morrigan yelled in a strained voice, her warning punctuated by another guttural screech and flash of light.

Too late he swung the spear up to knock away the hands that reached for him. The thing batted it away as if it were a mere nuisance, and the shadows wrapped around his wrists.

Screams filled his head. They were not the sounds of fighting that had moments ago surrounded him, but visceral sounds that froze his body in primal terror. All thought and logic left him in an instant. All he knew was fear.

Black filled his vision. Then as soon as it came, it was gone. The screaming, the fear … All of it just gone. The creature still stood before him, her predatory gaze watching his every breath with what he could only describe as hunger, but she had stepped back, her posture one of relaxed preparedness.

He risked a quick, confused glance to his left. Morrigan stood facing another three monstrosities like the one before him. She watched them warily, but though she was outnumbered, none made a move to advance on her.

When he could see no sign of Phoenix, panic gripped him. Before he could check his right-hand side, a man in an expensive grey suit stepped into the dim light cast by the moon, another of the creatures beside him.

Ethan did a double take.

It had been months since he and Phoenix had met the head of the Council Liaison Office, but the sanctimonious prick had made such an impression with his snide dismissal of Phoenix that Ethan would have recognised him anywhere. It looked like the CLO rep had undergone a few changes since they last met him – and Ethan highly doubted that they'd improved his personality.

"Please." Vicktor's voice rang clear in the sudden stillness, his eyes an eerie glow of red. "Let me be the first to welcome you home. I hope my friends here have made you feel comfortable."

"What the fu –" Ethan was cut off by a low moan from behind him. His blood ran cold and all other threats forgotten, he whipped his head around in search of Phoenix.

He spotted her on her knees, body bent double in the centre of the ancient ruins. The moonlight glinted off the sweat that beaded her pale forehead and her eyes were scrunched up in pain. He rushed to her, thoughts of the fae poison in her body filling him with a new source of terror.

It was only as he drew closer to her that his brain registered the rest of the picture. He slowed to a stop, and all coherent thought left him as he looked at her belly. No longer the gentle swell that had filled him with such pride in Faerie, it was now distended and straining against her tunic as if a full term had passed in minutes.

She looked up at him, eyes wide in shock. Then a contraction seized her and she cried out in pain.

That was all he needed to break through his own confusion, and he hurried the last few feet to her, dimly aware of Morrigan also backing towards them. He dropped down on his knees beside her. "Phoenix? What happened?"

A hoarse sob was the only response.

He cast his eyes around the ancient ruins of the Cathedral, counting six demon-Supe hybrids, Vicktor included. The odds were most definitely not in their favour. "We need to get you out of here. Can you stand?"

She shook her head, face twisting in agony. "There's no time," she gasped. "I think the baby's coming."

"Oh goodie." Vicktor clapped his hands. "It's time to get the party started."

Ethan watched in disbelief as the CLO rep pulled a phone from his pocket. He clicked his fingers and the five others with him spread out to form a rough circle around the ruins. Their red eyes glinted in watchful anticipation.

Vicktor raised the phone to his ear and stepped back into the shadows.

Phoenix's body clenched once more as another contraction took hold. Ethan looked up at Morrigan in desperation. "Do something. Open a gateway, anything."

The goddess gazed down at them with a mix of sorrow and acceptance, and he didn't know which terrified him more. She turned from him and her expression grew distant as she murmured a low chant.

There was a flash of light and a silver dome appeared around them before fading into the night. Morrigan's shoulders slumped as if drained by whatever spell she'd woven, but her eyes were alert as she stared out into the darkness.

"The ward will hold them back should they choose to attack again."

He looked at Phoenix and back to Morrigan, helpless. "How long?"

Worry tightened her mouth as she too looked down at Phoenix. "Long enough."

Darius ran his hands over the stone altar. Blood still stained its surface and there were dark patches visible on the stone walls too. He'd missed this chamber buried deep beneath the lair. For many years it had been the place he'd come to indulge his frustrations, biding his time while he waited for Phoenix to trigger the prophecy on her twenty-fifth birthday. It was fitting that his new beginning start here.

Footsteps echoed on the stone steps and he turned to face the witch. "It's time," she said.

"Do you have everything?"

She gave him a scathing look. "Worry less about what I'm doing and focus on surviving the ritual."

He raised an eyebrow, unphased by her warning. The witch would ensure his survival since it was the only way to guarantee her own.

Walking in a slow circle around the chamber, he took in the cell that had held Marcus and Aria for almost a decade, the chains that had held many a plaything, the spiderweb cracks in the wall from when Phoenix had used her power against him for the first time. He raised a hand to touch the rough scars that still covered the left side of his face. Everything he'd done had led up to this moment. Even his Sire's death had been necessary. He knew that now.

The witch waited until he returned to the altar before speaking again. "The power I'm going to transfer into you is unlike anything that exists in this world. You may be powerful, and old as hell" – she gave him a toothy grin – "but your flesh won't survive for long. You better be ready to finish this."

Silently, Darius unbuttoned his black shirt. He held the witch's gaze as he removed it and stepped up onto the stone slab. Carefully he picked up the skull that rested there and climbed up onto the altar. As he lay back, he looked into the skull's empty eye sockets and thanked his Sire for his sacrifice.

One by one, the witch lay out the offerings to the Horsemen. She took the skull he held out and placed it in the fourth and final position. A shock of electricity shot through Darius. His back arched and his muscles spasmed involuntarily. It passed within a second, but the dark excitement in the witch's eyes told him that worse was yet to come. Much worse.

The witch started chanting, and as she did, her voice changed. The words came faster and ghostly voices joined hers, echoing the chant until there was nothing else. Energy filled the chamber, sucking all the oxygen from the space until the pressure grew so great that it felt like it might crush him.

Darius clenched his teeth as every cell in his body was twisted and transformed. One minute particle at a time, he was changed. Fire burned through his veins, scorching him from the inside. He could feel all of them pulsing inside of him, their thoughts, their power, their thirst for destruction.

His vision turned black, and he screamed.

36

Pain lanced through Cassandra's abdomen and she gasped for breath. The contractions came quickly, shocking and sudden, the strength of the vision so forceful that the frosted glass walls of the Council office faded away and she could no longer distinguish reality from thought.

"The baby is coming," she gasped, curling in on herself against the pain that wasn't her own, but felt as real as if it were.

There was a distant sense of commotion around her as the Council members reacted to her cry. A figure crouched down beside her, and when she managed to blink the tears away, she saw William's kind eyes, full of concern. He reached out to touch her but stopped himself, realising the contact would only cause her more pain. The helpless look on his face warmed some part deep inside her, and she used his presence to ground herself back in reality.

When the world righted itself enough that the images faded to the background of her sight, she pushed herself up to her elbows. William quickly moved to right the chair that had toppled over with her, but before Cassandra could reseat herself, Méabh was shoving the wolf aside, her beautiful face tightened with tension.

"What did you see? Tell us."

Cassandra took a shuddery breath, conscious of the pensive stares fixed on her. Salty tears ran down her cheeks but she ignored them. In truth, she wasn't even sure what the tears were for – the pain or the child, as yet unborn.

"Phoenix has returned. The child will –" White-hot agony flared through her again, choking off her words. No images came, just pain. All-consuming pain. It set every cell in her body on fire, unmaking her and remaking her in its flame of eternal torture. She flung back her head and screamed.

Shouts of surprise. Hands grasping her. She was aware of it all, and yet of nothing. Her body was lowered to the ground, no longer her own. Uncontrollable tremors took hold of her and she could do nothing, see nothing. Nothing except for the devastation to come.

Her back arched and everything went black.

An eternity passed before Kam's soft voice reached her, calling her name, willing her to come back. It hurt to open her eyes, and she cringed back from the light that burned her. Instructions were snapped for the lights to be dimmed. Tentatively she eased her eyelids open once more.

For a moment, she could remember nothing. Then it flooded back in an instant. She opened her mouth to speak, but all that came out was a desperate sob. She curled her knees up to her chest as racking sobs took hold of her body. All the fear. All the pain. She'd felt it all. Everything that was to come.

When she'd finally been scraped raw of all emotion, she blinked the water – Were they tears? She wasn't sure – from her lashes and sat up. She looked around at the Council members who remained, seeing them, truly seeing them.

William, bless him, had gone from looking concerned to looking downright panicked. Méabh's expression was a haughty one of impatience at what she clearly classified as dramatics, but it did little to conceal her true worry. Even Kam's unflappable façade was ruffled.

Vlad was the only one not looking at her. His eyes darted nervously to the door of the office, and she was reminded of a scared rabbit caught between the urge to freeze or flee. She knew which he'd choose, and she knew the price they'd all pay for it.

There was no emotion in her voice when she turned to the others. "The Horsemen are here."

37

"You can do it, Phoenix. That's it. Just keep pushing."

Ethan's words barely registered through the haze of pain that consumed Phoenix. On all fours, her body tightened reflexively and she bore down with everything she had.

Sweat drenched her skin and her arms were ready to collapse as she dug her fingers deep into the earth. A scream, part desperation and part determination, ripped itself from her throat. Just when she had nothing left to give, she heard it: the cry a new life announcing itself to the world.

Her arms buckled, and she rested her forehead onto the soft ground. Tears of relief slid down her cheeks, and all she could hear was Ethan's repeated murmur of disbelief. "You did it. You did it."

Exhausted, exhilarated, numb, and still completely terrified, she raised herself up with Morrigan's help and turned for the first time to look at her baby.

The small red squished-up bundle was cradled in Ethan's arms and he was looking at it like it was both the most precious and most terrifying thing in the world. He smiled at her, his brown eyes wide with awe. "We have a little girl."

Oh so carefully, he placed the baby in her arms. Phoenix stared down at the little button nose, and the tiny hands. Her chest constricted with an aching joy. How had she gone from those small flutters of hope to this tiny little human?

As if seeking comfort from the harsh reality of the world it had been thrust into, the baby nuzzled in closer to her. She wrapped what she could of her tunic around her daughter, but her clothes were as sweat soaked as she was and gave little protection from the chill night air.

Morrigan bent and ripped the bottom of her flowing black dress. Gently she helped wrap the baby in the dry cloth. The goddess smiled and placed a hand over Phoenix's heart. "All she needs is your warmth."

Realising what Morrigan meant, Phoenix reached tentatively inside her. She was surprised to find the spark of her power burning so brightly when she felt so completely spent, but she was grateful as she carefully called the sun to her and wrapped its heat around them. When Ethan crouched beside them and held them both in his arms, she allowed herself that one moment of pure happiness. That one moment to just be.

It couldn't last though, because in the shadows, death waited.

She looked from the helpless human in her arms to the shifting darkness. "How long do we have before your ward fails?" she asked Morrigan quietly.

There was a long pause. "I can hold it a while longer. But the longer I hold it, the weaker I'll be when the time comes."

When the time comes to fight.

Ethan's arms tightened around her, a low growl rumbling through his body.

She looked down at the miracle she held against her chest, and the need to protect it overwhelmed her. A rage beyond words filled her at the thought of harm coming to her daughter, at the knowledge that Darius had sent these men and women, these things, to take her child. She would die before she let that happen.

"What day is it?" Ethan asked suddenly.

Confused, she looked from him to Morrigan. She had no idea. She hadn't even had time to register that they were home before the change overtook her body and pain made thought impossible.

"It's April. You've been gone three weeks," Morrigan said, her tone carefully neutral.

"So we did it?" Ethan sat up straighter. "We stopped the prophecy."

A shadow passed over the goddess's face, and a sense of dread filled Phoenix. "I fear it may not be that simple."

"What do you mean?" Phoenix forced herself to push back the panic clawing at her chest. "We did it, she's here. She was born before the deadline; it has to have worked."

Morrigan's smile was sad as she bent to run her fingers gently over the baby's cheek. "She is indeed a miracle, but her birth was not a natural one. I fear there are forces at play here that we haven't yet discovered." Her gaze flicked to the shadows, now moving more impatiently just beyond her ward. "Let us worry about first getting out of here before we concern ourselves with what is to come."

A soft gurgle drew Phoenix's gaze down to the baby that was looking up at her with wide, innocent eyes.

Ethan took one of the small hands in his, the tiny fist wrapping around his finger. "We need to give her a name."

An unexplainable sorrow filled Phoenix's chest. She'd never understood just how much it was possible to love a person. She realised now that this must have been how her parents felt when they'd first held her. They'd never seen a hybrid, or an abomination; they'd only seen their daughter. They'd seen the miracle that had been created by their love.

There was nothing she wanted more in that moment than to see this little girl grow up. To show her just how beautiful she was, and that her unique blood was something to be proud of. She wanted to help her daughter become a strong woman who would stand defiant in the face of all the hatred and prejudice she'd no doubt face and know she was not alone. She wanted her to live.

"Saoirse." Phoenix looked up at Ethan and saw all her emotions reflected back in the raw vulnerability of his expression. "I want to call her Saoirse."

He smiled, though his eyes remained sad. "Freedom. I like that."

Phoenix bent her head and placed the gentlest kiss on her daughter's brow. Tears blurred her vision as she said to Morrigan, "Promise me you'll keep her safe."

The goddess was solemn as she took Saoirse from her arms. "I promise."

With a wince of pain as her battered and spent body protested, Phoenix picked Claíomh Solais up from the ground beside her and rose to her feet with Ethan's help. She stared into the darkness that stood between her daughter and the life she deserved. "I'm ready."

The hardest part about facing death was not the thought that she might die, but what would happen to her daughter if she did. They all knew the goddess had the best chance of keeping Saoirse safe, yet as Phoenix stood at Ethan's side waiting for Morrigan to drop the ward, she wanted nothing more than to run back and pull her baby into her arms.

Ethan glanced at her, the Spear of Lugh gripped firmly in his hand, his eyes yellow. "Thank you," he said quietly.

She didn't ask what he was thanking her for; she didn't need to. Instead she just gave him a sad smile in return. "Let's make this count."

There would be moment, a split second between Morrigan dropping the ward that surrounded them all and erecting a new one around her and Saoirse, that their child would be in danger. As exhausted and spent as she was,

Phoenix was going to do everything in her power to buy the goddess that moment.

She cleared her mind and focused on the heat that burned inside her. She let it build, fuelled by a soul-deep ache at the knowledge of what she now stood to lose. Slowing her breathing, she held up a hand and gave Morrigan the signal.

The air shimmered, the ward becoming visible for a second before dissolving. Colours danced in her retinas and she blinked them away. She waited, the sense of being watched a palpable thing. The shadows were restless, but the creatures didn't move closer.

"Let's not make this harder than it has to be." Vicktor's pompous voice rang clear in the quiet of the night. "We don't want your child. Its purpose has been served. Give yourself up with the artefacts, and the baby will be spared."

Her throat went dry, her heart stuttering as the words caused it to miss a beat. It was a trap, she knew that. But still …

"Don't even think about it," Ethan growled low.

She didn't look at him as she nodded. Claíomh Solais's power thrummed through her arm like a magnet drawn to the power building in her solar plexus. It took all she had to keep her voice steady as she called out, "Okay, I'll do it. Just don't attack."

"Phoenix, what are you –" Ethan reached out to grab her with his free hand, but she slipped from his grasp, stepping forward to carefully angle her body in front of his.

"Drop the sword and throw it towards me," Victor ordered. "The spear too."

She moved as if to do what he asked, but at the last minute she swung the tip of the blade up and let loose the power inside her. White-hot light blasted through the sword's blade, illuminating the darkness in a blinding glare.

Inhuman shrieks of pain filled the night, but still she had less than a breath before a blackened figure leapt at her with fangs glistening from a gaping maw.

She slashed out with the sword, only just managing to deflect the vicious claws that swiped at her. Chaos erupted all around her, and though power thrummed in her veins, her assailant's attacks were relentless, and she couldn't get a reprieve to focus it.

Two more of the figures emerged from the darkness and stalked towards her. Their newly charred flesh, combined with their already hideous features, turned them into a thing of nightmares. Her fight or flight alarm blared a warning to run.

She edged backwards as the demon-Supe hybrids surrounded her. Their strikes came one at a time, attacks that would hurt but not be fatal. It was as if they were playing with her, when suddenly there was a blur of movement and a hand locked onto her throat from behind.

Vicktor's breath was rotten as he hissed in her ear. "You should have taken the easy option." His black tongue ran a slimy path up her cheek, and he gave a contented sigh. "I can taste your fear."

A gust of wind grazed her cheek and hot, black blood splattered the side of her face. Vicktor's body stilled, his grip on her throat loosening.

Shock held her frozen to the spot as Ethan carved an unrelenting path through the three creatures that had herded her into the CLO rep's path. Everywhere his claws struck, blood was drawn, and by the time he reached her side he was coated in the thick black substance.

It was only when he reached over to yank the spear from Vicktor's eye socket, the shaft of which she'd numbly noted in her peripheral vision, that her brain finally connected the gruesome dots. She shuddered as Vicktor's lifeless form slumped to the ground, the last of his limp grip sliding from her.

Ethan gave her a feral grin and spun the spear around, driving it back into a fourth creature that she hadn't even seen creep up on them.

A spark of hope kindled within her as she took in the bodies surrounding them. There had been five of the demon-Supes with Vicktor. Four now joined him on the ground and a little further away from them, near the edge of the ruins, she could just make out a fifth. Was that all of them? Had they done it?

"Shit."

She jerked her head around to look at Ethan and found him staring at the bodies that littered the ruins of the Cathedral, a look of horror on his face. Icy fear ran through her as she followed his gaze and saw what had elicited the snarled curse: the bodies were twitching. They weren't dead.

A chilling laugh carried on the wind and she turned in horror-movie-slow-motion to see Vicktor rise to his feet behind her. There was a great gaping hole in his eye socket where the spear had impaled him, but clearly his brain was small enough to have been missed and he grinned at her, very much alive.

Her tiny spark of hope was snuffed out in an instant. If they couldn't kill these things, they didn't stand a chance.

She was about to yell at Morrigan to get Saoirse the hell out of there when a strange, shimmering mist appeared in the space between her and Vicktor. The mist solidified and she had only a moment to register golden eyes before the world disappeared from beneath her.

38

Darius looked around with a curiosity that was not his own. The stone of the altar was solid beneath him, and the witch was slumped on the floor of the chamber, unconscious but breathing. He raised his hand to his face, turning it from side to side as he examined the lines covering the back of it.

This form was new to them. The Horsemen. The confines of flesh both a fascination and irritation.

Their thoughts vibrated through him. Not so much words as feelings. Their power filled his veins, crackling like electricity. It begged him to call it forth, a temptation unlike any he'd ever felt before. Desires that were alien to him battled for dominance until they all blurred into one loud demand.

To be set free. To consume. To destroy.

Slowly he slid from the altar, testing the responses of this new body. Their body. A smile stretched his lips – their lips – and he stepped over the witch's limp form. He walked a slow circle around the chamber, skimming his hand over the cool stone of the wall. Shadows trailed in his wake and as he passed the torches that lined the walls, their flames flared.

He instinctively knew that this world was different than they remembered. Much had changed in the millennia since they'd been banished. But here, deep in the earth, surrounded by the harshness of the stone and the smell of blood, this was familiar.

When he'd finally come full circle, he made his way up the stone steps that led from the chamber. A man stood guarding the door at the top. Erik, his mind informed him. Head of security. Vampire. Acolyte.

Erik stiffened as he noted Darius's presence. Recognition dawned in the red of his demon eyes and they widened in awe. He bowed his head in subservience. "My Lords."

Darius didn't acknowledge the gesture – it was no more than their due – he just continued down the long hallway, indicating for the man to follow. The surroundings had an odd sense of newness to him, even though he knew these eyes had beheld them for many years. He observed it all in silence, yet the voices still filled him, greedy, impatient. Attempting to focus, he turned to his head of security who followed just behind him. "Give me an update," he ordered.

There was a hesitation, and the voices inside him grew quiet. They were displeased.

"We have confirmation that the child was born, and indeed the ritual appears to have been a success." Erik gave a small bow of his head in acknowledgement of their presence. "Vicktor was there to intercept the hybrid and the artefacts, but it appears she had unexpected help."

"And?"

Another hesitation. "They got away."

It wasn't rage that filled Darius's veins in that moment. Rage was a human emotion – weak and insufficient. Fire burned through him as his vision turned red. Shadows swirled around the flame, seeking a target, someone to make suffer. The shadows shot out and wrapped around Erik's throat. His eyes bulged, but it was only when bones began to crunch that he uttered a choked protest.

The sound managed to break through the fog that had clouded Darius's mind. He blinked and the shadows dissolved.

Erik coughed out a breath and grimaced as he gave his neck a resounding crack. His face had paled, but he straightened to attention and met Darius's eyes. The Horsemen approved.

"There's someone here to see you," Erik said, returning straight to business, if somewhat hoarsely.

Darius raised an eyebrow and indicated for him to lead the way.

They made their way up to the ground floor of the building and into a small reception room. Two wing-backed chairs faced a blazing fire, and a tall man with greying hair and a stiff posture occupied one. At Darius's entrance he stood, smoothing his tailored black suit and pasting a politician's smile on his face.

He held out a hand. "Darius, good to see you again."

Darius looked at the hand and back up at the man, who flinched ever so slightly. The Horsemen watched with interest. *Vlad*, he informed them silently, *vampire head of the Council.*

Vlad cleared his throat and straightened his suit again. "Yes, well, I wanted to see you because I have information that may be of use to you."

Darius tilted his head, considering the other man coldly even as the voices inside his mind provided subtle suggestions of what he could do to the vampire with his new power.

When no response was forthcoming, Vlad continued. "If I understand correctly, you're looking for the four fae artefacts. I thought you might be interested to know that the Mists have returned to Ireland, and they have the missing cauldron in their possession."

The Horsemen stilled.

"And why would you tell me this?"

Some of the tension in Vlad's shoulders relaxed. "My colleagues in their esteemed wisdom have chosen to ally with the hybrid. They intend on uniting the artefacts and reinforcing the barrier to stem the influx of demons. I, however, can see the tide of change for what it is, and I bow to it willingly. I'm offering this information as a gesture of good faith, and I simply ask that you remember my support … when the time comes."

Darius was quiet for a moment. A smile crept across his face, and taking it a sign of gratitude, Vlad's shoulders relaxed even further.

Without turning around, Darius called to Erik, who had stationed himself at the door of the room. "See that our friend here is made comfortable."

There was a soft burst of static as Erik spoke into his walkie-talkie.

"I'm glad we've had this talk," Vlad said, the politician's smile returning to his face. "I really feel that you and I could do great things together."

Darius's smile never faltered as two vampire guards came to escort the Council head away. When the vampire was gone, he turned to his head of security. "You say the hybrid had help?"

Erik nodded. "We believe it was the Mists."

Interesting. That would support some of Vlad's information, at least. As for the rest …

"Send a healer to the witch," he ordered. "And prepare our army. We move at sundown tomorrow."

39

The world solidified around Phoenix. Two hands gripped her shoulders to steady her, and when her knees buckled, those hands stopped her from sinking to the ground. She looked up and found herself staring into the golden eyes that still haunted her dreams.

Maj watched her warily, as if expecting her to attack or bolt at any second.

Phoenix jerked back out of her grip, too panicked to process the conflicting emotions that came every time she saw or thought of the Mist. She swung her head around, desperately searching the unfamiliar wooded area for any sight of Saoirse or Ethan.

"My baby, where's my baby?"

The air to the left of her shimmered and Shayan, the youngest of the three Mists, appeared, holding Ethan's arm in a bruising grip. Ethan, for his part, looked ready to drive his spear through his handsome rescuer, and her heart skipped a beat at the sight of him. But her relief was short-lived as she turned frantically in a circle waiting for Morrigan to appear with Saoirse.

It was barely a second before a third disturbance appeared in the air to the right of her, but it might as well have been an eternity. When Jannah materialised with his arms around Morrigan and Saoirse, Phoenix's legs did finally buckle, and this time Maj let her slide to the ground.

Ethan rushed to them and pulled Saoirse into his arms before moving to Phoenix's side. He snarled a warning at the others not to come any closer.

Jannah's serious gold eyes met Phoenix's. "We gave our word that we would come to you. We are here to fulfil that oath."

Maj and Shayan moved to his side, their black robes shifting like shadows in the chill night breeze. They bowed their heads in acknowledgement of their older brother's words.

Phoenix's eyes flicked to their wrists, where thick gold bands had once rested before she'd freed them of their servitude to the Council. "How did you know where to find us?"

Morrigan stepped forward, her dark eyes glinting in the moonlight. "I contacted them before I came to retrieve you from Faerie; I needed them to return with the cauldron. Their oath allowed them to sense the danger you were in and find you tonight."

The idea that the Mists could track her did not sit comfortably, even though she was grateful that they had. So, she focused on the rest of Morrigan's comment instead. "The cauldron? You mean Dagda's Cauldron? My grandfather said it had been taken after the original banishment."

"It was," Shayan answered quietly, an odd tension settling between him and his siblings.

Her next question was cut off by a soft gurgle from Saoirse. She shook her head; the questions weren't important. They needed to focus on getting out of here before those things found them again.

For the first time since the world had rematerialized, she looked around and actually took in their surroundings. Tall trees circled them, blocking all but the view of the moon, near full overhead. She scanned the shadows for any sign of danger.

"Where are we? Can those things find us here?" Because they hadn't been dead, and she had absolutely no idea what that meant for their group if Darius decided to send even more in their wake.

"We brought you as far as we could from the Cathedral," Jannah answered, his calm golden eyes doing a sweep of the darkness also. "It takes a lot of power to transport others with us, so we couldn't move you far. It will take them a while to track you, but we shouldn't delay here."

Ethan looked up suddenly from where he'd been soothing the baby cradled in his arms. "How *did* they track us?"

A heavy silence fell around the group.

"We used Eoghan's gateway," Phoenix said softly as realisation struck her. She looked at Morrigan, and the goddess met her gaze with an unwavering one of her own. "You knew. You knew that the baby was coming." Her throat tightened even as her voice rose. "Why did you bring us home? We could have stayed in Faerie. You brought us back here knowing they'd be waiting for us at the time I'd be completely defenceless."

"Some things need to happen. The details are not always revealed to me, nor the reasons why, but you needed to be here for the final pieces of the puzzle to come together. What picture we make from those pieces still remains to be seen."

Frustration and anger flared in Phoenix at the goddess's cryptic response. She was so sick of being a pawn in some stupid game the fates were playing. And if it wasn't bad enough that her life got fucked around for their amusement, her child had been forced into this world surrounded by monsters and death.

Burning tears pricked the back of her eyes. "I trusted you," she said hoarsely.

She turned and held her arms out in a silent request for Ethan to give her the baby. He placed Saoirse in her arms without a word. Phoenix cuddled the small bundle to her and let the tears roll down her cheeks as she ran her fingers along the soft skin that was still so pure and untouched by the world.

It should have been different. She should have been able to experience her child growing within her, should never have had to be ashamed of such a miracle. Instead, she'd had that time ripped away from her and her little girl had been violently thrust into this world. Well, she was done with it. She was done playing by everyone else's rules.

She rested her forehead gently against Saoirse's cheek and made the silent promise that she wouldn't let this be their life. And when she lifted her eyes to Ethan's, she could see the same solemn promise mirrored back at her.

"We need to get moving," Jannah said finally.

Ethan moved towards her but froze at the sudden sound of a car engine in the distance. He tensed, hand instinctively gripping the spear that rested on the ground beside him. She reached for the sword on her back even as her other arm hugged Saoirse tighter to her.

Jannah held up a hand, urging them to wait. His solid form turned to a wisp of shadow and he disappeared. Barely a minute passed before he returned, but to Phoenix it was one of the longest of her life.

"It's okay," he said, his posture showing no sign of the tense readiness the rest of them held. "It's your family."

Phoenix looked at Ethan in confusion, a mild sense of panic darting through her before she realised it was unlikely Jannah had meant her family. But still, how would any of their friends have known to find them here?

A car door slammed, closer now. She moved to Ethan's side, careful not to disturb Saoirse, who seemed to be blissfully unaware of her mother's frayed nerves as her tiny, red-tinged eyelids drifted closed with a sleepy yawn. He wrapped an arm around her waist, his other still holding the Spear of Lugh ready despite Jannah's reassurance of safety.

There was no stealth in the crunching of feet approaching them, no attempt to catch anyone unaware in the low mumble of voices. The signatures of Ethan's parents hit her a moment before they crashed through the trees. Ethan let out a gasp of disbelief.

She didn't blame him when he let go of her waist and ran to them, but she'd have been lying if she said she wasn't a little envious. Cormac and Fia enveloped their son in a great big bear hug, their laughter and relief ringing clear for all to hear.

"Phoenix!" A third figure stumbled through the trees, and Phoenix let out a shocked sob at the sound of her best friend's voice.

Abi dashed towards her, arms open wide for a hug, but she skidded to a sudden stop, her eyes going wide at the sight of the small bundle cradled in Phoenix's arms. She looked from the bundle down to Phoenix's belly and back again. "Is that …"

Phoenix choked out a laugh that was half sniffly sob, half joy, and nodded. A shocked silence fell as the others were distracted from their reunion long enough to notice what Abi had.

Ethan tugged his parents over to join her and Abi. His eyes glistened with pride as he said, "Everyone, we'd like you to meet Saoirse."

40

The car rumbled down the motorway, taking him away from creatures that would haunt his nightmares for a long time to come, but all Ethan could focus on was the little girl nestled in Phoenix's arms beside him – their little girl. It was only now that the danger had passed, however temporarily, and they were surrounded by family and friends, that the reality was truly hitting him.

He had no words for the feeling that stirred in his chest as he looked at her, no measure for the love, or the fear. Because this tiny human was their responsibility now, and didn't that just highlight to him exactly how much trouble they were in.

When the tearful reunions were finished and he'd introduced his parents to their new grandchild, Cormac updated them briefly on the situation. His parents had sent Morrigan to retrieve him and Phoenix from Faerie, but the goddess had only just left when a panicked call came through from William warning them of Cassandra's newest vision; Darius had somehow found a way to pull the Horsemen through to their world.

His parents had wasted no time in calling on Izzie to perform a tracker spell so that they could pinpoint the exact place and moment when he and Phoenix crossed back over. The witch it seemed had grown significantly from that young, frightened little girl he'd saved from being sacrificed all those months ago.

Realisation had dawned on Morrigan's face as his father had spoken, as if she then understood why Saoirse's birth hadn't resulted in the shift they'd all expected. Ethan had been too exhausted by that stage to make sense of what it all might mean, but when the goddess had gathered the Mists and left to make preparations for the ritual, he knew any reprieve they'd gotten would be short-lived.

Leaning back against the headrest, he forced his eyes to stay open even as his eyelids grew heavier by the minute. In front of him, Cormac focused on the road with the determined caution that only came from driving with a newborn baby in the car. His mother cast surreptitious glances back at Saoirse from where she sat in the front passenger seat, and a smile tugged at his lips as he imagined what they'd be like as grandparents. On the far side of Phoenix, Abi too kept looking at the baby with a wide-eyed awe, and it struck him just how loved this tiny little person was already.

For a while there was nothing other than the lulling roll of tyres over asphalt, then suddenly Phoenix jerked beside him. "Oh no. We haven't bought any baby stuff. Where the hell are we going to find anything at this hour of the night?"

He looked at the clock on the car's dashboard and grimaced. It wasn't yet midnight, but it was late enough that shops would be closed, even if it happened to be a late-night shopping day. But wait ... What bloody day was it anyway?

Abi cleared her throat, the colouring of her cheeks noticeable even in the dim light of the car. "Actually, I may have bought a few bits. Just some basics ..." She held up her hands in defence. "I know you're not meant to buy things too early, but I needed to keep busy and some of the stuff was just too cute."

Phoenix burst out laughing, and Abi's relief was obvious as she too joined in. "You're going to love the crib I got. The only thing I don't have is baby formula. I figured it was too early, and I didn't know if you were planning on feeding her yourself."

The laughter disappeared from Phoenix's face, and she looked down at Saoirse, sorrow shadowing her eyes. "I don't know if I can feed. My body didn't exactly go through the natural developments. And if something happens to me ..."

His heart broke as he looked at her, and he wanted more than anything to swear he'd never let anything happen to her. But how many times now had her life been put at risk and he'd been powerless to help?

Fia turned to look back at them, her brown eyes sympathetic. "We can stop at an all-night chemist and get some formula so that the option is there if you need it. She's sleeping soundly enough for now; you don't have to make the decision until she wakes."

Ethan stared out at the lights of the city as the car idled on the side of the road. Apparently, it took three people to decide on the most appropriate baby formula, and he and Cormac had been left in the car with the sleeping Saoirse while the women went into the all-night pharmacy to stock up on milk and "other supplies," as they cryptically stated.

Cormac glanced in the rear-view mirror at him and his Alpha smiled. "You look good with a baby."

Ethan snorted. "Are you mad? I'm afraid to breathe too hard in case I break her."

"She's stronger than she looks, trust me."

Hell, he really hoped so because when he looked down at his little girl, the thought of her growing up in their world terrified the life out of him.

He was quiet for a few minutes as he thought about that. What must it have been like for his parents? They hadn't just had him and Sasha to worry about; they had the whole pack. Their every decision decided the fate of the wolves under their care, and sometimes even the best leaders got things wrong.

"How's Sean doing?" he asked quietly. Cormac had filled him in on the basics of the Omega's rescue, but he'd been so focused on getting Saoirse somewhere warm and safe that he hadn't had the mental capacity to really think about it before now.

Cormac stared out the window, lines of worry showing at the side of his face. "The witches did better than we could have hoped with the separation spell, but even with the demon gone, it'll be a long road. You don't go through what he has and come out the other side unchanged."

A weighty silence fell, broken only by the steady hum of the car's engine. Ethan was just about to admit how nervous he was at seeing his friend again, when his mother, Phoenix, and Abi emerged from the pharmacy laden with bags. Cormac jumped out to help them put everything in the boot, and then they were on the road again, his confession left unspoken.

The lights that were a constant in the city even at this late hour added an eerie glow to the silhouette of the Dublin City skyline. The traffic was light and it wasn't long before they pulled to a stop in front of the converted warehouse he'd come to call home while in Dublin. It seemed like a lifetime since he'd been back, and the feeling was only heightened by the fact he now held a brand new person in his arms.

They'd barely climbed from the car when a familiar figure came running towards them from the doorway. His sister grabbed Phoenix in a tight hug before turning to him, smile wide and brown eyes glistening. Though he knew his mother had sent word ahead about Saoirse's surprise arrival, Sasha's expression was still one of awe as she took in her little niece.

"She's actually cute!" she said, genuine surprise in her voice. "Like, I know everyone says to the parents that their baby is cute when they're just being polite because the kid looks like a squished up old man, but I really mean it." Her smile turned mischievous. "She must take after her mother."

Ethan chuckled, giving her a gentle nudge with his foot. "Don't forget we're twins, so you've got the same gene pool as me."

She tilted her head back and laughed, the sound acting like a balm to his soul. When she demanded to hold her cute new squishy niece, he handed Saoirse over obediently, even if something inside him rebelled at the thought of letting her go.

He helped his dad grab everything from the car and followed the others inside. As he made his way upstairs to the apartment, his steps slowed. He hadn't thought to ask who would be here, and though he was grateful beyond words to be able to come home to his family and friends, a tinge of apprehension tightened his chest.

On the top floor, the door to the apartment swung open to reveal a glowering Shade. Ethan grinned at the vampire, and the glower broke into a lip twitch that was the closest semblance of a smile he'd ever seen from his friend.

Before he could utter a hello, Nate shoved past the vampire and threw himself at Ethan, wrapping arms and legs around him in an enthusiastic embrace that almost sent them both stumbling to the ground. "Good to have you back. I'm sick of being the mature, sensible one around here."

Cormac cleared his throat behind them, and Nate unwrapped himself from Ethan with a cheeky grin. "Sorry, Alpha."

Lucas, at least, allowed them to enter the apartment before greeting them, something akin to pride in his grey eyes as he looked at the sleeping baby now back in Phoenix's arms.

For a few minutes, everything was in chaos as they rushed about setting up the basics they'd need for Saoirse. Ethan had no idea what half of the stuff was for, but he couldn't keep the smile from his face as he watched his friends and family work with an efficiency that would make any tactical squad proud.

They'd just finished organising the crib when the room suddenly fell silent.

The signature that reached him was achingly familiar. He turned slowly towards the hallway.

Sean's white hair was cleaner than the last time he'd seen it, though still long and unruly. The solid jaw that, in the past, had always been clean-shaven was now covered in a light stubble. But it was the eyes that were the biggest shock of all.

The blue eyes he remembered were now tinged with the red remnants of the demon that had tried to claim Sean's body. Tried and failed. That wasn't the cause of his shock, however. It was the haunted look behind those eyes.

"I wanted to leave before you got back, but …"

"We wouldn't let him," Abi said in a firm voice, moving to stand at the Omega's side.

Ethan couldn't look away. His father had tried to warn him that it would take a long time for Sean to heal, but staring at his childhood friend now, Ethan wondered if healing was truly possible after everything he'd been through.

Words caught in his throat. All the things he'd wanted to say for so many years, yet nothing would come. "Are you …"

Sean gave a bitter smile that looked wrong on his kind face. "Okay? Evil? Angry at you? No." His shoulders slumped, and he suddenly looked world-weary.

Ethan swallowed past the emotion choking him. "It's good to see you."

41

It was like a surreal dream. Not just to be back in Ethan's apartment again, but to be surrounded by her friends and family. It was more than Phoenix had truly hoped for. When she'd stood in the ruins of the Cathedral facing off with Vicktor and the rest of the demon-Supes, she'd been fully prepared to die.

Of course, some of the reunions had been more difficult than others. She couldn't quite look at Sean without having the unnerving sensation that Darius was somehow watching their every movement through him. She kept her feelings to herself for Ethan's sake, but she made herself scarce while he and Sean had their awkward reconciliation.

A hot shower and a change of clothes seemed like a luxury she couldn't afford given they still had a ticking time bomb hanging over them – if Cassandra's vision was to be believed. So she got Saoirse fed and settled with Abi's help, and rejoined the others in the living area. Izzie had arrived at some point while she'd been in the bedroom, and Phoenix was struck by the strange mix of youthful features and experience-aged eyes. She'd never met Annabelle's friend before, but as she looked at her now, she was reminded of the night Ethan had landed on her doorstep with Annabelle's limp body. The night that had changed it all for her.

When everyone was gathered, Cormac finished the private phone conversation he'd been having with William and placed his mobile on the table in the centre of the group, pressing the button to switch over to loudspeaker. "Everyone's here," he told William.

There was a moment of static, then William's voice rang clear in the room. "The Council – or what remains of us – has been considering what Cassandra's vision might mean for our plans. We've agreed to go ahead with the ritual, but without the adjustments we'd planned. If Darius has managed to pull across some element of the Horsemen, we need to recreate the original banishment, preferably before we have to face him or any more of his abominations again."

"How do we know it will work if we can't even confirm exactly what he's pulled across the barrier?" Shade asked, his usual scowl unchanged by their predicament.

"The ritual is tied to their magic," William said. "Four artefacts for the Four Horsemen. It shouldn't matter what form they're in here – so long as their magic is here, the artefacts will find them."

"But if their magic is here, doesn't that mean Darius has access to it?" Abi visibly paled as she asked the question. Phoenix reached out and squeezed her hand, but no one offered any comments of comfort.

"Like I said, we need to complete the ritual before we're forced to engage him again."

Phoenix looked around the room, feeling a bit lost. She'd been dimly aware of Cormac and Fia giving an update on the plans they'd agreed upon with the Council during the drive back to the apartment, but in truth she'd been focused only on Saoirse's sleeping face. She didn't remember any magical solution as to how they were going to avoid Darius, however.

She cleared her throat. "How exactly are we going to do that? I mean, he's always been a step ahead of us. How can you be sure he won't just attack us while we're conducting the ritual?"

"The witches will hold a barrier with the Mists," Izzie said quietly. "Only one witch is required for the actual spell itself, and the rest of the coven will buy us whatever time they can."

Phoenix's breath caught in her throat and she felt Ethan tense at her side, but they both stayed silent. The young witch might have been little more than a child to them, but she'd more than proven her worth already and she had as much right to be there as any of them.

Lucas pushed away from the window he was leaning against and looked around the room. "We all know what's required of us for the ritual. The Mists will bring the final artefact with them to the Hill of Tara tomorrow, so that just leaves the question of defence. If we are attacked and the witches' barrier falls – which we should assume it will – we're going to need people who are able to fight and hold back whatever Darius sends our way. My clan will be here before night's end to help in whatever way they can."

"The Donegal pack is in transit too," Cormac confirmed. "And the Dublin werewolf pack have also pledged their aid."

"I'll contact my aunt. She promised the fae would come." Phoenix reached into the pocket of her blood splattered clothes and wrapped her hand around the smooth crystal resting there.

"Well shucks," Nate chimed in. "I'm afraid I don't have any shifter friends to offer up, but I did manage to acquire a few of these babies." He reached behind him and pulled out a small black ball that was completely nondescript except for a single button on its surface.

When no one fell at his feet in congratulations, he huffed out a martyred sigh. "How are we friends when none of you have a clue what this is?"

"Because you just can't resist our charming wit?" Shade suggested, rolling his eyes when Nate looked even more forlorn. "Please do enlighten us."

"*This* is a top of the range incendiary device, filled with pure silver. Shove it down one of those demon thing's throats, and I'm sure even they are going to be a little too preoccupied to bug us."

The vampires and wolves in the room winced, subtly shifting away from the small silver bomb. Even Phoenix grimaced, despite the fact that her hybrid nature meant silver wasn't as lethal to her.

"The Council are securing whatever forces we can without triggering all-out panic across the Lore," William said. "But there's still one more species needed for the ritual."

They all looked around the room in confusion. It was only when Phoenix's eyes fell on Abi that she froze, her lungs forgetting to expand for a minute. "Human," she whispered.

William's silence was all the confirmation she needed. It made sense, she supposed. This prophecy, the Horsemen – it was about their world being destroyed, not just the Lore. How self-absorbed had they been to forget they weren't the only ones who would suffer if things went wrong? Hell, Abi had reminded her of it more than once when she argued for her place at their side. But still …

Phoenix shook her head. "It can't be Abi. She needs to stay and protect Saoirse. We'll find someone else. We'll –"

Abi turned to her, blue eyes looking sad but determined. "Let me do this. Please. Morrigan can protect Saoirse. If this all goes to hell, she'll be able to keep her safe better than I ever could."

Phoenix just continued to shake her head, the thought of her best friend standing in the middle of such danger impossible for her to accept. "You can't, Abi. You'll die! William, tell her. What happened to the human who stood in the original banishment?"

"He died." There was a long pause. "As did many of the Supes that stood at his side."

A heavy silence fell over the room as they considered what they knew to be the truth: not all of them would make it back tomorrow night.

Phoenix hung her head. The hopelessness of the situation burned her throat. She clenched her fists, wanting to scream or punch something. Anything, just to release the frustration. But it wouldn't change facts.

In the quiet of the room, Izzie spoke softly. "I may have another way to keep Saoirse safe."

Ethan watched Phoenix's eyelids droop as she struggled to stay awake. It was past two in the morning, and after everything she'd been through, he had no idea how she was still functioning. With the plans for the ritual agreed upon, everyone in the room had fallen deep into their own thoughts. They all knew what was on the line, and they all knew how uncertain the outcome was.

A small cry from his bedroom shocked his body to attention at the same moment that Phoenix jerked her head up. Their eyes met across the room and the ghost of a smile tugged at her lips. "I think someone wants to be fed."

He pushed himself away from the kitchen island that had been propping him up and offered her his hand. "Come on, let's get her settled and get some rest."

There were mumbles of "Goodnight" from around the room, but his only focus was on the woman at his side. The woman who, against all odds, had given him the most precious gift. He kept hold of her hand as they walked the short distance to his room, relishing the feel of that simple touch.

His heart both lightened and clenched in agony when he saw the little red screwed-up face wailing for food and comfort. He picked Saoirse up from the crib and realised he had no idea how he would leave her tomorrow. If Izzie could do what she said she could, he could think of no better protection for his daughter. But to leave her knowing he might not return … the thought hurt in a way he couldn't put into words.

When Phoenix offered to take Saoirse from him, he shook his head wordlessly and took the bottle from her, ushering her into the ensuite bathroom for the shower she more than deserved. Carefully he settled down on the king-size bed, leaning back against the headboard. He held his little girl as she fed and memorised every inch of her. She was perfect.

He'd just finished winding Saoirse when Phoenix emerged from the bathroom looking clean, if not exactly refreshed. With a tired yawn, she settled down on the bed next to him. She reached out to touch Saoirse's tiny little feet, staring at them with the same wonder that he no doubt had on his face.

"She should have ended this," she said softly, her green eyes darkening with pain. "She should be enough."

Once more his heart clenched. He wanted more than anything for that to have been true, for it all to be over so they could just enjoy this miracle together as a family.

"She is enough. She should never have had that responsibility fall on her. Just like you should never have had the blame fall on you. No child, no one person, can be responsible for the lives of every person in this world."

When Phoenix spoke again, something changed in her voice. Gone was the uncertainty that he'd always sensed under the surface of her confidence. In its place was one thing: strength.

"I know that now. I know they were wrong."

Shifting Saoirse into his right arm, Ethan wrapped his left around Phoenix and pulled her close. He kissed the top of her head and closed his eyes. "I love you," he whispered.

42

Darius stared at his hand, watching as the flesh and bone melted before his eyes. The slow-motion decomposition was mesmerising, if not a little disgusting; it would make a neat party trick. Pity he couldn't keep the power. He concentrated until the process reversed, the cells reforming and skin knitting back together. A small patch of skin on the back of his hand refused to cooperate, the flesh remaining blackened and charred even as he willed it to repair.

He snarled and threw his whiskey glass at the stone wall of the chamber. It shattered into pieces, and the golden liquid glistened in the dim light. Flames erupted on his hand, flickering with insatiable hunger. He closed his eyes, and when he opened them the fire was gone.

The voices were louder in his head now. *Use the power,* they ordered. *Let it fill you. Let it become you. Devour. Consume. More.*

Slowly he stalked over to the body that hung from chains, back against the chamber wall. No blood or wounds marred Vlad's naked chest, but sweat drenched his clothes, and the moan of agony as he sensed Darius draw near was a drug unlike any other.

"Maybe we'll try this one again." Darius placed his hands on either side of the vampire's face. He closed his eyes and let the power fill him. Fill him and unmake him.

His body turned to shadows, and in the shadows came fear. In an instant he knew every nightmare Vlad had ever had, his worst fears. He took that knowledge and turned it into something tangible and real, then he let it flow through his hands.

The vampire screamed in pure terror.

Darius inhaled, they inhaled, breathing in his fear. The Horsemen's power fed on it, growing and growing until the world swam around him. Only when it felt like he might not be able to piece himself back together again did Darius let go of the shadows.

Every cell of his body was electric, alive. The voices inside him purred in pleasure. He extended his fangs and with the sweet scent of fear filling his nostrils, he struck. The vampire's normally poisonous blood tasted like honey to them, and they savoured its power. When the body was finally drained dry, he opened the manacles holding the limp meat sack aloft and let the body flop to the floor. More. He needed more blood to feed the power.

This time when he held his hand out and called the fire, he smiled and watched it burn. Everything was in place. His army was finally ready. Soon it would all be his for the taking.

43

The night passed far too quickly. One minute Phoenix was lying in Ethan's arms listening to Saoirse's soft breathing, the next she was standing in a circle of candles, preparing to raise the dead.

"Do you think she can do it?" she asked Ethan quietly.

He looked up from the centre of the circle where he was busy fussing over Saoirse's crib and glanced at Izzie as she carefully placed the last candle. "I've only ever heard of necromantic magic in legends. I want to believe she can, because I don't know if I can do this without knowing Saoirse is safe." His eyes were pained as he looked down at his daughter once more and gently caressed her cheek.

Phoenix's heart clenched. Of all the things she'd encountered in her life, watching him with his child was the most magical thing she'd ever seen. She let that magic ignite a small spark of hope in her, and she held it close, tucked away in a private little part of her heart.

"We're ready," Izzie said, composing herself as she picked up a black candle that seemed to absorb the light around it. She looked so much older than her sixteen years, her face sombre and focused.

Ethan hesitated. Every muscle in his body telegraphed his reluctance to step away from his child.

Izzie gave him an understanding smile. "You saved my life, Ethan. Let me do what I can to repay the favour."

He closed his eyes for a minute, then nodded. With a final look at Saoirse's sleeping form, he stepped away from the crib and placed himself on the opposite side of the circle facing Phoenix.

Izzie began chanting, softly at first, her words growing stronger as she continued. The hairs on Phoenix's arms stood on end, and a shiver ran down her spine. The saying that someone had walked across her grave was completely inadequate for the creeping sensation she now felt. It was more like a stampede.

In the dim light of the bedroom, Ethan's yellow eyes glowed. As Izzie's power expanded, filling the room, her own power responded. A ball of light flared to life in her chest and the sun's energy flowed through her.

The whispers were the first thing she heard. The ghosts of memories. She heard her mother laughing, her father calling her name. There were other voices too. Some she didn't recognise, but they called to something familiar inside her. They were her past, her present, her future. They were part of her.

Across the room Ethan's eyes widened in surprise and she could only assume that he was experiencing something similar.

Izzie's voice changed as her words took on a power of their own. The chant filled the room, mirrored back by the ghostly echoes. Phoenix closed her eyes and focused on the voices of her parents, on the fact that she got to hear them again one more time.

When someone touched her hand, she didn't jump. She opened her eyes slowly, her breath held. The warmth of the sun embraced her, the glow of light blinding for a minute before it faded to reveal the smiling face of her mother. Tears glistened in Aria's luminous green eyes, and her smile was one of pride.

Slowly, as Phoenix watched, Marcus appeared next to her. He reached out a hand and brushed a tear from her cheek, his face full of love.

So many emotions roiled inside Phoenix that they threatened to choke her. She knew from the transparency of the forms that her parents weren't really there. But in that moment, they felt so alive to her. She could feel their touch, she could breathe in their scent, she could see them.

Other shadowy figures filled the room, but Phoenix refused to take her eyes away from her parents for fear that they might disappear. "I miss you," she whispered, not sure if they could even hear her.

"We're so proud of you," her father answered. "We're always with you."

As one, Aria and Marcus turned towards the crib in the centre of the circle. Their faces seemed to glow with love and happiness as they moved to Saoirse's side. They looked down on their granddaughter, and in that moment

Phoenix knew that no matter what happened, her child would be safe.

Hot tears burned tracks down Phoenix's cheeks and she tore her gaze away to look at Ethan. Similar emotion blazed in his eyes as he lifted his head from the two young girls who stood with him to look at her.

When the oldest girl turned to smile at her, Phoenix let out a soft gasp. Lily looked younger than she remembered. The heavy weight of her grief had finally lifted, taking away the pain that had been her constant burden in the final part of her life. Her blonde hair glittered in the light of the candles, and there was a life to her green eyes that seemed almost contradictory to her current state.

Lily whispered something to the girl beside her, who also turned in her direction. Phoenix wasn't surprised to see Annabelle's smiling face, and her heart filled with happiness to know the sisters had found each other again.

Annabelle gave her a shy wave and mouthed "thank you". Two other figures moved to stand at their side, their forms not quite as defined as the girls', but visible and very much present. They pulled the girls into a tight embrace, and there was the faint echo of laughter and joy as the family reunited.

Phoenix blinked away the tears that clung to her eyelashes and looked around her. So many people filled the room. Most were little more than whispers of a thought, their features indistinguishable, but somehow she knew they were all there for the same reason.

As if reading her mind, Aria looked back at her from where she stood by Saoirse's crib, her eyes sad. "All of

309

these people have been hurt by him. Because of his greed. We can't stand with you, no matter how much we want to, but we can do this for you. Let us protect her while you protect the innocents of this world who cannot defend themselves. Be their voice when they have none and bring them light in this darkest of times. Go. Show him what hell really looks like."

44

Phoenix squinted at the sun as she waited at the bottom of the Hill of Tara. It seemed wrong somehow for the sun to be shining so brightly given what lay ahead of them. Her body wasn't complaining, however, as it soaked in the healing energy and tried valiantly to recover from the trauma of the past twenty-four hours. In truth, she'd have happily found herself a hole in the ground to curl up into if she'd had the choice. But she didn't have the choice, so here she was.

Ethan stood by her side, keeping a watchful eye on their surroundings. The tension in his body was as evident as her own, and no amount of slow breathing or restless pacing seemed to help either of them.

The Hill of Tara was eerily quiet. There was no sign of the dog walkers or cyclists that often frequented the spot, and the tourists wouldn't be quick to venture this way thanks to a subtle spell the witches had placed at dawn that morning. They wouldn't know quite what deterred them from the place, but it would be enough to keep innocent people from becoming cannon fodder if things went badly.

A shiver ran through her at the thought, and she looked over her shoulder to reassure herself that Claíomh Solais was still strapped to her back where it should be. Though where exactly she thought the sword might disappear to, she had no idea.

Beside her, Ethan had a firm grip on the Spear of Lugh and she could tell by the whites of his knuckles that he too was taking what comfort he could from the tangible weight of the artefact. Now all they needed was the cauldron.

Where the hell are they?

She scanned the broad expanse of green that surrounded the small hill where Lia Fáil sat. The Stone of Destiny. Would it decide their destiny here today?

The witches had already formed a wide perimeter around the hill. Once the Mists arrived with the cauldron, Maj and Shayan would join them and erect a ward, effectively sealing off the hill from any possible attack. It wasn't foolproof of course, so groups of Supes were gathered behind the witches, ready to form a second line of defence should the ward fail. She didn't want to think about what might happen if they were needed.

"What if they don't show?" She bit her lip and shuffled restlessly from one foot to the other.

"They will."

As if summoned by his words, there was a soft flutter overhead. They both looked up just as a large crow swooped down from the sky and Morrigan shifted to her human form to land beside them. Her black training gear shimmered with the same oil-slick effect that Phoenix had grown used to seeing on her feathers, and the clothes clung to her almost as they were a second skin.

Morrigan turned three-sixty, her watchful eyes checking their surroundings. Then she raised her fingers to her lips and let out a low whistle that vibrated through Phoenix's bones.

At her call, a light mist fell around them. It coalesced, solidifying to form three bodies. The Mists' golden eyes glowed, and their bronzed skin shimmered in the sunlight. Shayan stood in the centre between his older brother and sister, a small cauldron in his hands.

The sword on Phoenix's back sent vibrations rattling down her spine. Even without holding Claíomh Solais, she could feel the power thrum through the blade as like called to like. From the shocked expression on Ethan's face, she assumed he was feeling something similar from the spear gripped in his hand.

Dagda's Cauldron was remarkably nondescript. It bore a striking resemblance to an old-school cast iron pot, though she assumed it wasn't actually made of iron, given it was a fae artefact. She eyed it with curiosity. Had it been worth it? The price the Mists had paid for keeping it safe?

"We need to get into position," Morrigan said. "The sun will set shortly and there's much to do."

Without another word, they made their way to the perimeter where the witches were making the final preparations to raise the ward. Jannah stopped a little behind them, pulling Maj and Shayan to the side to speak quietly to them.

Phoenix watched the exchange closely, paying particular attention to Shayan's tense expression. It was he who had taken the cauldron, but they'd all agreed that it was best for Jannah to stand as the Mist representative in the ritual. In order for that to happen, the youngest Mist would have to be willing to hand over his ownership of the cauldron, like Aoife had the spear. For a moment she wondered if he'd refuse to do it. Her hand twitched on the leather strap holding her scabbard as he seemed to hesitate, but then he gave a solemn nod, said the words needed, and handed the artefact to Jannah. She released a breath.

Maj looked over at her, an unreadable expression in her golden eyes. "We'll hold it as long as we can." With that, she and her younger brother stepped back to join the witches and close the circle.

An ominous chill ran through Phoenix, but she pushed it away. She'd promised herself that no matter what happened, she'd find some way to get back to Saoirse. She intended on keeping that promise. Still, she had to fight the urge to turn around and flee as the near-translucent ward flared to life like a dome around them. Together, she, Ethan, Morrigan, and Jannah continued their way up the hill.

Immediately behind the ward circle, the Council's troops dotted the field. They were easily identifiable by their matching fighting gear and professional-looking badassery, but she paid them little heed.

The werewolves were stationed next in the line of defence. Some of the faces she recognised from the Donegal pack, others she assumed were the Dublin wolves who'd pledged their aid. She scanned the field but couldn't see Ethan's family among them. They must be helping to prepare for the ritual, she realised with an anxious twist of her gut.

In the limited tree cover that dotted the field, she spotted Lucas's vampires. Though many of the vampires were strong enough to withstand even the glaring sun that beat down on her now, it would weaken them unnecessarily. The shade allowed them to conserve their energy until the sun began to set, or someone tried to kill them all, whichever came first.

She continued to search the horizon, hoping.

She told herself it was stupid to feel let down, but still the pang of disappointment settled in her chest like an ache.

Just as they reached the bottom of the hill where Lia Fáil awaited them, Cormac and Fia intercepted them. "Everyone's in place," Cormac informed them.

A quick glance around showed Nate off to their left, his attention firmly fixed on the silver-laden explosives he was checking. Sean stood close to him, staring into the distance with grim determination while Sasha bounced restlessly on her heels beside him. Shade was nowhere to be seen, and she assumed he was taking shelter with the other vampires.

"The Council came," she noted as she spotted William prowling along the base of the hill. He looked every inch the wolf, even in his human skin.

Cormac grimaced. "They're all here except Vlad. Apparently, he never resurfaced after the botched attack on Darius."

She'd never met the vampire head of the Council, but no one around her seemed too surprised by the revelation, and since they weren't short on vampires, she guessed it didn't really matter too much.

"Did my aunt …"

Cormac shook his head, but Fia gave her shoulder a reassuring squeeze. "They'll be here."

She took a shuddery breath and squared her shoulders. If they had to, they'd make do without the fae's support.

They all looked towards the rock that sat atop the hill and the others who waited there to start the ritual. Ethan opened his mouth to say something, but before he could speak, Cormac pulled him into a firm embrace, turning to Phoenix and bringing her in close as well. Fia kissed them both on the forehead, then took her mate's hand and stepped back with a nod of encouragement.

"I guess it's time to get this show on the road." Ethan placed a hand on Phoenix's back. She gave him a nervous smile and together they followed Morrigan and Jannah up the last stretch of hill.

Lia Fáil was nothing like Phoenix had expected. Sure, the fae artefacts all seemed to have been designed in an understated way, but this was just ridiculous. She tilted her head as she assessed the rock that was said to have heralded the rightful king of Ireland. All she saw was a random stone pillar sticking out of the ground. It reminded her of those strange phallic-like artefacts ancient civilisations used to encourage fertility.

But the power. Holy shit, the power!

The tug she'd felt from her sword when she was close to the spear or cauldron was nothing compared to what she felt now. One look at the surprise on Ethan's face told her he felt it too.

As she, Ethan, and Jannah stepped closer, a bright light flared to life, seeming to come from within the stone itself. Familiar Celtic symbols appeared on its surface, and her hand reached out involuntarily to touch them. A slender hand with red tipped nails grasped her wrist in a vice-like grip, and Phoenix looked up to be greeted by Méabh's sardonic smile.

"I wouldn't advise that."

Phoenix snatched her hand back, and with an extreme effort of will, forced herself to step away from the stone and turn to face the others gathered on the hill.

Izzie watched them with interest and gave a small nod of acknowledgement as their gazes met. Abi stood quietly at the witch's side, as they'd agreed. Phoenix had made her swear on every god and goddess in existence before leaving the apartment that morning that she'd stay with Izzie and allow the young witch to keep her safe, no matter what happened. She was simultaneously terrified for, and fiercely proud of, her best friend as she took in the fierce determination that shone in Abi's blue eyes. She may have been scared shitless, but she was sure as hell going to stand here with her head held high.

Lucas was waiting with the group despite the bright sun that was only then beginning to drift towards the horizon. His expression was carefully schooled, but she could feel the weight of his concern as he watched her. She knew he felt a responsibility to her father to keep her safe, and they both knew it was something that wouldn't be possible.

Remembering the love that filled her on getting to see her parents again, she stepped up to her father's Sire and took his hand. She stood on her toes so that she could speak quietly in his ear. "He forgives you."

She squeezed his hand and stepped away, but not before she caught the emotion glistening in his eyes.

On the far side of the stone, an Asian man stood next to Méabh. Though he was clearly a Supe, his appearance somehow made him seem the least threatening of all – Abi included. But the energy that oozed from him almost took her breath away. When his eyes met hers, something ancient stared back. Kam, Phoenix guessed. She swallowed hard.

A sudden darkness fell around them as heavy grey clouds rolled in to block out the sun. Morrigan raised her face to the sky and her eyes turned stormy. "It's time."

45

Ethan scanned the horizon as the sun set beyond the hills. Adrenaline buzzed through his veins, fuelled further by the power that emanated from the spear, down his arm and into his very core. Some distant part of him knew he should be afraid, that in reality, none of them were guaranteed to survive the next couple of hours. But he wasn't.

Only two things mattered to him in that moment: Phoenix and Saoirse. If he had to give up his life this night so that they could live, he would without a thought. He'd find a way, for them.

With Dagda's Cauldron in hand, Jannah went around to them one at a time requesting a blood sacrifice. His own blood to represent the Mists, Méabh's to represent the fae, Kam's for the shifters, Izzie's for the witches, Lucas's blood for the vampires, Ethan's for the wolves, Abi's for the human, and finally, Phoenix's as the only hybrid.

An oddly sweet odour mingled with the metallic tang as the combined blood settled at the bottom of the cauldron. The metal changed colour wherever the blood made contact, and faint Celtic symbols glowed around the outside.

Once it was done, the others formed a circle around Lia Fáil, and Ethan and Phoenix moved to opposite sides of the stone. Morrigan gave the order and he turned the Spear of Lugh upside down and stabbed it into the ground. Opposite him, Phoenix did the same with Claíomh Solais.

A shock of power shot through him and for a moment he couldn't breathe. It receded as quickly as it came, but the low hum of energy remained, and something told him that he'd need to brace himself when the fourth and final artefact was added.

He looked up and met Phoenix's wide eyes. The connection that had been formed between them when he gave her his blood in Faerie was still faintly present. Enough so that he could have spoken to her without saying a word. He could have told her how much he loved her, how amazingly strong she was, and how proud he was to call her the mother of his child. Instead, he gave her a cheeky wink and got a wry smile in return.

Morrigan stepped back out of the circle and gave them a solemn look. "So long as you all hold together, the power will distribute evenly through you. If you break the circle …"

"Don't break the circle," Kam ordered, his voice heavy with warning.

Ethan rolled his shoulders and gave his neck a resounding crack. Hold the spear, don't move. How hard could it be? Unease settled in the pit of his stomach as he looked out over the hilly landscape once more. It was quiet. Too quiet.

Izzie's words were low and indecipherable as she began to chant over the cauldron. Ethan held his breath for the sudden whammy of magic that would likely hit when the witch completed the blood circle. A heavy silence fell. And nothing happened.

He turned in confusion to see what was going on. Izzie was kneeling by the cauldron, her eyes wide with panic as she stared at it.

"It's not working." She looked up, frantically seeking out Kam. "Why isn't it working?"

"What do you mean it's not working?" Méabh snapped, an edge of fear tingeing her impatience.

"I did it exactly how he told me," Izzie said, indicating to Kam as her voice grew higher pitched. "There's something wrong. I can't feel any power." She took a deep shuddery breath in an obvious attempt to calm herself and closed her eyes. With her hands splayed above the cauldron, she repeated her chant and waited.

When nothing happened for a second time, she opened her eyes and shook her head. "Tell me the steps again," she demanded. "We must have missed something."

Kam frowned, and his ancient eyes took on a distant stare. "The blood of each species was mixed in the cauldron. An incantation declared the intention and infused the blood with power, then a circle –"

"Wait," Lucas interjected. "Have we got everyone's blood?"

They all looked around in askance, but no one stepped forward to claim they'd been missed. They'd covered the same basics as the original ritual: witch, vampire, fae, shifter, werewolf, Mist, human. The only difference this time was that Phoenix's hybrid blood had been added.

Abi raised a hand, blushing a little as all eyes turned to her. "Are we sure Phoenix's blood should be included? I mean, if there's never been a hybrid before, it can't have been included in the original banishment."

There were low murmurs as everyone debated the logic. On the one hand, her birth had technically created a new species and therefore was required as a representative of their world. And on the other, her blood was simply a mix of two species already represented – fae and vampire – so it shouldn't do any harm even if it wasn't required.

It was this last idea that caught Ethan's attention. A cold sense of dread crept through him as a terrifying thought formed.

Any hybrid created from existing species did, in fact, carry the blood of their parentage and should therefore be covered within the group gathered on the hill. But there was one exception to that logic; there was another hybrid, less natural, but no less present this side of the barrier.

"Shit," he whispered, causing everyone to fall silent around him. "I think I know what species we're missing."

Phoenix listened to Ethan's theory with a sense of foreboding. She didn't want what he was saying to make sense, but it did. Her blood was just a combination of two species that had already offered up their blood willingly. But Darius's new creations, they were something different.

Demons weren't of this world, and as such, their blood hadn't been necessary to fulfil the original requirements. Now that the blood was mixed with a species natural to this world, however, it was a different story.

She was just about to ask what the hell they could do when movement in the periphery of her vision distracted her. The light was growing low in the evening sky and eerie shadows danced around them, but as she squinted into the distance, she saw it again: movement beyond their perimeter.

The ward flared blue, and surprised yells came from down the hill.

"What the fuck was that?" Ethan asked.

"They're here," Morrigan answered, her tone resigned.

The ward flared again, and the field turned into chaos around her. None of it registered though, because the familiar sense of wrongness hit Phoenix. It stole her breath away and left her gasping even as her vision swam black. She gritted her teeth and forced herself to focus.

Suddenly, it was like a veil was lifted. The movement she'd seen only moments before hadn't been her imagination. She turned in a slow circle and beheld the swarm of black that surrounded them on all sides, held at bay only by the ward. There must have been hundreds, maybe thousands.

"How long will it hold?" she asked in a whisper.

Jannah's expression was grim as he stared out at the sea of writhing bodies. "Not long enough."

Even as he said it, a blast of fire lit up one side of the protective circle. The witches cried out, but the ward held firm.

Phoenix's heart hammered in her chest. If what Ethan believed was true – and she was convinced it was – what they needed was beyond that protective barrier. But if they dropped it now, there would be no going back. They were outnumbered, and if their previous experiences were anything to go by, outmatched. They'd all die.

"I hate to rush you guys," William roared from the base of the hill, "but I think we've got a situation here. Any chance you can hurry up and do the damn ritual?"

Lucas turned to Jannah, his voice tight with urgency. "Can you materialise beyond the ward?"

The Mist shook his head. "We had to make it airtight. We didn't know what Darius might have at his disposal."

And just to punctuate his words, fire struck the wards again, spreading to cover the entire surface of it. The ward glowed red hot and cracks formed across its surface.

The cries of pain were more than Phoenix could bear. She spun to Morrigan and pleaded. "Is there any way to complete the ritual without the circle?"

Morrigan's expression was sorrowful as she stared at the field below as if already mourning the losses to come. "The artefacts and the intention are what is important.

The circle is to bind you all so that the power can be dispersed through you. It can be done without the circle, but not without the blood." Morrigan turned to her. "Phoenix, if there is no circle, then the power will be channelled solely through the holders of the artefacts."

The look in her guardian's eyes told Phoenix everything she needed to know: the fewer the people to absorb the power, the lower their chances of surviving its force.

Phoenix looked to Jannah, who met her gaze unwavering. He would keep his oath to her, even if it meant his death. It was harder to look at Ethan, but she did, and when her eyes met his, she found comfort and surety.

With a deep breath, she yanked Claíomh Solais from the ground. "Let's start by getting the missing blood."

46

The Horsemen observed from deep in the recesses of Darius's mind as their army launched a relentless assault on the ward that formed a wide circumference around the Hill of Tara. Shrieks of pain followed each strike against the ward, and a vicious smile split his face. It wouldn't be long now.

At his side, the witch watched silently. Her power crackled around her, ready and waiting to be used when the time came.

They'd wanted him to turn her, the Horsemen. To combine her with one of their most powerful acolytes. But there was something about her humanity – or natural lack of it – that appealed to the person he had been. They'd been displeased with him for his decision, and they'd made sure he knew it.

Unconsciously his hand pressed against his side where rotten flesh covered his ribcage. Oh yes, they had an interesting way of conveying their displeasure. But right now they were pleased with him, and he bathed in the warmth of that feeling, in the satisfaction that soon he would prove to them just how worthy he was of their praise.

A flash of fire lit the sky, flaring out over the dome of protection covering Phoenix and her foolish friends. The flame called to the power that welled inside him, caressing and tempting him, demanding to be set free. The will to hold it back was growing weaker by the hour. The Horsemen wanted chaos. They wanted fear. They wanted everything to burn.

But it wasn't time yet.

His eyes scanned the mass of bodies that rushed about the field, preparing for the moment when the ward would fall and they'd meet their inevitable death. So many willing to sacrifice themselves for a cause they believed to be worthy. They had no idea they were doing all the work for him.

Then he saw it: the flash of red. Anticipation rippled through him and he licked his lips. "There you are."

His smile widened.

47

Phoenix sensed the others falling in behind her as she raced down the hill, Claíomh Solais gripped tightly in her hand. Ethan kept pace with her every step of the way, his expression grim but determined. Her own heart thundered in time with the pounding of her feet and terror threatened to crush her, but she pushed the feeling as far down as she could.

Cormac intercepted them as they reached the second line of defence. "What the hell is going on?"

"We need blood from one of the demon hybrids." Ethan pointed to the swarming mass of black. "We can't complete the ritual without it."

A blur of movement came from the right and Shade skidded to a halt beside them. "The ward can't hold much longer. They've surrounded us on all sides. I don't know how long we'll be able to hold them back once it falls."

"How many?" Phoenix could see Cormac doing the mental calculation as he assessed their best strategy.

"Hundreds."

Ethan let out a low whistle. "Might as well tell the witches to conserve their energy. We need to let them through."

If Shade had been pale before, he turned positively see-through at Ethan's words. "What? Are you fucking crazy? They'll —"

A look from Ethan halted his rant and he shook his head in disbelief. He muttered under his breath, "I should have found me a less crazy family," and disappeared in another blur of movement.

Despite herself, Phoenix smiled and some of the tension eased from her. Shade was right, this was a fucking crazy idea, and yet a part of her was just grateful to be standing here with these people at her side.

There was a ghost of a smile on Ethan's face too when he turned to her and held out his free hand. "Let's go make some new friends."

They left Cormac to organise the wolves as all around the field, the other teams were preparing. Phoenix made a point of not looking at the creatures surrounding the ward, but that same sense of wrongness choked her as they grew closer to the outer circle.

Even from a distance, she could see the beads of sweat running down the back of the witches' necks and the tremble of their muscles as they fought to hold on against the onslaught. "We need to do this quickly," she said.

Ethan grimaced. "Jannah has gone ahead to warn the other Mists. When we give the signal, they'll drop the ward."

Morrigan swooped through the sky above them, once more in her crow form. The sight called to something primal deep within Phoenix, and she squared her shoulders and gathered her resolve. All around the field their friends and allies stood ready to fight, despite the possibility that their idea was, in fact, crazy.

She allowed herself to look back, just once, towards the top of the hill. Her eyes sought out Abi, and she spotted her best friend standing sandwiched between Sasha and Izzie. All three looked fiercely defiant as they stared down at the hoards below them. In front of them stood a lone wolf: Sean.

He met her gaze across the distance and gave her a barely perceptible nod. Only then did she let herself turn and truly face what was to come.

Phoenix looked beyond the witches and hissed in a sharp breath. She'd known it was bad, but she could never have prepared herself for the nightmare that was before them. Snarling faces and crazed red eyes belied the methodical way the creatures moved. There was restraint and logic in the way they relentlessly attacked the ward, and that terrified her more than anything else. At their centre, a broad man stood barking orders. They all obeyed without question.

She scanned the sea of faces. There was no sign of Darius on this side of the field, but she could feel his eyes watching her. He was there somewhere, she knew it.

"We find the easiest target and get out," Ethan said, his tone brisk. "We need to complete the ritual, or all this will have been for nothing."

She swallowed hard and nodded, not so sure there would be an easy target.

He moved to give the order, but she grabbed his arm and pointed to the man at the centre of the crowd who had caught her attention moments before. "Tell the others they need to take him out. He's in charge."

He followed her line of sight and nodded. He was quiet for a moment as he conveyed her message to the pack via bat – wolf – signal. That done, he raised his hand in the air.

Morrigan let a loud "*Caw!*" and the wards came down.

For all of her bravado and insistence that humans be considered equal in determining what happened to their world, Abi was about ready to piss herself as she watched the sea of bodies swarm onto the field. So many. How had Darius gotten so many Supes?

At her side, a feral growl rumbled from Sasha. The wolf held herself tensely, muscles twitching with the desire to help her packmates, but still the other woman didn't move from the hilltop. On her opposite side, Izzie had closed her eyes and was murmuring unintelligible words. Abi didn't know what it was the witch was doing exactly, but the air was charged around them and the hairs on her arms stood on end.

Sean stood in front of them. He hadn't looked at her before moving into that position, but she'd seen the nod he'd given to Phoenix, and she knew from the stubborn set of his jaw that he'd die before he let anyone past him.

Screams of pain filled her ears as bodies collided below. There were flashes of light and bursts of flame, all punctuated by the clash of metal on metal. And blood. There was already so much blood.

It was clear from her vantage point just how outnumbered they were, and as she reached for one of the throwing knives strapped to her waist, she felt utterly helpless. She'd wanted to be treated equally, had demanded that humans were every bit as capable even if they didn't have the same natural advantages. Now look at her, cowering at the top of the hill while everyone else risked their lives.

A deep rumble came from overhead and a streak of white lightning forked through the sky. The two women at her side jerked their heads up, worry clouding their features. Then, suddenly, they were both on their knees, screaming as they clasped their heads in their hands.

"Sasha? Izzie!" she cried. There was no response other than their screaming, and she frantically looked around for Sean.

But there was no sign of the Omega. In fact, there was no sign of the field surrounding her, or the battle she knew was raging even now. All around her was a wall of black shadows.

Ice-cold fear bathed her, freezing a scream in her throat. Tendrils of darkness crept towards her, sinuous and seductive in their movement. Every instinct in her body screamed not to let them touch her, but she could see no way of escape as the shadows closed in from all sides.

One of the snake-like ropes lapped at her foot and she jerked back, only for another to caress the back of her neck. Every muscle in her body tensed, locked in place by fear. She was dimly aware that Sasha and Izzie were still kneeling on the ground, their screams now hoarse.

It was this sound more than any true sense of bravery that finally got her moving; she had to help them.

She spun on her heel and found a spot in the wall of shadows that looked – if even just to her imagination – less dense than the rest. She held her breath and ran straight for it. The darkness wrapped around her, welcoming her. But suddenly it was gone, and she could see everything around her with startling clarity.

She saw wolves she recognised from the Donegal pack being viciously struck down by the demon-Supe creatures. She saw friends fleeing with no true chance of escaping. She saw Fia on her knees in the middle of it all. The wolf's kind eyes met hers a moment before her head was separated from her body. Abi watched it all, impotent.

"Abi! Abi, help me."

Phoenix's desperate cry shocked her out of her frozen state of horror. She swung around and found her friend standing at the bottom of the hill, a small bundle cradled in her arms. Fire blazed around her, and the terrified wail of a baby joined the screams that filled the field.

"No. No. No." Abi shook her head in disbelief. Saoirse shouldn't be here; she was meant to be safe.

Wait, something inside her said. *That can't be Saoirse. She is safe. The spirits are protecting her.* With that thought, everything around her faded, leaving only darkness. She stumbled backwards out of the shadows, gasping.

A low chuckle came from behind her, and when she spun around, she was met by the face that haunted her nightmares.

"Hello, Abi." Darius smiled widely. The gesture caused the rotten skin and scars on his left cheek to contort, showcasing the gleaming white of his teeth between the decrepit flesh.

Fear clawed at her throat, choking her. Memories of that dark chamber swamped her mind.

Darius tilted his head, assessing her with intrigue. "Fear is an interesting thing, is it not? It can incapacitate us more wholly than any other means I've come across in my long life. Of course, I've never had quite the level of control over it as I do now, but I did okay. I think you'll agree?"

He stalked towards her, and though Abi tried to order her body to move, her muscles were paralysed, frozen in a strange limbo between flight or fight. He walked a slow circle around her, the shadows following in his wake.

"It seems appropriate that you will yet again be the reason Phoenix gives herself up to me."

The words sent a jolt through Abi, and in an instant his hold on her mind was gone. She was weaker than him in every way possible; there was no denying that. But she was damned if she was going to let herself be his victim again. Slowly she moved the fingers of her right hand, inching them towards one of the three remaining throwing knives at her waist. Her fingers closed around the cool metal and she held her breath.

Darius came full circle to gloat face-to-face, and that was when she struck. With a scream filled with all the anger and frustration and helplessness she'd felt for the last few months, she plunged the blade into his eye. Darius roared and stumbled away from her, grasping for the knife.

It took only a moment for him to yank it free; then he wheeled on her, his rage terrifying to behold. She knew in that moment he was going to kill her, but that suited her just fine. If he killed her, he wouldn't be able to use her against her friends. She squared her shoulders and looked him in his one remaining eye.

The shadows coalesced around him, swirling into a maelstrom of fury as blood streamed down his face. She was distantly aware of someone yelling her name as she said a silent goodbye to her friends. Darius held up a hand and closed his fist.

Her throat constricted as if all the oxygen had been pulled from the space around her. She gasped for breath, her hands scratching at her throat. The burning in her lungs intensified. Her vision blurred and started to turn black when suddenly a flash of white shot past and barrelled into Darius.

Abi had only a second to register Sean's blue eyes before oxygen flooded her lungs and the world spun.

48

Fire lanced through Phoenix's arm as razor-sharp claws tore through her flesh. She whirled, lashing out with Claíomh Solais. The blade cleaved through her attacker's neck, as it had cleaved through every other attacker before this one.

A swarm of maggots burst forth from the stump where the creature's head had been only seconds ago. She shrieked and jumped back, stamping her feet in a panicked attempt to squash any that came near her.

It had seemed like such a straightforward plan – get the blood and get the hell out. But the sheer numbers and strength of Darius's army had overwhelmed their defences in seconds. Her hands were slippery with the black blood she'd spilled, and not all of the bodies dotting the field around her were their enemies.

A sudden explosion came from her left and despite it all, she had to grin at Nate's exhilarated "Whoop!" Ethan was buried in a flurry of bodies to her right, but no matter how much she tried to carve a path to him, she kept running up against another obstacle.

They couldn't keep this up forever; they needed to get the blood back to the cauldron.

Even as the thought passed through her mind, another attack came from both sides. She dived just in time to avoid the flame that shot over her head. She rose to her feet and as she did, something caught her eye on the horizon.

A sea of bodies crested the hill from the west, heading straight for them. Rather than the black undulating hoard of Darius's army, this group rode magnificent horses and were led by two riders bearing a banner displaying a symbol of the sun – the symbol of her mother's people.

She ducked to avoid another strike, but something inside her began to lighten. They'd come. Aoife had kept her promise.

With renewed focus, she dispatched the two demon-Supes attempting to turn her into a shish kebab. She slashed and ducked, dodged and stabbed, every move getting her closer to Ethan.

She'd almost made it to him, when Morrigan's warning *"Caw!"* came from above. Phoenix swung around and her gaze fell on the hilltop where Abi and Sean now stood alone, facing an all-too-familiar figure.

Terror gripped her. All thoughts of getting to Ethan forgotten, she moved as if her life – her best friend's life – depended on it.

Oddly, none of the creatures moved to attack her as she sprinted for the top of the hill. A distant part of her knew that could only mean she was running straight into a trap, but she didn't care.

Despite the fact that they stood little chance against Darius, Abi and Sean had settled into an effective pattern of attack. Though she doubted they were causing true harm, their alternating strikes were enough to distract and irritate their foe.

It seemed, however, that he'd finally had enough of humouring them. Black shadows swirled around him as he held out a hand and let loose a blast of power that sent both Abi and Sean flying through the air. The ground rumbled with the force of the power.

He turned and smiled at her.

A sickening scream bubbled up in Phoenix's throat as she took in the rotten flesh covering one side of his face, and the gaping hole where an eye had once been. The man who she'd once called uncle opened his arms wide in welcome, and she ran straight for him.

Ethan drove the Spear of Lugh home time after time. Its aim never once failed him, but try as he might, he couldn't stave off the attacks long enough to get one of the bodies – or even body parts – back up to the cauldron.

He spun, plunging the tip of his spear through the chest of yet another demon-Supe and caught a flash of red in the corner of his eye. He cursed, then cursed more ferociously when he turned for a proper look.

Phoenix was almost to the top of the hill, and Darius stood there waiting for her with open arms. What the fuck was she doing? She couldn't face him alone.

"Shade!" he yelled to the vampire to his right. "Get the blood." He didn't wait for an acknowledgement before turning back to the hill, more than prepared to kill anyone stupid enough to get in his way.

A huge vampire with glowing red eyes stepped into his path. Ethan recognised him immediately as the one Phoenix had pegged as the leader, and he swore; he really didn't have time for this.

To increase his frustration further, the solid wall of muscle that was the vampire's chest obscured Phoenix from Ethan's view, and he knew he had only seconds before she reached Darius. He gritted his teeth. "Can we at least make this quick?"

The vampire gave him a slow, terrifying smile that promised a world of pain.

Ethan glanced to his left, trying to calculate his chances of getting past the demon-Supe without a fight, and quickly surmised the odds were not in his favour. He darted right.

A shadowy tendril shot out from the vamp and grabbed hold of him. Ethan lashed out with the spear and shattered the ethereal restraint, but not before the sickening sense of wrongness had seeped deep into his soul from its touch and given him a taste of what awaited them should they fail.

With renewed determination, he spun the spear around and drove the tip through the vampire's chest. True to its nature, the fae weapon found its mark.

He yanked the spear out, his mind focused again on getting to Phoenix, but then he froze in disbelief. The gaping hole in the vamp's sternum swirled with shadows

339

and before his eyes, the tissues knitted back together and he was fully healed.

"You've got to be shitting me!"

Life flared in the vampire's red eyes and his grin widened. He looked down at his chest, then back up at Ethan. His hand shot out, and before Ethan could recover from his shock, it clamped around his throat in a crushing grip.

Ethan's brain screamed for oxygen. He slashed at the hand with elongated claws, knowing it was pointless trying to pry the fingers away; any damage he caused simply repaired itself in a swirl of shadows. His head swam, and his vision grew black around the edges.

His vision had almost faded entirely when a blinding white light seared his retinas. There was an inhuman screech of pain and the pressure released from his throat. His knees buckled beneath him.

"Ethan, are you okay?"

He recognised Aoife's voice as someone grabbed his arm to keep him upright. He blinked repeatedly, as if that might return his vision quicker.

"Phoenix," his said urgently, as the light cleared enough for him to make out Aoife's features.

"Go. We'll cover you." She pushed him towards the hill, her order punctuated with the clang of metal on metal.

He didn't look back to see what had happened to the vampire. He just ran.

Everything else around him was inconsequential as he zeroed in on Phoenix. She stood alone on the top of the hill, facing off with Darius. Claíomh Solais glowed brightly in her hand as if she was channelling the power of the sun through it. Shadows oozed from Darius and lashed out at the sword. Anywhere they touched the blade, they seemed to swallow the light it cast. Phoenix hacked and sliced at the shadows, but they kept coming.

Darius laughed, a crazed look on his half-rotten face as he held his arms out wide, taunting her. "You fool. You think you can kill me? No one can kill me. I am eternal."

Fire flared in his hands and engulfed his arms in blue flame. A maniacal scream filled the air and a ring of fire burst to life around Darius and Phoenix.

"No!" Ethan roared, skidding to a stop just out of reach of the flames.

The heat was too much. It burned his skin without touching him, and the smoke clogged his airways with each searing breath he took. His body screamed at him to stop, but still he pushed forward.

Through the flickering flames, he saw Phoenix tear through Darius's abdomen with her sword. Hope surged inside him. But then he saw Darius smile – and time fractured.

Phoenix drew her sword back to drive the blade into Darius once more, but she hadn't noticed the shadows moving behind her. They shot out, wrapping around her arm and throat. The sword fell from her hand as she clawed at her neck with her free hand, her face a mask of shock.

No! This couldn't happen. He wouldn't let it.

There was no way Ethan could reach her in time, even if he could get through the ring of fire. So, he did the only thing he could do.

He drew his arm back and prayed to every god that had ever existed, whether in truth or only in the hearts of those who believed. He prayed to all those who had gone before him, to the loved ones who were even now fighting to the death at his side, to all those who were going about their lives in blissful ignorance of the fight that was raging to decide their fate. And he let his spear fly.

49

The witch stood watching from a distance. She felt no sympathy as the spear found its mark in Darius's heart. She had tried to warn him. Had told him time and again that the power was too much for anyone on this earth to hold for long.

And now, his once-powerful body was rotting from the inside out. The strength that had taken him millennia to develop was being consumed by the insatiable hunger that was Greed.

The spear wouldn't be enough to kill him, of course. Not with the Horsemen's essence still inside him. But his body was weak and broken now. He was no use to her.

Slowly, she dragged the blade of a curved dagger down the inside of her forearm. As the blood welled, she closed her eyes and started chanting. It was time to find a more suitable vessel.

50

Phoenix saw the exact moment that the spear lodged in Darius's heart. She saw the fury in his black eyes as the shadows swirled and coalesced to close the wound. Then she saw his expression change.

The flames that had been blazing at her back disappeared, leaving only icy cold where there had seconds ago been a wall of heat. The shadows binding her arm and throat loosened their grip, and she gasped in a lungful of air.

An odd silence fell around them, the sounds of battle seeming muted. Surprise flickered in Darius's eyes and he looked around, confused.

For an instant he looked almost human. Something akin to vulnerability broke through the crazed look that had twisted his features until they were almost unrecognisable, and in that moment she was reminded of a time when this man had been more than a monster to her.

Something inside her died a little, but she didn't hesitate; she lunged for Claíomh Solais where it had fallen on the ground between them. With a single, clean strike, Phoenix brought the blade up and severed his head from his body.

Darius's head hit the ground with an echoing thud. She watched it with a numb detachment, as if seeing it through someone else's eyes.

"Phoenix? Are you okay?" Ethan was at her side in an instant, his eyes wide with panic as he frantically checked her for injuries.

"Is it over?" she whispered, unable to look away from Darius's fallen body.

Ethan reached down and yanked his spear free from the now-headless chest and looked back towards the field, his expression grim. "I don't think so."

The roar of battle seeped back into Phoenix's consciousness with a sudden clarity. And with that roar came a low, keening wail drifting on the wind. She looked around at the bodies that littered the field, her breath catching as she spotted William slumped at the bottom of the hill, covered in blood.

It hadn't been enough. She'd cut the head from the snake, but still the swarm of creatures surged forward, bringing death and destruction.

"We need to complete the ritual." She grabbed Ethan's hand, intending to drag him back to Lia Fáil, but pulled up short as Sean stepped into their path.

Abi! She couldn't believe she'd forgotten what had drawn her up the hill to start with – the sight of Abi and Sean facing off against Darius. Frantically she looked around for her friend.

Phoenix's knees buckled as she caught sight of Abi's prone figure on the ground behind Sean. She didn't seem to be fully conscious, but was clearly stirring. Phoenix moved to run past him and help her friend but stumbled.

The air around the Omega felt wrong. It felt empty, like a black hole that had absorbed every bit of light and happiness that existed in the world. Simply being close to it sucked away every shred of hope she held until she too was empty. An empty, useless husk.

"Are you …" Ethan's words trailed off. "Sean?"

Dread filled the place where hope had once been, and she turned to look properly at the Omega. Ancient, inhuman eyes stared back at her. She hadn't noticed in her panic to get to Abi, didn't know Sean well enough to notice the difference in his demeanour. But now she saw it. Now she saw them.

"Did you really think it would be that easy? We are eternal."

The voice that came from Sean's mouth was not his own. It came from all around her, filled her. She stumbled backwards, shaking her head, and he smiled.

A low rumble filled her ears and the ground beneath her shuddered. She fought to hold her balance, but a crack split the earth between her feet. She leapt to the side barely a moment before the crack ruptured, forming a large fissure.

Even as she landed, more spiderweb cracks were spreading out around the hill. A thick acrid smoke oozed up from the gaps in the earth and reached up towards the sky. She choked as the smoke burned the lining of her throat, and from one breath to the next her visibility all but disappeared.

Ethan called out to her and she tried to reach out for him, but the ground undulated and rolled again, knocking her sideways and further away from his voice. Tears stung her eyes and try as she might, she couldn't blink them away. In the heavy grey of smoke, the shadows came for her.

Desperate, she grasped for the spark of power inside her and called the sun. The light came slower than it ever had before, but it came nonetheless. For a moment, the flare of white drove back the smoke and the shadows lurking within it, but then they started pushing back against her power.

Sweat ran in rivulets down her neck and chest as she tried to hold that small spark of light. Suddenly, the light surged outwards.

A new, almost familiar power joined with hers, and her own light flared with renewed force. Through the glare of white, the shadows, and the smoke, she saw a huge white horse galloping towards her. Aoife sat atop the animal, her face strained as she focused all the power she had to drive back the shadows.

Her grandfather appeared at Aoife's side on his own chestnut steed. His violet eyes glowed and when he held out his hand, a gale-force wind rose up around them, pushing back the smoke.

"Go!" Aoife yelled at her.

Before Phoenix could speak or even think, Ethan was at her side. He grabbed her hand and pulled her towards the top of the hill. She had only a second to glance back to where Sean faced off against Aoife and her grandfather in the centre of a raging whirlwind.

"No! We have to help them," she yelled, terror gripping her.

"We have to complete the ritual. It's the only way to stop this."

He tugged on her hand again and, with difficulty, she turned and left her family to their fate. Together, she and Ethan cleared the remaining distance to where Lia Fáil sat inert at the top of the hill.

As Phoenix stood at the highest point and looked down on the hill, a crushing sense of dread filled her. The blackness surged towards them from all sides, growing closer by the second. There was no time left.

A blur of movement came from their right and Shade appeared beside them, covered from head to toe in blood, and a grim smile on his face. He held up a severed head with lifeless red eyes. "Someone request some blood?"

She gasped as she recognised the face of the large vampire hybrid that she'd pointed out to Ethan before the wards had dropped.

Ethan gave a low whistle, taking the offered head. "I don't know how the hell you pulled that one off, but this'll definitely do the trick."

Shade attempted a nonchalant shrug, but his legs buckled and he only just managed to remain standing. "Was a piece of cake."

"We need Izzie and the cauldron." The words had only left Phoenix's mouth when she spotted Izzie stumbling up the hill towards them. The witch had her arm around a limping but conscious Abi, and Nate was supporting her on the other side. All three were coated in blood and had visible wounds, but still the tightness in her chest eased just a touch at the sight of them.

"Has anyone seen —" She didn't get a chance to finish her sentence before a shimmering mist coalesced to leave a grim-faced Jannah standing before her with the cauldron in his hands.

"Do you have what we need?" he asked, his voice rushed.

Ethan held up the head, thick black blood dripping from the jagged stump that used to be a neck.

"Good." Jannah thrust Dagda's Cauldron into Shade's hands. "I do solemnly pass ownership of this artefact to you, to act as a guardian to its power, as witnessed by those who stand here now."

The vampire gaped at him as if the Mist had lost his marbles, but Jannah just turned to Phoenix. "Our defences are failing. We can't last much longer. I will do what I can to hold them off, but if you don't finish this now, it will be too late." Without waiting for a response, he turned to mist and disappeared.

Izzie, Abi, and Nate reached them a moment later, and Phoenix flung herself at them, grasping her friend in a tight hug. "Are you okay?"

Abi gave her a crooked grin. "I cut the bastard's eye out."

Phoenix choked out a laugh that was partly a sob of relief. "You sure did. You did amazing."

"Where's everyone else?" Nate asked, looking around at the significantly smaller group. A long gash ran down one side of his face and he was holding his left arm oddly, but his amber eyes were alert.

"I think we're on our own," Ethan answered.

Phoenix looked at the cauldron now resting in Shade's hands and at the people who stood with her at the top of the hill. Everyone with her now had been with her from the beginning. Even Izzie, in a strange sort of way, had set her on this path. They'd become a weird, fucked-up kind of family to her, and some selfish part of her was glad they were with her now.

"It'll have to be enough," she said, squaring her shoulders and stepping into her position at the east side of Lia Fáil. She flipped her sword over and drove the blade into the ground.

Ethan helped Izzie add the final ingredient to the cauldron before taking his place opposite Phoenix and driving his spear into the earth. Their eyes met, and a world of emotion passed between them.

Izzie's chant started, and Phoenix looked at Abi. "Stand clear of the circle. You've done your part; now I need you to be safe."

Stubborn blue eyes glared at her, filled with anger and frustration and sorrow. Abi bit her lip but stepped back to watch.

Izzie's words grew louder and as they did, the power rose with them. Claíomh Solais thrummed in Phoenix's hands and she had to clench her jaw to stop her teeth from rattling. The air around them became electric.

The witch nodded in confirmation: it was working. Nate and Shade stepped into position at the North and

South points of the circle. Four points of the compass, four of them to absorb the power. Would it be enough?

As the final word was spoken, the cauldron flared to life.

51

"It worked," Izzie whispered in disbelief.

Fear and resolve all warred within Phoenix as she looked at the cauldron, now glowing with intricate symbols. Izzie took a shuddery breath and gave Shade a nod. She stepped back on shaky legs and joined them in the circle.

Shade sucked in a breath as he held the glowing cauldron in both hands. "Ready?"

When they all nodded, he carefully tilted it until the blood dripped over the edge. The first drop landed on the ground, sizzled, and left a scorched mark. With slow, deliberate steps, he completed the blood circle around them. He placed the cauldron on the ground and returned to his position.

Nothing happened.

Phoenix focused all of her will on their intention – the banishment of the Horsemen and all demons from this world. But she felt nothing other than the power that had already been thrumming through her sword from the artefacts being reunited.

Then it hit.

The power crashed over her like a tidal wave, and the whole world turned white. In that instant, she could feel it all: the death, the destruction, the possibility.

Her body was torn asunder, made and unmade. No longer flesh and bone, now just energy floating on the air. She looked down on the battlefield that was little more than dull images moving within a haze of white, and she was filled with such unspeakable emotion that she felt it crush her.

So much death. So, so much death. What kind of people were they if they could do this to each other? She saw it all, every life lost, every life irrevocably changed, and she hated it. She hated that it wasn't the demons who had caused this, not really. And what was more, she hated that there were people out there this very moment who were blissfully unaware that any of this was happening. They were cocooned in their safe, comfortable lives, oblivious to the fact that others were sacrificing themselves so that they could keep that oblivion.

In that moment, she knew.

Yes, they could banish the demons again. The power was theirs to harness that way, should they wish it. But it wouldn't stop the pain. It wouldn't stop the death. Because they were death. Not the demons, and not the Horsemen. Them.

The power lashed at her, bringing with it glimpses of what the future might look like. The future where the demons remained, and the one where they were once again banished. In one of those visions, fires burned and destroyed everything she'd ever loved. But in the other, people destroyed everything she'd ever loved.

So much pain. So much hatred. It could all end now. They could let the Horsemen end it quickly and save themselves the heartache. They could be at peace and leave the rest of the world to fend for itself, no more running, no more fighting.

And then a single name came to her through the haze. Saoirse.

Every molecule in her body screamed for the horrors to stop, but within the devastation, there was something else too. There was love.

She focused on the name like it was a beacon. With all her will, she pushed back the fear and the thoughts of succumbing. Giving up was not an option; so long as they lived there was hope. So, she repeated the intention over and over again. *Banish them. Banish them. Banish them.*

Still she floundered within the power, drowning in it. Even as she tried to channel it into her intention, it consumed her. She was made and unmade in an endless cycle until she didn't believe she could ever be whole again.

A voice called to her from a distance. "I'm here, Phoenix. Just listen to my voice, okay? Hold on."

The voice was familiar, someone dear to her. But it was only when Abi's hand touched her shoulder that Phoenix managed to claw her way up through the power enough to recognise it.

Abi kept talking, and though the words seemed to fade in and out, she listened. She let her friend's voice guide her as Abi told her all the reasons why this world was worth saving. Why she would stand with her to the end, magic or no damn magic.

Piece by painful piece, Phoenix's body reformed. The magic filled every cell within her, flowing through her to find her own magic settled at the centre of her solar plexus.

With extreme effort, she opened her eyes.

Izzie was on the ground beside her, blood running from her nose as she gritted her teeth and struggled to keep her head up. Shade was kneeling next to her, one hand stretched out as if he wanted to help the witch, but his head was thrown back and his face frozen into a mask of agony.

To her right, Nate's body was stretched taut. His arms and legs were pulled wide as if some force was tearing him in two, and his whole body shook with the strain. Veins bulged at his temple, and sweat ran in rivulets down his face, which was now a worrying shade of red.

And across from her, Ethan stood. Barely. He slumped against the spear, his body clearly failing, but his eyes were open and he had them fixed on her. The life and sparkle they normally contained was missing. Instead, they were glassy with pain, and sweat covered his pale skin. His muscles trembled with the effort of holding himself upright.

Phoenix let out a sob as his knees buckled and his eyes fluttered closed. She wanted to call to him, to give him her strength, but it was taking all of her energy to hold onto the power. Soon she'd have to let it go, and she didn't know what would happen once she did.

Finally, she twisted her head to look at Abi. Rather than standing a safe distance away as she'd been instructed, Abi now stood behind her, a hand on her shoulder. How she'd crossed the circle, Phoenix had no idea. All she knew was that her human best friend now stood caught in the torrent of magic that was near to breaking point.

Abi's long hair blew around her, and her expression was fierce as she met Phoenix's eyes. "Do it," she demanded, no fear in her voice.

Phoenix's heart screamed in defiance, but she nodded, tears streaming down her cheeks. She closed her eyes one final time and reached deep down within herself, further than she'd ever reached before. She called the sun, let it fill her, surround her, become her. And then she let it go.

52

Blinding white seared into Ethan's eyelids. He could hear nothing, see nothing. Was this it? Was he dead?

It was strange, really; he'd never considered what death might be like. Even knowing when he stepped onto that hill that he might not walk down it again, he hadn't stopped to imagine what waited for him. He'd been prepared to give up his life so long as they might live. What happened after was irrelevant.

He tried to open his eyes, but a searing pain shot through his head so he scrunched them closed again. Voices drifted into his consciousness. Familiar voices. His mother. His father. They called to him, and a deep sorrow filled him at the realisation that they must be dead too.

Something shook him, and his whole body roared in agony at the movement. Dammit, surely death wasn't meant to hurt so much?

"Ethan. Ethan. Open your eyes, Mo Faolán."

He recognised his mother's voice, closer now, beseeching him. He couldn't deny her, even in death, so he forced his eyelids to open despite the pain in his head.

The white persisted for a moment, but the glare began to slowly fade until he could start to pick out shadows.

Bit by painful bit, things came back into focus: the grass that tickled his cheek, the cold air brushing his skin, the hands that touched his shoulder. His mother's face appeared before him, and something about the overwhelming relief in her expression, told him that he'd been wrong – he wasn't dead.

He sucked in a breath. He was alive?

He tried to push himself up from the ground, but his arms were like jelly and merely collapsed under him. Strong hands grasped his shoulders and helped raise him to sitting. Ethan looked up to see tears glistening in his father's eyes before Cormac cleared his throat and looked away, fussing to make sure Ethan wouldn't fall over before he let go.

Disbelief prevented him from speaking, so he just stared at his parents' bloodstained faces and let it all sink in. He was alive. They were alive.

The realisation pierced the fog of pain that clouded his mind, and he jerked his head around, overcome with a sudden panic. "Phoenix?" The word came out as little more than a rasp.

On the far side of Lia Fáil, he spotted her bright red hair fanned out across the ground. A renewed sense of terror gripped him and he struggled to rise, growling with frustration when his legs refused to obey.

Cormac was at his side in an instant. His father wrapped an arm around him and hefted him to his feet. Ethan didn't dare breathe as they crossed the distance to where Phoenix lay on the ground, unmoving. Abi crouched by her side, her face pale and expressionless. She didn't look up as he approached, and an icy chill settled deep in his heart.

He collapsed at Phoenix's side and with a shaking hand, he reached out to touch her cheek. It was so cold.

It struck him just how peaceful her face looked. For so long he'd watched her try to hide her fear and worry from everyone. He'd seen the tightness that tugged at the corner of her smile, the furrow of her brow when she thought no one was looking. Now, all the tension was gone. Washed away on the tide of magic that he'd felt surge from her just before the world had disappeared.

He looked around now and realised with surprise that the first rays of dawn were cresting the horizon. Soft light bathed the field around them in an eerie red that seemed suited somehow to the blanket of bodies covering the grass. Those who had survived wandered about aimlessly, some checking for loved ones in the carnage, others just looking lost.

It was quiet now that the sounds of fighting had gone. The ritual had worked. It had torn the demons from this world and put them back beyond a fabric that now seemed far too insubstantial to stave off the nightmares he knew would come.

A strange numbness settled over him as he looked down at Phoenix once more. Ever so gently, he lifted her head into his lap and wrapped his arms around her. "We did it," he whispered and bent his head to kiss her forehead. "We did it."

Her body gave a sudden twitch, and her eyelashes brushed against his cheek. He jerked his head up in shock and almost let her head roll from his lap before he caught her.

So slowly it was like torture, her eyes opened. She blinked up at him, winced, and closed her eyes again. She swallowed and ran her tongue over her chapped lips. "Really?" she wheezed. "That's how you kiss me after we save the world?"

One minute Phoenix was standing at the centre of the sun, heat and light blazing around and within her, the next there was just him. The thread of life, so tenuous now, connected her to him, and she knew that she could follow it back if she chose. But she also knew that in doing so, she'd leave behind the comforting numbness that cocooned her. Slowly, she blinked open her eyes.

The look of shock on Ethan's face would have made her laugh if not for the crippling pain that came with her return to consciousness. Every inch of her body felt like it had been scorched from the inside out and her nerves screamed in agony. She closed her eyes, half-wishing for oblivion to take her again, but he held her to him, refusing to let her go.

She had no idea how much time passed as she lay there. She was dimly aware of people talking around her. Their voices were familiar, but their words meant nothing. Mingled with the voices, there a low, keening lament. It drifted on the wind, its sound both beautiful and sorrowful. She wondered distantly who the song was for.

Someone came and spoke low to Ethan. There was a moment of jostling as he seemed to adjust the position of her body in his arms, and then she felt a gentle pressure on her sternum. Heat sparked in her solar plexus in response to the touch and trickled through her body. The pain didn't disappear exactly, but the warmth dulled it enough that she could once more breathe without wanting to die. Her eyes flickered open, and she found herself looking into the smiling face of her mother.

No. It wasn't her mother. It was Aoife.

Her aunt placed a gentle hand on her cheek, her eyes glistening with tears as she crouched before her. "You did it, Phoenix."

For a moment Phoenix wasn't sure exactly what Aoife meant, then she heard it: the silence. She looked around and realised for the first time that she was no longer surrounded by the sounds of battle. Instead, there was just the quiet aftermath of death. So many bodies littered the ground that it was almost impossible to see the green of the grass, and not all were dressed in the black of Darius's army.

"Is it …"

Ethan's arms tightened around her. "It's over," he reassured her in a whisper.

She looked again at the fallen who coated the field. How many? How many of their allies? In the distance, near the original ward line, she spotted Maj and Shayan standing together. They seemed to be staring back at her, and she cast her eyes around, wondering why Jannah wasn't with them. The two Mists stood there for a moment longer, then dissipated into the wind.

361

At the bottom of the hill, she spotted Kam and Méabh lifting a body between them. She wondered if it was William as a vague recollection flitted at the edges of her consciousness, but was afraid to voice the question. All around them people tended to the wounded, and high up in the sky, the black crow soared, drifting on the sorrowful notes of death's lament.

Finally, she turned back to her aunt, unable to look at such immense loss anymore. "You came."

A sadness tinged Aoife's smile. "I promised you we would. You're our family, and no matter what, you will always have a place with us. No matter how my mother may feel."

Clíodhna. Had she been here? Had she put aside her bitter prejudice enough to fight at their side? Phoenix couldn't remember seeing her, and something told her she didn't want to know the answer. So instead, she asked, "Where's grandfather?"

Aoife dropped her eyes, but not before Phoenix saw the crushing pain shadowing them. Even before her aunt spoke, a part of her knew.

"He's gone." Aoife raised her head, composing herself. "He gave his last breath to help us survive. I need to leave now to bring his body back to Faerie. I must … I need to make sure he passes." She took a shuddery breath and stood. "I'm sorry to have to leave you again so soon, but I meant what I said. You'll always have a place with us." She turned her gaze to Ethan and gave him a fond smile. "As will you, wolf."

Ethan gave her a nod of gratitude, and Phoenix watched quietly as her aunt turned and made her way to a small group of fae soldiers who were standing guard around one of the fallen. Her grandfather, she realised now.

Phoenix was too exhausted and numb to feel sorrow for the man she'd barely known. But later, when she had the strength, she'd remember his face and mourn what could have been. For now, it was enough to acknowledge his sacrifice.

Bone-deep weariness settled over her, but also something else: hope. Yes, she had seen what the future might hold for them if they didn't find a way to all live in harmony together, but for now it was enough that they lived. She didn't want to be surrounded by death anymore; she wanted to get back to her little girl and start their lives properly.

She turned to Ethan. "Take me home. Please."

EPILOGUE

3 months later

Phoenix's jaw dropped as Ethan pulled the car over to the side of the road and killed the engine. She couldn't believe it – the pub looked exactly as it had before the fire had destroyed it. The front door was a replica of the one she'd first walked through almost five years before, and an odd sense of nostalgia caused her throat to tighten.

"They've done a great job," Ethan said with no small hint of pride in his voice.

She just nodded, unable to speak.

Once the dust had settled after the banishment, and everyone had had a chance to say goodbye to their dead – of which there were far too many – Cormac and Ethan had arranged for a group of wolves from the Donegal pack to come back to Dublin to help with the rebuild of Abi's pub.

Phoenix had been unspeakably grateful, especially considering it was her fault that her best friend's livelihood had been destroyed in the first place. She'd insisted that she pay for the work, but Cormac had refused, saying that Abi had more than earned the help with her bravery during the ritual.

She wasn't sure if he realised just how right he was. Phoenix hadn't told anyone how close she'd come to giving in that night when she'd been caught in the maelstrom of the artefacts' power. If it hadn't been for Abi stepping across that circle and lending her strength when she did, she might have made a very different choice.

The door to the pub swung open and before Phoenix could even get her seatbelt unbuckled, Abi was pulling open her car door. "You're here! Oh my god, I'm so happy to see you!"

Her friend was positively glowing with joy as she caught her in a crushing hug. Phoenix laughed. "Wow. Have you been working out?"

Abi gave her a playful shove and moved aside so that she could get out. Ethan climbed out on his side and took the car seat and sleeping baby from the back of the car.

Abi's squeal dropped to a whisper but contained no less excitement as she peered down at Saoirse. "Oh, would you look at her! She's getting so big already." She beckoned them towards the pub. "Come on, Sasha's inside. She's going to want to see her niece."

Ethan followed obediently and was ushered up to the living area where Sasha was busy unpacking her things. Phoenix trailed behind them, taking in the newly refurbished pub. It was exactly as she remembered it.

Slowly she walked around the interior of the pub, trailing her fingers over the smooth wood of the new tables and breathing in the familiar aroma of Guinness hops. She came to a stop behind the bar and looked out on the room.

Abi came to stand at her side, leaning her elbows on the bar. "I honestly never thought I'd get to stand behind this bar again."

Phoenix's throat tightened once more. "Abi, I'm –"

Abi held up a hand, cutting her off. "Don't you dare apologise again. None of this was your fault, and I wouldn't be standing here now if it wasn't for you. Even if I had a chance to go back and do it differently, I wouldn't."

Phoenix nodded. "I'll miss working here with you."

"I'm excited that Sasha decided to come help run the pub, but it won't be the same without you." Abi nudged her shoulder and smiled.

At the mention of Ethan's sister, a shadow fell over Phoenix. "Has she said if they've managed to track down Sean yet?"

The Omega had been last seen walking away from the Hill of Tara after the ritual had been completed. They knew he'd survived the banishment of the Horsemen, though what toll it had taken on him was anyone's guess. The pack had been searching for him ever since, but as yet they'd had no luck tracing him. Ethan put on a brave face anytime she asked him about it, but she knew it was eating him up inside.

Abi frowned, worry dulling the sparkle in her blue eyes. "All of their leads so far have turned out to be dead ends. I have a feeling he'll only be found when he wants to be."

They were silent for a few minutes, each lost in their own thoughts. Then Abi shook herself and smiled broadly. "One last drink for old times?"

Phoenix stared out the passenger window as the green peaks of the Wicklow mountains rolled past and the roads shifted from motorway to narrow backroads. Ethan followed her directions with ease, taking the sharp twists and turns with extra care now that they carried precious cargo in the car.

They'd driven this route together once before. It had been little more than six months since they'd first gone on the run from the Mists, but it felt like a lifetime ago. So much had changed since then. She had changed.

Twisting her head to look at the back seat, she smiled as her daughter blinked back at her with wide, curious eyes.

Ethan slowed the car and came to a stop with the engine idling when they reached a half-hidden lane that led to a small white house. Unlike last time, she didn't tell him to keep driving. She stared at the house where she'd grown up and this time, instead of being bombarded by painful memories, a familiar warmth wrapped around her.

She'd never truly be able to forget the days she spent alone in that house, hoping beyond hope for her parents to walk back through the door. But she realised now that holding onto those memories did a disservice to her parents. This had been their home, and for however brief a time, they'd been happy.

Ethan gave her a questioning look, and she nodded. He swung the car up the tree-lined lane and came to a stop in front of the house, killing the engine.

"Are you sure you want to do this?" he asked gently.

She took in the rainbow-coloured roses that edged the house's white façade, and tears pricked the back of her eyes. Her mother's flowers. How had they survived?

Ethan's expression turned worried and she forced herself to swallow past the lump in her throat to answer his question. "I want this to be our home. I want Saoirse to grow up here and know the love that I did."

He reached over and squeezed her hand, then climbed out of the car and set about freeing Saoirse from the confines of her car seat.

Phoenix climbed out of the passenger side. She looked towards the lush forest that bordered the property and saw a large crow perched in a tree, watching them. She smiled and met Morrigan's gaze for a moment, then turned and followed Ethan into the house and the start of their new life together.

*****

Not ready for it to end?
Find out how it all began ...

Join Phoenix in a FREE bonus short story exploring her life in the lead up to her parent's disappearance and her residency with the Dublin vampire clan.

Get your copy at

Author Note

Thank you for joining me on this new adventure through Ireland's hidden supernatural world. If you enjoyed this book, I would be very grateful if you could leave a brief review (it can be as short as you like) on the site where you purchased your copy.

As an author, reviews are the most powerful tools in my arsenal when it comes to getting attention for my books. Honest feedback goes a long way in increasing visibility and helping me to reach other readers like you, so thank you in advance!

A Quick Thanks

It's safe to say that this book was the hardest of the three to write. The journey that Phoenix needed to go on challenged me almost as much as it did her, but we got there in the end.

Thank you so much to the readers that have embraced this new magical world with me. Rest assured that, though the trilogy is finished, there's still plenty of life left in the Lore yet.

I couldn't have made this the trilogy it is without the team at Three Point Author Services, so I'll be forever grateful to Bre, Michele, and Andrea for helping me grow as a writer. I look forward to torturing you all further in the future with my terrible understanding of comas!

And as always, I owe a huge thanks to my partner and baby girl. It takes a significant amount of time and commitment to write and publish a book. They've not only supported me through this whole journey, but they continue to be my biggest cheerleaders, and I'd be lost without them.

WHERE TO FIND ME ONLINE

LMHatchell.com

Facebook.com/LMHatchell

Instagram.com/lmhatchell

Just want to be notified when I've a new release?

Follow me on:

Bookbub

Amazon Author Central

Made in the USA
Columbia, SC
30 March 2022